The Tree Shepherd's Daughter

"One of those remarkable tales in which the reader becomes completely immersed ... It will be enjoyed not only in its own right, but also will have readers eagerly anticipating books two and three in the promised trilogy."
—*KLIATT*

Into the Wildewood

"Compelling and beautifully written ... a great follow-up to an already breathtaking first novel. Fans of the series will be very satisfied."
—TeensReadToo.com

"*Into the Wildewood* brings a fresh perspective to the genre with a crackerjack plot and razor sharp writing."
—*ForeWord Magazine*

The Secret of the Dread Forest

"The pleasant mix of fairy dust and romance—hallmarks of the previous two books—is still present in *The Secret of the Dread Forest*. The book zips along—fans of the series will not be disappointed."
—*VOYA*

"New and old characters combine in a breakneck plot that will have readers turning pages in class and long after bedtime."
—*ForeWord Magazine*

The
Goblin's
Curse

With endless love to my children, a constant source of inspiration, aggravation, and much delight.

THE FAIRE FOLK SAGA: TRILOGY 2

The Goblin's Curse

GILLIAN SUMMERS

THE SCIONS OF SHADOW TRILOGY

flux
™
Woodbury, Minnesota

First Edition
First Printing, 2012

Book format by Bob Gaul
Cover design by Kevin R. Brown
Cover illustration by Derek Lea
Cover images: Borgund Stave Church © iStockphoto.com/Dainis Derics
            Urnes Stave Church © iStockphoto.com/Dainis Derics
            Man © iStockphoto.com/Renee Keith
            Fire flames © iStockphoto.com/Selahattin Bayram
            Smoke © iStockphoto.com/Paul Senyszyn,
               iStockphoto.com/David Mantel,
               iStockphoto.com/AlexPitt
            Scots pine © iStockphoto.com/Alexander Dunkel
            Pine tree © iStockphoto.com/DNY59

Flux, an imprint of Llewellyn Worldwide Ltd.

Library of Congress Cataloging-in-Publication Data
Summers, Gillian.
  The goblin's curse/Gillian Summers.—1st ed.
    p. cm.—(The scions of shadow trilogy ; #3)
  "The Faire Folk Saga: Trilogy 2."
  Summary: Sixteen-year-old Keelie is glad to be back at Colorado's High Mountain Renaissance Faire for the summer but her pet goblin, Cricket, is not welcome, especially after rumors spread of a nearby goblin army and even Sean, Keelie's boyfriend, holds her responsible.
  ISBN 978-0-7387-1572-8
  [1. Magic—Fiction. 2. Elves—Fiction. 3. Fairies—Fiction. 4. Goblins—Fiction. 5. Colorado—Fiction.] I. Title.
  PZ7.S953987Gob 2012
  [Fic]—dc23

                                      2011052167

Flux
Llewellyn Worldwide Ltd.
2143 Wooddale Drive
Woodbury, MN 55125-2989
www.fluxnow.com

Acknowledgments

Many thanks to my wonderful editors Brian Farrey-Latz and Sandy Sullivan, whose keen eyes catch every opportunity to improve a story. I'm constantly amazed at Sandy's knowledge of Keelie's world. She remembers every nook and cranny of the faires, the Dread Forest, and Under-the-Hill and could probably lead guided tours while singing the festival songs of the elves. It's a treat to work with such talented folk!

Also, thanks to the great folk of the National Park Service, who have always been ready with answers to tree questions, especially Keelie's great friend Wyndeth Davis. To Rennies everywhere—huzzah! You make me happy.

one

The Colorado night air smelled dry and spicy as Keelie Heartwood picked her way up the twisty, unlit dirt path toward Heartwood, her father's furniture shop. It perched at the top of the hill, with a good view of the jousting field below. She felt like she was coming home.

"Ow, Cricket." She tugged on her T-shirt to dislodge her pet goblin's tiny claws, which were digging into her shoulders.

The quaint, medieval-looking cottages and tall, sprawling structures she passed were shuttered and quiet—the

High Mountain Renaissance Faire was closed until the weekend and many shops were empty, their owners gone to buy supplies or visit friends in Fort Collins. But the shops that served as seasonal homes for the shopkeepers showed signs of life, their upstairs windows glowing golden against the starry night sky. It was lovely. And on the other side of the faire, the night was filled with flickers of light and bursts of song from the distant campground.

Still, Keelie thought the grounds were a little spooky at night. It didn't help that some of the shops were painted in fantastical colors, or adorned with dragons and unicorns and cartoon fairies. Fairies that looked like tiny people with wings, that is … Keelie knew the real ones looked very different.

Crickets called out in the shrubbery that bordered one side of the path, and the slight weight between her shoulder blades chirped metallically in response. "Friends of yours?" Keelie asked. No answer, but she hadn't expected one.

She'd come this way almost a year ago, following a fast-walking attorney from her mother's law firm. She'd been grieving and angry at her mother's sudden death, adrift and about to be delivered into the hands of a man she didn't know. She'd sworn never to call him Dad, but he'd won her heart.

The fact that he wasn't human had little to do with it.

As she turned the last bend of the path, her heart clenched at the sight of Heartwood across the wide, moon-lit clearing. A medieval-looking two-story building, with an open-air furniture showroom downstairs and her father's apartment upstairs, the shop had been Dad's home at this faire for years, and now it was Keelie's as well. A sturdy, narrow staircase on one side climbed up to their apartment. Keelie headed toward it, glancing at the shops on either side of the clearing.

A light glowed from the shop on her left. Last summer, it had been a costume shop called Galadriel's Closet, but since then the building had been totally transformed. Now it was an open structure with a two-story, stacked-stone chimney jutting above a metal roof, with a shed at the rear. Tools hung from iron hooks all around, and a huge pile of coal gleamed blackly in the moonlight. It seemed to be a forge, which was strange, since there was already a forge down by the jousting ring where the horses could be easily taken to be shod. On Heartwood's other side was the mask shop, with a new name to complement its new location. A few weather-proof masks hung outside, disturbingly reminding Keelie of ones she'd recently seen.

With a shrug, she skirted Heartwood's flagstone floor and started up the stairs to the apartment. She lifted the ribbon with the key and squinted at the door, wishing she'd brought a flashlight. She finally stuck a finger over the keyhole, then guided the key to its rightful spot by following her finger with her other hand. With a click of its well-oiled lock, the door swung open.

Immediately, the weight on her back vanished and a small black shadow fell to the floor, moving quickly and silently into the room.

Keelie lit a candle with matches that were kept by the door and walked toward the kitchen. The apartment was one large area, divided into rooms by cloth hangings and wall screens. Dad had made her a bedroom in one corner, with a window that overlooked the jousting ring far below. She opened the closest window, then crossed the room to open another. The temperature was starting to drop, but the breeze would help banish the stale and dusty smells that had built up in the closed space during the weeks that Dad was with her in the Northwoods.

The dark shadow that had been on her shoulders now leaped onto the windowsill and stared out into the darkness, its body shiny black like an insect's. It turned its big yellow eyes to her and chirped.

"That's the faire. Stay out of sight, okay? Most folks can't see you, but if they do, they'll freak out. Goblins aren't much loved among the elves."

The little goblin ran back to her and climbed her leg.

"Watch the claws," Keelie hissed. "I swear, you're worse than a kitten."

Cricket stopped at her shoulder, his usual perch, a hank of her hair snagged tightly in his little clawed hand.

Dad didn't like the goblin. Who could blame him? After all, he'd recently worn armor for the first time in a hundred years because of goblinkind. But the little guy was a gift to Keelie from Herne the Hunter himself, and she could hardly refuse him. Besides, Cricket was handy to have around since he subsisted on garbage.

Keelie placed her candle on the tiny counter in the kitchen area, then put another on the small square dining table. Dad had told her to run the water for a bit to warm it up, so she opened the tap in the little kitchen sink, then the one in the huge claw-foot tub in the curtain-enclosed bathroom.

Footsteps sounded on the stairs outside and Keelie called out, "Dad?"

A grunt answered her, and she looked out cautiously from behind the bathroom curtains. Dad was bent over, carrying a huge trunk. Her clothes. She ran to help.

"Are you smuggling trees from the Northwoods?" he gasped. He dropped the trunk and fell on it, winded.

"Of course not, silly. They would have talked to you if I had."

"True." As a tree shepherd and Lord of the Dread Forest, their elven home in the Oregon woodlands, Dad spoke to trees all the time. The elves had been surprised and unhappy to discover that even though she was part human, Keelie was also a tree shepherd. Of course, the whole elves-are-real thing had been a shocker for Keelie. Mom had never said a word about it. She had kept lots of other secrets, too.

"I'm going to make one more trip, and then I'm done for the night. Leave the candle on the table and blow the others out." Dad kissed Keelie on the forehead, careful to stay away from the goblin. "I love you, daughter. Get some sleep."

"I was hoping to catch a bite to eat with Sean at the Poacher's Inn. Want to come?"

"No thanks. I'm going to talk with Davey, but stop by Janice's shop. Raven is here."

Janice ran Green Lady Herbs, and Keelie had met her last summer. Janice and Dad dated sometimes, which Keelie found very creepy even though she knew it was natural. Raven was Janice's daughter and Keelie's friend. They'd only been able to exchange emails over the past year, since, when Raven joined her mother at the Wildewood Faire in New York, she'd stayed there—permanently. It's not every day a girl finds out she's the intended mate of the Unicorn Lord of the Forest.

"I will definitely stop by and pick up Raven." Happiness surged through Keelie at the thought of having a friend here. She hadn't realized how much she missed female companionship.

Keelie suddenly felt the need to hug Dad and wrapped her arms around him, squeezing. He didn't seem surprised, and he held her for a long moment.

"Missing your mom?" he said softly.

"Yes. But I'm okay, really. It's just being back here." She waved her arms around to include the room, the faire outside, all of Colorado.

"I figured. Hey, your overnight bag is in the trunk. I didn't want to balance it on top." He turned and walked to the door.

"Say hello to Sir Davey for me. I'll see him tomorrow." Keelie smiled and waved him off. Sir Davey was her father's best friend, and one of hers too. At three feet tall, Sir Davey was as diminutive as he was handsome, and a master swordsman as well as a geological expert. And, as one of the ancient race of dwarves, he was an expert wielder of Earth magic.

"You bet." Dad closed the door behind him and went downstairs humming an Irish tune, probably one that had been playing in the campground.

As she turned off the water in the big tub (still cold), Keelie wished she could grab a hot shower in Sir Davey's RV. She was heading toward the kitchen to shut off the water there, too, when a pebble hit her arm. "Ow!"

"Sorry," a voice called up from the clearing below. "Thought the window was closed. Can I come up?"

She went to the window, still rubbing her arm, and her eyes met the rueful gaze of a tall, wide-shouldered boy with blond surfer looks that seemed out of place in this medieval fairy-tale land. But he belonged here, more than she did in the opinion of some. A full-blooded elf, Sean o' the Wood was the head of the Silver Bough Jousters. Better yet, he was Keelie's boyfriend.

"Dad's gone back to the campground. I'll come down." Keelie didn't have a problem asking Sean up, but Ren Faire gossip was worse than the gossip in small towns.

She put Cricket on the ground, skipped down the wooden steps, and flung herself into Sean's arms. He held her off the ground and kissed her deeply before setting her on her feet again.

"Ready to go? I'm starved."

"Raven's here. Can we stop by Janice's to see if she wants to join us?"

"Sure. Raven is fun."

They held hands as they crossed the clearing. Keelie felt flushed and happy to be with Sean. Their relationship had been rocky at times, but she'd recently discovered an answer to a troubling question about her future, so she felt that nothing could come between them now.

Okay, so she was sixteen, and though Sean looked about nineteen, he was actually eighty-six. But he'd looked like this for most of his very long life, and, as Keelie had found out on her recent trip to the Northwoods, she too would live an elven lifespan—six or seven hundred years. With that much time ahead of her, there was no rush to do anything.

At the Green Lady Herb shop, light glimmered from the windows in back. Keelie and Sean walked around to where a small stone patio held two chairs and a worn bistro table. Potted plants were everywhere, and the stimulating green smell of the growing herbs energized Keelie. She knocked on the back door as Sean hung back to avoid crowding the little space.

Janice opened the door, brows raised in inquiry, then immediately grinned.

"Keelie! Oh, honey, you've grown."

Keelie hugged her. "Thanks." Why did adults always say that? She hadn't gotten any taller.

A whoop sounded from the dim interior and Raven appeared, black curls twining over her shoulders, skin glowing pale.

"Keelie!" She pulled Keelie from her mother's arms and they danced a fast whirl of welcome that spun them out the door and onto the patio.

"And Sean!" Raven grinned at him. "I hear you went on a heroic mission to the North Pole."

"Not that far north," Sean admitted. "But close."

Raven hooked an arm around Keelie's neck. "I've missed you so much. Hubby fills me in on all of your adventures. Giant trees, goblins, the fairy High Court. You don't rest, do you?"

Keelie shrugged. "If I stop, Lord Elianard stacks the homework even higher—may as well stay busy," she joked. "It was kind of scary at times, though."

Raven's smile faded. "I'll bet." Elianard's name had probably reminded her of his attempt to steal the horn of the Wildewood unicorn, now her husband. "How is old Elianard, anyway? I noticed that his snooty daughter isn't lording it over the girls in the court this year."

Sean cleared his throat. "Lady Elia is close to term, expecting her first child." Keelie heard the note of wonder in his voice. Births were rare among the elves, who considered themselves a dying race, but Elia had gotten pregnant right after her marriage, giving elves all over the world hope for their future.

"Fab." Raven didn't seem excited at the thought of a mini Elia. "Want to come in and sit down? Cramped quarters, but I can put the kettle on for tea."

"We're headed to the Poacher's Inn for dinner and thought you might want to come along," Keelie said.

She hadn't finished speaking the words before Raven vanished inside, returning with a black denim jacket.

"Headed to the inn for dinner, Mom," she called. "Bring you back something?"

Janice's voice drifted back from the front of the store. "No thanks, hon. Be careful."

Raven closed the door. "Mom's been getting a strange vibe from your new neighbor. Have you met Hob?"

"Not yet. We just got here."

"Hob the Hottie we call him." Raven laughed as Sean growled at her words.

The three friends swapped stories as they headed toward the Poacher's Inn, which sat on the shores of a little lake used for pirate battles. Its broad decks provided a great view of the watery hilarity. At this hour, the boats were tied up, oars in racks, and fiddle music wafted through the air, adding extra sparkle to the golden glow from the inn's windows.

Except for crickets and the neighs of horses from Equus Island, where the elven stables were, the music was the only sound tonight.

Keelie cherished this quiet moment, walking with friends, the sounds of the night around her. It was peaceful, and she hadn't had much peace lately.

Sean pulled open the door to the inn and all peace vanished in a blast of rowdy laughter, drums, and bagpipes. The fiddle they'd heard must have been somewhere on the faire grounds, because it would have been inaudible in this racket.

Keelie and Raven shared a grin and waded into the crowd of Rennie revelers. A curving sweep of bar had been added along the wall facing the lake, and it was full, as were the tables that filled the floor space.

"I'll find us a table." Sean had to almost shout to be heard over the din of voices and music.

Raven dragged Keelie to a table where a group of girls were laughing as one of them tried to meld belly dance with a Highland fling.

"Guys, do you know Keelie Heartwood?"

The girls turned to them with smiles and Raven introduced them. The three closest were Marcia, Lily, and Tracy.

"Fairies," Raven said, rolling her eyes.

The three giggled.

"Wait till you see our wings. Glittery," Tracy said. "I play Lavender Lollipop."

Keelie thanked the Great Sylvus that she'd never had to don wispy costumes and glittery face paint and pretend to be a fairy, though the girls seemed proud of their jobs at the faire.

"Your cat's here," Raven shouted in her ear. She pointed toward the bar, where a fat yellow tail hung down. The rest of Knot was obscured by a blond giant with long dreds and iridescent dragons tattooed on his mighty arm muscles.

"Who is *that*?"

Raven gave her a playful shove with her shoulder. "Vangar, your other new neighbor." She licked her lips. "If I weren't married..." Then she laughed. "Just kidding."

Vangar. A guy that big could not work in the mask shop, and those giant muscles seemed likely to be the result of much hammer-wielding, so he must own the forge. Keelie congratulated herself on her brilliant deduction.

"Your other new neighbor, if you can drag your eyes away from mighty Thor, is Hob the Hottie, the mask maker. He's over there with his fan-tourage."

A dark-haired, handsome man was speaking to a group of women who seemed to be enchanted by his words. This was the guy that gave Janice a "strange vibe"? He seemed pretty normal.

"Add your dad to the mix, and your hill is the place to be. You can look forward to lots of low-cut bodices and hip-waggling action in front of Heartwood," Raven said, laughing, no doubt at the dismay Keelie was sure was plastered on her face.

Sean waved his arms and Keelie led the way to a table by the bar. From here she had a great view of Knot, who was listening intently to Vangar, a shot glass of golden liquid in front of him.

"Does your cat drink Scotch?" Sean's tone implied that he'd believe it.

"Oh no. Strictly mead." Keelie watched as the bartender poured more of the thick, sweet liquid into Knot's and Vangar's glasses. Vangar touched his glass to Knot's and the two drank.

Keelie wondered what Knot's toast would be. "To many mice," perhaps, or "Capture a *bhata* and shred it for luck." He didn't get along with the little sticklike fairies. Luckily, unlike mice, the *bhata* could rebuild their bodies out of found materials.

A platter mounded with grilled chicken, vegetables, and brown rice appeared on the table and the three of them dug in, enjoying the antics of their fellow faire workers. Performers of all types took turns on the tiny stage, playing everything from fiddles and Celtic harps to spoons and buckets.

At midnight the cook chased everyone out, claiming that whoever stayed had to clean up for the next day. Keelie found herself on the road again, arm around Sean's waist, as Raven told them about life with a husband who turned into a unicorn part-time. It reminded Keelie that Raven had some fairy blood, and she might need to use any skills that came with that.

"Would you like to come to the meadow with me tomorrow morning?" she asked.

"Sure," Raven said. She had her head thrown back and was staring at the stars as she walked. "What time? And why?"

"After breakfast. And why—well, because of the goblin blood that was shed there." She didn't add, *because I killed a Red Cap*. Raven knew.

"So you want to see if the taint is still there, in the soil?"

"Yes."

"Do you think it's safe to go there?" Sean's smile had vanished.

"Probably. It's the tree I planted that I'm worried about."

Raven pushed back her black curls. "Okay, sure. Come by the shop and get me."

Sean's teeth flashed in a moonlit grin. "Have fun revisiting the scene of your glorious and victorious battle."

Was he being a jerk on purpose? Keelie decided to laugh it off. She pretended to shudder. "Scariest day of my life. No wait, that was in New York, when the trees went crazy. No no, that would be in California, when the Redwoods kidnapped my grandmother. Or maybe—"

Raven laughed. "I get it. Life as an elf is crazy." They'd arrived at Green Lady Herbs. She waved good night and disappeared around the back of the building.

"Elf lives don't seem to be crazy for everyone. Just my family," Keelie said glumly to Sean. "We seem to attract trouble."

"We?" Sean looked around. "I see no one else. You're the one that draws trouble like a flame draws moths. It's all that power."

Keelie held out her hands and looked at her fingers, slim and pale. Kind of puny-looking, actually. "I don't feel powerful."

"And yet you are. You've always had the power to solve problems, and that's put you in great danger. It attracts formidable beings. But I want you to know I'll always have your back and protect you."

"Sean." Keelie detected fear emanating from him, and she wanted to reassure him she could take care of herself.

"We'll talk later." He kissed her lightly on the forehead. "What do the trees tell you now, Keelie?"

She closed her eyes and lifted her face to the pine-scented air. "They're grumbling about the parking in the campground. And someone has an open fire. Dad heard. He's taking care of it." She opened her eyes and smiled at Sean. "Elf girls can be normal, right?"

"Most elf girls don't talk to trees."

A *feithid daoine*, a fairy shaped like a black beetle, droned by and squeaked a greeting, which Keelie returned.

"Most elf girls don't talk to bugs."

"It was a fairy."

"Elves can't see fairies." He looked serious now. "It looked like a bug."

"But I'm part fairy." Keelie counted off on her fingers. "And part elf. And part human. I'm a total mongrel." She sighed.

The grim look vanished and Sean smiled his brightest. "*My* mongrel." He leaned forward, eyes on her mouth again, and she jumped away. She didn't need the trees to tell her that another scorching kiss and she'd be asking him upstairs for more. Bright yellow eyes were watching her from the upstairs window, another reason not to invite him up.

"I plan to get up early tomorrow," she said, edging toward the stairs. "Want to have breakfast at Mrs. Butters'?"

"Sure. Six thirty?"

She gulped. She was thinking "early" meant eight. "Okay. Six thirty it is. Good night, Sean."

"Good night, Keelie. And I forgot to tell you—we have a new faire administrator, and she's supposed to be making rounds tomorrow."

Keelie shrugged. "Dad's got everything in order, I'm

sure. I'm just anxious to get to the meadow to make sure everything's okay."

◆ ◆ ◆

Keelie awoke in the dark before dawn, with the sky turning lighter to the east. She opened her eyes and took in the sleepy, early morning sounds of the faire. Murmurs and doors opening and shutting. Later would come the hammering, and voices, and laughter.

"Ah, my sleepyhead is up." Dad, brown hair loose and curling over his shoulders, pushed aside the bedroom curtain and set a steaming mug of tea on the nightstand by her bed (cypress, from Florida).

He was in Ren Faire mode all right. Usually he had his hair in a loose ponytail that hid his pointed elven ears.

"Dad, did Knot come home with you? I haven't seen him at all. "

"He's around. He was sleeping at the foot of your bed when I got home." Dad pulled the curtain shut so that she would have privacy as she dressed.

Keelie sat up and reached for the mug, looking around the area that was her bedroom. The sun's first rays shone against the many-paned windows, illuminating the wooden wardrobe, her battered Wellingtons, the trunk of clothes Dad had brought from the Dread Forest. The thick leather Elven Compendium of Household Charms lay on top, a dozen colorful sticky notes protruding from its pages, her massive and never-ending homework assignment.

She wondered where Knot had gone. Cricket was nowhere to be seen, either. He didn't get along with Knot and was probably hiding somewhere, chewing on a plastic bottle. Goblins ate paper and plastic, which was why cities were infested with them. During their brief layover in the Dread Forest, Grandmother Keliatiel had compared Cricket to a cockroach and offered to stomp it.

Keelie had to scramble to keep the little guy safe, although Grandmother's cockroach analogy had given her pause. Would she have kept a roach as a pet? Yuck.

She also didn't understand why she was missing Knot-the-obnoxious-feline when he wasn't around. She hoped it wasn't backwash from the spell they'd put on the Redwood Forest sign in California. One of Knot's bits of furry orange fluff had fallen in at the last second, and the spell-cast compulsion to love and respect the forest now included the love of cats, too.

More likely, she missed him because he was always around—as her appointed fairy guardian.

"Garb today, or jeans?" she asked loudly. "Garb" was the faire folks' word for "costume," and at the Ren Faire some people lived and breathed earlier times. Others donned jeans at the end of the day. The High Mountain Faire always had a pirate theme, and Keelie was looking forward to being all piratey. Last year she hadn't known anything about faire life and missed out on a lot of fun.

"Jeans are okay," Dad replied. "Did you see that Galadriel's Closet moved?"

Keelie jumped out of bed and pulled the curtain aside.

"Yes! I saw the mask shop and the new forge, too. I was surprised to see a forge up here."

Dad, busy in the kitchen, frowned. "We've been assured the fire source is not a concern. And you're going to like Hobknocker's. I've heard Hob is quite the ladies' man."

"I saw him last night at the Poacher's Inn, surrounded by ladies. Two of you in one clearing. Chick Magnet Central."

Dad smiled and ruffled her hair.

"Where is Galadriel's Closet now? I want to get a pirate-wench corset." Keelie took a sip of the tea and curled her toes with pleasure.

"They're at the front gate. You should go down and say hello to Mara. They decided to rent costumes to mundanes, like that shop at the Wildewood Faire does." The kitchen was so small that Dad was almost at arm's reach from her bed as he assembled the supplies for a pot of oatmeal. The man lived off the stuff, though Keelie had to admit that the way he fixed it was very tasty.

"I promised Sean I'd meet him for breakfast, so don't make any for me," she said.

"Knot will eat your share." Dad eyeballed the water level in the pot and turned up the flame. "I haven't seen him around, but he'll enjoy it even if it's cold."

"You know, I never got to see all of Wildewood," Keelie said. "Between my hideous dragon costume and the faire shutting down early when the forest went nuts and the power plant exploded, it wasn't the best experience." She grabbed her third-best pair of jeans from the trunk, along with a T-shirt printed with cartoon-like panda bears.

"We'll be there in a few weeks." Dad's voice was a pleasant rumble. "You'll get a better look this time."

Keelie flipped her curtain shut and yanked on her clothes, then rummaged under the bed for her shoes. Yesterday's socks were hanging out of them and she jammed them onto her feet. Showers and clean clothes later—first, she'd go meet Sean, and then pick up Raven to head to the meadow.

"Don't make plans to be out late tonight," Dad called. "You'll have an early start tomorrow. I heard the new admin wants us to rehearse the royal parade, and then the pirate's parade. And I may be busy because I have to meet a tow truck driver in the campground. Someone noticed a big puddle of oil under the pickup truck's engine."

"Oh my." Keelie fought a grin. She knew it was serious and possibly very expensive to have car trouble, but the thought of a tow truck dragging the Swiss Miss Chalet—their tiny, gingerbread-festooned house perched on the bed of Dad's aged pickup—down the road was hilarious.

She stepped past her curtain and pulled it closed behind her, enjoying the familiar rattle of its wooden rings. "I think I might go down to the meadow this morning," she said casually. "I want to check out where the Red Cap died."

Dad filled in what she hadn't said. "Because of the blood in the ground? There's nothing around there that could be harmed by the taint."

Keelie knew he was worried, though, because suddenly he was stirring the oats on the stove much faster. She bit her lip and hurried to the bathroom, shielding her mind because sometimes Dad could read every thought as it scrolled through her brain.

"Why don't you take Lord Elianard with you?" he called. "He's anxious to get started with your lore lessons again, and he can check if the goblin taint might be threatening the elven village."

"Maybe." She could sense the spread of the goblin's toxic magic herself.

She did need to see Elianard sometime, though. Keelie thought of the enormous Compendium, which was basically a magical recipe book containing the collected spells and charms of generations of Dread Forest elves (they really needed to get it online). She would study it later.

Elianard would surely give her a huge lore lesson if he knew she'd planted an aspen branch right in the center of the disturbed earth where the evil Red Cap had died. The branch had immediately put out a leaf, and Keelie hoped it would thrive, but just this spring she'd learned a lot about what goblin blood could do to trees. If the little sapling was still alive, its roots would have drunk deep of the evil goblin's blood—blood spilled by Keelie when she'd called up the combination of tree and Earth magic that had blasted the evil creature to fragments.

She was glad Raven would be there with her. She didn't want to return to the site of her battle alone.

two

"Okay, Dad, I'm headed to Mrs. Butters'." Keelie kissed her father goodbye and trotted down the stairs. She started across the clearing toward the path down the hill.

A door closed nearby. "Hey, neighbor!"

She turned to see Hob walking toward her. He was even better-looking in the daylight.

He grinned at her. "Heading my way? If I don't get a muffin in the next ten minutes, I'm going to eat a squirrel."

Keelie laughed, and as they walked together down the hill, she couldn't help wishing that all the mean elf girls could see her walking with this studly specimen.

"I can't wait to see your shop," she told him.

"Come by any time." He shrugged. "My wares are not the caliber of your father's, but they're amusing."

"Lots of people like masks and disguises."

He looked a little startled, but then his smile broadened. "They do indeed, if they have a mischievous streak."

"My cat should be your first customer, then." The thought of Knot in a mask was funny. In a creepy way.

"No pets allowed. But you can buy the kitty a toy if you wish." He bowed as they arrived at Mrs. Butters' tea shop and held her fingers to his lips. "Milady, have a lovely day."

"You don't know how nice it is to meet a normal person here. Thanks for walking me down." She curtseyed, and turned to see the women on the crowded deck of the tea shop assessing her. It made her day.

Take that, she told them silently, and went inside to get her tea.

Mrs. Butters' tea shop was already crowded, even though the morning was barely started. The tantalizing smell of fresh-baked goods made Keelie's stomach growl as she hopped onto the plain wooden deck that surrounded the little bakery. Sean leaned against the railing that ran along the back and sides of the deck, separating it from the forest. He was holding a mug and laughing with his jousting friends. They were all tall and muscular, but Sean was the best looking. Every female on the deck glanced at him, secretly enjoying his presence.

Keelie entered the little shop and waited while one of the burlap-and-leather-clad mud men ordered his breakfast. Mrs. Butters' little brown face, like a living version of the gingerbread man's wife, split into a smile when she noticed Keelie, and she placed a utilitarian white mug of hot water on the counter. Keelie put a dollar down and edged past the mud man to choose a tea bag from the assortment in a basket at the end of the counter. Today seemed like a "Sweet Orange" day. She tore the top of the little square paper pouch and tossed it into the recycling bin, then dunked her tea bag in the hot water and went to join Sean.

The jousters greeted her like an old friend. Since she'd spent the winter in the Dread Forest, they were as old as any other friends she had—with the exception of Laurie, who still lived in L.A. near where Mom's house had been.

Keelie felt envious glares bounce off her back as Sean leaned over to kiss her. "Hope you didn't buy any food," he said. "We ordered extra muffins."

Keelie examined the picked-over plate and chose what was left of a bran muffin. Breakfast with Sean had sounded romantic, but she hadn't counted on the rest of the jousting team. After a few minutes of listening to their jokes and stories, she excused herself.

"Don't leave yet. Are you coming to the practice this afternoon?" Sean put an arm around her waist and pulled her to him. He felt strong and safe, and she wished he could come with her to the meadow.

"I'll be fine," she said. "See you tonight."

He placed a soft kiss on her rounded human ear, and she felt her other ear blush red all the way to its elven tip.

Mrs. Butters waved as she jumped off the deck and

headed toward the meadow. Before Keelie even got to the pony ride area, she saw Raven striding toward her, wearing jeans, soft tall boots, and two layered tank tops, the top one featuring a unicorn head.

"Ready to return to the scene of the crime?" Raven squeezed Keelie's arm.

"Thanks for doing this." Keelie didn't want to admit that she was feeling apprehensive.

Raven waved at the folks still lingering at Mrs. Butters'. Sean was gone, but some of his guys were still finishing their breakfast, joined now by girls who this weekend would probably be dressed up as fairies and princesses.

They went through the gate to the meadow and down the wide, unpaved path. The meadow was dotted with a few trees, and on the far side was the forest where the elven village was located. Keelie had never felt welcome there—even though she'd now mastered the Dread, the elven spell that made humans fearful and back away from the woods, not knowing why they didn't dare go in. She fingered the rose quartz keychain clipped to her belt loop, then pulled out her extra one and offered it to Raven. "You might need this."

"Thanks," Raven said. "Einhorn and I have been talking about adding the Dread to the Wildewood Forest. I'm not sure we need it, but you can understand why he's a little paranoid about keeping it safe, now that the trees have recovered."

Keelie quickly briefed Raven on Sir Davey's Earth magic lesson about how to keep the Dread from overwhelming her by using the rose quartz. It had been a life saver for her, literally.

"When we're done with the treeling, can we go up the lane to the bridge?" she asked Raven. "I want to see if the water sprite is still there."

"Sure." Raven laughed. "You know, I always thought Water Sprite Lane was named that because it sounded medieval, not because there's a real sprite."

The sprite had helped Keelie during the Red Cap's attack, and she recalled her shock when she'd first seen the little creature's fish-like face. She'd certainly seen stranger things since then ... she'd even befriended another sprite back home in the Dread Forest.

Ahead, she saw the tall aspen that spread its branches over the center of the meadow. Keelie ran to him. *Hrok, I'm back.*

Greetings, Tree Talker. The forest sings of your return.

The tree's face pushed up through its bark, and Keelie once more saw Hrok's handsome features. Inexplicable tears choked her. She hugged the tree and kissed his bark-covered cheek. Raven stood nearby, watching. Keelie couldn't tell if her friend could see the tree's face. Although Raven's drop of fae blood allowed her to feel magic, Keelie didn't think it extended to the tree spirits.

She focused her tree speak so that only Hrok, not the other trees, could hear her. *I came to say hi, and to check on ... that place. How is the sapling doing?* She glanced at a tiny tree that grew between Hrok and a great boulder. No grass grew beneath it, although the rest of the meadow was green. Raven headed toward it.

Greetings, Tree Shepherdess. The treeling does not thrive as we had hoped. The bitterness of the goblin's blood has tainted its rings. You have changed since you were last here, Keliel Tree Talker. You have grown in power. Hrok seemed pleased.

A shriek split the air, heard only by Keelie and the fae who suddenly abandoned their bushes and hidey-holes to fly into the air—a humming, droning cloud of sticks and buglike creatures. One of the *feithid daoine*, the bug fairies, tried to dig into her jeans pocket.

Keelie covered her ears and closed her eyes, as if that would help deflect the piercing sound that went on and on. After a moment she opened one eye and tried to find the source of the sound.

Raven was touching the treeling's leaves and examining its trunk. "This looks like a healthy sapling," she called back, oblivious to the din.

Keelie could barely hear her. She kept her hands over her ears, becoming accustomed to the brain-melting scream. It seemed to be coming from the little sprout of a tree that Raven was looking at.

Keelie marched up to the sapling, wary of the soil beneath her, although it felt normal. *What is your problem?* she asked the treeling.

The sound stopped, and the sudden silence was almost a sound as well. Keelie felt the young tree's confused and angry thoughts, and a pang of guilt went through her. She'd stuck a lifeless branch into what she'd thought was nourishing earth, unaware that the blood that soaked the soil was poisonous and alive with energy. The little twig had revived and grown, but he had sucked up the goblin blood to feed himself.

I'm Keliel, called Tree Talker, and I can help you, she said to him in tree speak. *Are you hurt?*

No, the treeling shouted. *I hate to be ignored. I can remember being powerful, but I'm not powerful now.*

That's because you were once part of the Queen Aspen, she who was central to many of the trees on this mountain. When she died, we had a Tree Lorem for her near here, and one of her branches was given to me. I planted it, and you came to life. You probably share memories with the Queen Aspen. Do you not see me in her memories?

Keelie felt the little tree pout, his anger deepening. "This is one furious tree," she said aloud.

Raven looked surprised. "Really?" She glanced around at the peaceful meadow. "Everything seems so normal now. What do you plan to do?"

Before Keelie could answer, a roar filled the air. This time Raven could hear it too.

The surrounding trees' leaves shook in consternation, and Keelie recognized the sound—a motorcycle. Weird. The folks who worked the faire were usually very good about keeping to the medieval theme and not bringing in mundane sounds that would break the faire's ambiance.

The motorcycle zoomed up from the players' campground, roared onto the path that crossed the meadow, and zipped past before Keelie could do more than frown.

In a second, it had crossed the bridge and disappeared into the woods at the crest of the hill.

"Who was that idiot?" Raven frowned. "If the faire admin catches him, he'll be toast."

Keelie didn't answer. She was busy casting mental feelers around, calming the trees that bordered the meadow. With the Dread firmly in place, they hardly ever saw humans up close. Keelie turned to stare up the hill, at the woods shielding that entrance to the faire. Something about the biker had been a little inhuman, but she didn't know what. She turned back to the young tree.

I'm going to replant you. Pick any spot in the forest, and I'll move you there. What do you think of that?

She felt the trees' disapproval all around her. They didn't care for the bratty twig, but still, her offer seemed high-handed to them. A person did not ever offer to move a tree—trees were forever. People, even long-lived elves, were just a sneeze in the cosmic nostril.

Keelie remembered how pleased she'd been when the branch she'd jammed into the churned earth had immediately sprouted that leaf. She felt she'd given new life to the Queen Aspen, and then she'd left with her father on her own new path.

She turned to Hrok. *I'm sorry. I didn't know what goblin blood could do when I planted the treeling. I only meant to give you a companion. But our elven charm book may suggest a way for me to counteract the evil effects of the Red Cap's blood.*

Then consult your wise book. Hrok gave a green, breezy sigh. *I have tried to like the twig. I really have.*

Keelie stared at the belligerent sapling. *I hope I can help.* She hugged Hrok, not sure if her tree friend really understood human hugs, and pulled Raven back toward the path.

"The trees aren't loving that little guy. I wonder if your mom might know some herbal remedy for his anxiety?"

Raven shrugged. "She knows a lot, though she's no tree psychologist. I'll bet if you tell her what the symptoms are, and what results you want, she might be able to put something together."

"I hope so." Keelie's other option was the Compendium, and though she hated to bother her dad when he was busy setting up Heartwood, he needed to know what was happening in the meadow. After their experience in the Redwood Forest, the presence of a goblin-tainted tree at this faire would be scary enough to bring him running.

Dad? We have to move that aspen sapling I planted where the Red Cap died. I'm getting bad vibes from it. She let him see the treeling and its surroundings.

Her father's thoughts were momentarily visible to her as she connected with his mind, and she saw a file, a bowl of oil, and a neat array of carving implements. Dad was sharpening his tools.

I'll come and see for myself, but I trust your judgment. I'll get some help to dig it up. Maybe we can plant it by the shop later, where we can keep an eye on it.

She communicated that this was a great idea, then told

Hrok and Raven the plan. The two girls continued on toward the bridge.

"So, you don't know who that motorcyclist was?" Keelie asked. Raven had looked as annoyed by the noise as she'd been. The faire folk were probably buzzing about it.

"No. Plenty of the folk are bikers, but they keep their bikes in the campground."

When she reached the middle of the bridge, Keelie stopped. Raven watched curiously as she leaned over the railing and called, "Hello? Anyone down there? I've met another sprite. Her name is Plu. What's your name?"

The water below gurgled between the rocks, but aside from the quiet murmur of the trees, there was no other sound.

A discordant jangle stopped Keelie's feet as she was about to step off the bridge. She knew that sound. It wasn't the sprite, and it was no cowbell either. It was the sound of the bells that Peascod the jester wore on his hat. Peascod, who had served Herne the Hunter, dark lord of the hunt, then had betrayed him. Peascod the goblin baiter. Peascod, who had almost killed her.

"Did you hear that?"

"Hear what?"

"Jester bells." Keelie shuddered.

Raven's eyebrows rose. "Keelie, we're at a Renaissance Faire. If you freak out at jester bells, you need to find a nice mall job. What next? Fear of turkey legs or archers?"

Suddenly the bridge was humming with twiggy curses and Knot appeared, a smear of orange as he streaked toward them, *bhata* clinging to his fur. He looked like a frightened porcupine.

"Knot, come here." Keelie didn't care for the squeaky thread of fear in her voice. She cleared her throat and tried for a lower timbre. "Knot, leave the *bhata* alone."

Beside her, Raven was doubled over with laughter. "He can't resist trying to annoy the fae. He deserves whatever he gets."

Keelie tried to pick the fairies off Knot as he staggered past, but he hissed and she drew back. He bolted into the meadow, looped around Hrok, and headed back toward the gate.

"Whatever." The morning was full of grumps, both cat and tree. She hoped the people she ran into would be more pleasant. How could anyone be upset on such a beautiful morning? Despite the treeling's bad manners, she was back at the High Mountain Faire, the sky was blue, and the stream gurgled romantically. Maybe Sean would forget his beloved jousting later on and take a break to stroll with her.

They headed up the hill to the faire, saying hi to old friends as they passed the shops. At Janice's, a gangly boy in black leggings and a long-sleeved tunic sat outside in a folding chair.

"Who are you?" Raven parked her fists on her hips and stared at the boy.

The kid ignored her. "The new faire administrator is inside. Inspection day for Green Lady Herbs." He laughed rudely. Keelie's skin prickled in premonition.

"I'll see what's going on," Raven said. "See you later."

"Yeah, thanks for coming along." Keelie had been glad for Raven's company even if her friend couldn't hear trees. She turned to leave.

Janice dashed out of her shop, clutched her cap over her head, leaned backward, and gave a long silent scream. Then she ran back inside choking out the words, "Faire admin."

Knot yowled.

"The day is getting stranger by the minute, Knot."

A woman dressed in colorful skirts and scarves stepped past Keelie and pushed the shop door open a crack. "All quiet," she hissed over her shoulder. Keelie recognized her as Sally, the tarot card reader whose popular shop was by the front entrance.

She also noticed that a crowd had gathered.

"Everyone's getting inspected this year," one grizzled man said. Keelie remembered that he'd been a pirate the year before. Then all voices stopped as a familiar female voice rose in anger.

"I don't have time for your petty problems. We have to have the faire in order. I asked for an inventory. I get a scribbled sheet. Who are you, Leonardo? Is this a secret code?" The tirade grew louder, and the voice more familiar.

"The new faire admin," whispered the old pirate.

No... Keelie thought desperately. There were three Ren Faires in Colorado—no way she could be so unlucky.

The door to Janice's shop banged open. Janice charged out, red-faced, her hair in wisps around her face, her cap gone. Close behind was the faire's new administrator.

This was much worse than goblins.

Keelie staggered as the crowd shifted to allow Janice to pass. She strode rapidly up the path. Keelie watched her go, then turned to face her fire-breathing nemesis.

The new faire administrator was in fact her old boss from the Wildewood. Finch.

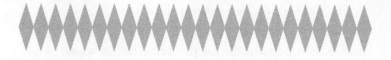

three

Keelie's feet solidified on the ground, goose bumps of fear adding a physical element to her mind's conclusion: *Run. Run as fast as you can.*

Sylvus help them all.

The fairy girls she'd met at the pub were hovering at the corner of Janice's shop, their faces frozen in fear. It was as if they'd seen one of the four horsemen of the apocalypse strolling through, searching for its next victim.

Before Keelie could bolt, Finch sighted her. She stopped and pointed. "You. Heartwood. Walk with me." She turned to the boy and held out a sheaf of papers. "You, kid, take these to my office."

The boy frowned. "I'm Eric the Bold."

"You'll be Eric the Bald if you don't hurry."

The boy raced away, papers under his arm.

"Don't dawdle, Heartwood." Finch marched up the path.

"Okay," Keelie managed to squeak.

Sympathy flickered in Raven's eyes. "Good luck," she mouthed. "I need to go and help Mom." She hurried away as if her pants were on fire.

Two fencing instructors, walking with a trio of belly dancers, darted to the side when Finch passed them in a blazing fury. "There is no fraternizing on my watch! Less cleavage, ladies," Finch yelled as she passed them. "Heartwood, keep up."

Keelie scurried to Finch's side.

"I'm going to bloody kill whoever dared bring a motorcycle *into* the faire." Finch came to a sudden stop in the middle of Ironmonger's Way, then whirled around to glare at Keelie. "Do you know what the penalty is for bringing machinery into the faire?" She lowered her voice, as if it hurt her to say the words, and pounded her fist into her hands.

Keelie shook her head.

"Death." Pivoting on her leather-clad boots, Finch strode determinedly toward her victim.

Keelie didn't know whether to take this opportunity to run to Heartwood and stay there until the end of the faire, or to follow Finch. She didn't want to witness what the faire administrator was about to do.

"Heartwood. Move it."

No choice in the matter. Keelie ran after Finch. She had to jog to keep up—the woman could cover a lot of ground in a short time. Keelie kept an eye on Finch's fists, which kept opening and closing as she stormed up the path. Booth owners paled as if a demon had erupted from the bowels of Hell and now walked among them, controlling their destinies.

A group of pirates in full garb stood outside the pottery booth, where they were teasing a new belly dancer who needed to rethink her attire. Keelie grimaced as she anticipated Finch's reaction to the large sparkly green halter top, cleavage overflowing and on the verge of spilling out.

But Finch veered off the path. They were going to cut through the woods. The trees tapped into Keelie's mind, their speech hivelike. *Who is this woman with the flaming hair?* They sent a rush of green energy to Keelie, and she sent them reassurance. She didn't need freaked-out trees scaring the rest of the forest as she tried to keep pace with the draconic faire director.

Behind her, she heard jingling belly dance scarves, stomping feet, and occasional murmurs. Glancing over her shoulder, she discovered that the now eerily quiet crowd of pirates, belly dancers, and other faire workers was following them, flitting between the trees, hurrying to stay close. Most of them wore frightened expressions, but still they followed, swept along by macabre curiosity. There was nothing like a possible murder to brighten up the day.

They left the leafy woods path and stepped out into the hilltop clearing. The shop that had once been Galadriel's Closet bore a rustic sign that proclaimed it to be the Flames and Skulls Forge, and in front of it was parked the largest, most beastly looking motorcycle Keelie had ever seen in her life.

It was shiny, covered in chrome, with gargoyle heads sculpted along the front of the handle bars and metallic ribs that formed a funky-looking frame. The midnight-black gas tank sported an airbrushed red dragon flying over a burning building. The motorcycle was as tall as Keelie. No wonder everyone had heard it roaring into the faire.

Finch growled. Keelie thought she saw small tendrils of smoke trailing from the faire administrator's ears. Finch's mother, Ermentrude, had a problem with smoking; she'd taken up knitting as a way of controlling her cravings. But knitting and Finch wouldn't go together—yarn was too combustible.

The scent of smoke and metal wafted in the air as the crowd of followers trooped into the clearing. The silence was suddenly broken by the clanging of metal on metal. Under the forge's shed roof, a broad-shouldered silhouette hammered over glowing coals.

Keelie saw Dad stop at the edge of the Heartwood shop, a rag tossed over his shoulder. She should be helping him polish furniture. He hadn't spotted her. His eyes were on the forge, and on the angry faire administrator who looked as if she was about to change into a dragon and flame the place.

Hob came out of the mask shop and joined Dad. He looked even more handsome than before, if that was possible, and his blue eyes sparkled with mischief as he eyed the scene, seemingly pleased by the crowd. Then his gaze caught Keelie's and he bowed his head slightly. She nodded in return.

"That's a really big motorcycle," Finch growled, although Keelie thought she heard a hint of admiration in her voice.

"And that's a really big guy," Keelie said, eyeing the figure in the forge.

The clearing rang with metallic peals as the smith picked up the pace of his hammering.

"Yeah! I'll be able to take him." Finch said to herself, as if readying for a challenge.

"Are you going to fight him?" Keelie asked. The crowd pressed closer.

Finch's answer was a growled cry that sounded like a cross between an elephant and a wolf with a twist of dinosaur thrown in.

The clanging stopped, and a shadow stretched out from behind the Flames and Skulls. Keelie saw Vangar, the wild man from the Poacher's Inn.

Today Vangar was bare-chested and wearing thick leather pants and boots fastened with rows of metal clasps. He carried a double-headed hammer marked with runic symbols, which he spun like a baton twirler in an impressive display of strength and dexterity as he approached Keelie and Finch. Keelie stepped back. But Finch stared the giant down until he grunted, dropped the hammer head to the ground, and leaned on the handle.

"Is this the welcoming committee?" Vangar's voice was deep and rumbly like a volcano. His gaze swept over the crowd but settled on Keelie. She stepped backward trying to disappear. He'd know soon enough that she was his next-door neighbor.

Finch snapped her fingers. "Heartwood, now." She pointed to the spot beside her.

So much for escaping. Keelie stepped forward.

Finch's hair curled in tendrils as sweat dripped from her neck and forehead. Keelie wondered what that meant for dragons. She figured Vangar was sweating because of his hot work in the forge, since the day was still cool.

Finch gestured to the motorcycle. "What were you thinking? Do you need to be taught the rules?"

"Darling, don't be so uptight." The blacksmith smiled, looking her up and down appreciatively. "You're a fiery wench."

Darling. Fiery Wench. Keelie wondered if Vangar had a death wish or was just dumb. She was going to have to keep Finch calm. She didn't want the faire director transforming into a dragon in front of the human booth owners and faire workers. Some of them knew about the magical beings at the faire, but some didn't.

A wave of heat rolled over Keelie. It was like being on a hot asphalt parking lot in July, and it was coming from Finch. She gripped Keelie's upper arm tightly. Keelie winced but tried to give off soothing vibes, as if Finch were a tree.

Vangar smiled at Finch, revealing several gold teeth that matched his molten yellow eyes. "Darling, do I detect a temper?"

Finch squeezed Keelie's arm even tighter. She bit her tongue to keep from screaming in pain.

"Mundane vehicles aren't allowed on the fairground," Finch said between clenched teeth. Keelie was pretty sure that whatever was going on was not about the motorcycle. She'd seen Finch swear and yell, but the woman seemed to be trying to hold herself in check this time.

"Babe, it's a weekday, so what's the big friggin' deal? There're no mundanes around to see my motorcycle. You need to relax. Wanna go for a drink over at the Poacher's Inn?"

Finch turned several shades of crimson as she dug claw-like fingers into Keelie's biceps. Time to intercede before she lost her arm. "The shop owners aren't ever allowed to bring motorized vehicles into the fairegrounds," Keelie gasped.

"Hell, I'm at the back of the faire, so how am I supposed to haul my metal and other supplies to my forge? Get a mule?" Vangar turned his molten gold eyes on Finch.

"You weren't hauling materials on a motorcycle." Finch leaned forward, her eyes sparking. "Didn't you read the guidelines?"

There were whispered conversations going on behind Finch and Keelie. She caught snippets: "you know he's right"—"why can't we drive our vehicles onto the faire ground?"—"where can you get a mule?"

Finch whipped around and glared at the crowd, which immediately went silent. Her attention back on the blacksmith, Finch's eyes flashed angrily. "I need your promise that you won't do this again."

"I think you came for a ride." Vangar glowered at her, but Keelie thought she saw a hint of smile. The man was suicidal. "You'll need to ask nicely."

Finch raised her arched red eyebrows and laughed, a rusty sound. Keelie flinched. She's never heard Finch laugh.

Vangar stood tall, hand on his hammer. His lips curved up and he leaned forward. "You'll have to hang onto me."

"Not likely. I'm going to pull your contract, and believe me, I'll find something I can use to kick your leather-clad ass out of here." Finch's eyes narrowed.

"You'll find everything in order. There is nothing that can close down my forge," he answered confidently.

"I beg to differ," a voice proclaimed from the crowd. The girls around Keelie sighed as Hob pushed his way through until he stood by Finch and Keelie. He regarded the blacksmith, who was head and shoulders taller.

"I think if you have three or more shop owners complain about the forge, then a vote may be taken to release you from the contract." Hob spoke as if he were a lawyer.

"Aha!" Finch pointed at the blacksmith.

"I have concerns about the forge being so close to me." Hob gestured toward his shop with its flammable, papier-mâché masks. "What if it catches on fire? One random spark from the forge and I could lose everything."

Whispers erupted from the crowd.

Vangar strode over to Hob and glowered down at him. "My forge is safe. Be reassured, I use every precaution to keep the fire contained. If you would like to look at my safety record at other faires, I can provide them, along with references. I've never had any trouble with my fire." The blacksmith turned to the crowd. "Please, if you have any concerns, I can give each and every one a personal tour to calm your fears."

Finch relaxed her grip on Keelie, but when she attempted to pull away, the faire director tugged her back. She was stuck here, and whatever happened, she was going to be in the thick of it.

"So, that's two shop owners who are against you. Just one more"—Finch held up her index finger—"and you and your metal beast, and your fire, and your swords, are outta here."

"I know he has something against me," the blacksmith said, motioning with his chin at Hob, "But who else has lodged a complaint against me?"

Finch pushed Keelie in front of her. "Heartwood has."

Sacrifice the elf. Keelie stared at Finch, mouth open, though she shouldn't have been surprised.

"Hey, back off." Dad pushed through the crowd, his eyes blazing.

The blacksmith ignored him, squinted at Keelie, and shouldered his hammer. He lowered his face until his broken nose was inches from hers. "You have a problem with my forge, kid?"

Behind him, an oak tree shivered nervously as the hammer swung close. No one but Keelie noticed the tree raise its lower branches out of harm's way.

"No." Keelie forced the word out. "I only saw your shop last night."

Finch erupted angrily. "You do too."

Dad was suddenly there, glaring at Finch. "Do *not* use my child as a pawn in your game."

To Keelie's surprise, Finch was unable to meet Dad's gaze. "Maybe I was mistaken."

A familiar loud purring motored at Keelie's feet. Knot rubbed his head up and down her leg. Thank goodness he was here. He'd get her out of this. He'd claw the mean blacksmith.

Instead, Knot walked away and hopped onto the motorcycle. She cut her eyes over to him as he sat on the wide leather seat and began to wash his tail.

The jousters and elves had arrived and were gathered on the left edge of the crowd. Elianard frowned disapprovingly when his eyes made contact with hers.

Vangar noticed Knot on his bike. "Hey, there's my drinking buddy. You. Me. Down to the pub. I need a mead."

Knot meowed.

Vangar gave him a thumbs-up in agreement and turned back to Keelie. "So, kid, why are you and Hobknock in league with the administration?"

Hob scowled.

The blacksmith hefted his hammer and smacked it against his giant, callused palm. "At some of the faires I attend, when a shop owner sides with management, it's like turning against their kind—the other merchants."

Grumbles came from the crowd.

Keelie's cheeks burned red and she was beginning to understand how the French aristocrats felt during the revolution. "I didn't side with anyone."

Finch stepped on Keelie's foot. "Quit trying to incite the vendors against me. It won't work." Finch's voice had gone low and dangerous.

From the corner of her eye, Keelie saw Cricket crawling toward the elves. They frowned in disgust. A bit of paper stuck out of its mouth, probably a discarded napkin. The little goblin turned and made its way to Keelie.

Hob bowed his head. "G'day to all. I must tend to my business." And he wove his way back through the crowd. Some of the belly dancers squealed and jingled with delight.

Finch forced a smile. "Vangar, get your motorcycle out of the faire, and if you dare ride inside the premises again, I'll kick your ass through the front gate." She had a delighted gleam in her eyes. Keelie knew that despite her complaints, Finch thrived on conflict.

"I like a challenge," Vangar retorted. He leaned against a beech tree. Keelie saw the tree push its face out of the bark. It sniffed Vangar and then crinkled its barky face, as if it couldn't quite place what it was smelling.

"Me too," Finch raised her chin in answer to Vangar's declaration. She turned to the crowd. "If anyone else has a complaint about the blacksmith, then I will personally file it and you in the privies. I've had enough whining for one day." Everyone stared open-mouthed at Finch. She placed her hands on her hips. "Don't you people have things to do?" The crowd dispersed silently, hurrying back through the woods, back to their jobs, back to their shops.

Vangar walked over to Keelie. "You kept your cool. I like that. When you work with fire, it's an important attribute. If you need a job, I could use some help in the forge. I could train you."

"This is the last person that needs to be working with fire," Finch said with a panicked look. "She doesn't follow orders, and disaster follows her."

Although she felt insulted, Keelie didn't want to pass the insult on to Vangar. It would be better to take a lets-be-nice-to-the-neighbor approach. "Thanks! But I have a job with my Dad." She held out her hand. "I'm Keelie Heartwood, and Knot is my cat." She motioned toward the big orange furball who needed a lesson in loyalty.

"If you belong to Knot, then you're good people." A big grin broke out on Vangar's face, transforming him from scary giant to friendly troll.

"Meow." Knot hopped onto the motorcycle.

"Sorry, buddy, I can't take you for a ride like I promised."

Knot shot a baleful glare at Keelie as her goblin scuttled out into the open with a plastic bottle hanging from its mouth like a huge cigar. Keelie motioned for Cricket to come to her, but it seemed to be checking out Finch. It crawled toward her, shiny eyes fixed on the woman's boot buckles. Not good. Keelie bit her fist.

"Take the motorcycle and the cat to the performers' campground and leave them both there," Finch suggested, cutting her eyes over to the goblin, who offered her the plastic bottle.

Keelie wasn't surprised that Finch could see Cricket, unlike the humans here. Finch was a dragon, after all.

The goblin climbed up Finch's legs and moved his arms back and forth as if saying "hi."

"If you don't get this thing off of me, I'm going to roast it," Finch snapped, although she'd let Cricket climb up without complaint.

Keelie gently removed the little goblin and sat it on the ground, where it proceeded to munch on the plastic bottle, chewing busily.

"He eats plastic. Huh." Finch studied the goblin. "He can have a job in clean-up. Walk with me, Heartwood. We have things to discuss." She turned to Vangar. "You get this machine monstrosity out of here."

Vangar winked at Finch. "If that is your desire, I shall surely comply. But babe, I'm going to need to drive my motorcycle out of here. You gonna have a cow if I do?"

"If I have a cow, then I roast it and eat it," Finch said under her breath. She glanced at Keelie. So the faire admin knew Keelie was onto her secret.

Finch straightened. "You can drive it out," she said to Vangar, "but if I see it by the forge again, then it's going to be impounded for the duration of the faire."

"Well, I'll be. I'm growing on you." He flashed her a debonair smile.

Finch's face flushed red.

If Keelie didn't know any better, she'd think there was a thing going on between these two. She thought of her bruised arm. All that squeezing—maybe it was excitement, not anger, that Finch was feeling. She wondered what other ghastly and dangerous surprises awaited her in dragon courtship.

Vangar was looking at Finch through hooded eyes. "You're no longer threatening to kick me out. You're falling for my charm. Before this faire is over, you'll be wanting to date me."

Finch laughed, then wiped the tears that had squeezed from the corners of her eyes.

Vangar didn't seem insulted. "You'll see. No one can resist me."

"Always a first time." Finch grabbed Keelie by the arm and tugged her away.

"What was that about? I didn't say anything about protesting against the forge," Keelie hissed at her.

"You're with me, and when you're with me, you agree with me," Finch said matter-of-factly.

"This is the United States of America," Keelie said, rubbing the circulation back into her bruised arm. "You can't make me agree with you."

Finch looked over at her. "For the humans it is, but not for us."

Keelie rubbed her sore arm. "It's going to be days before I have feeling again."

"Quit being a drama queen. I have other matters to discuss with you."

"Like what?"

"Let's take a walkabout to the meadow. There's something I want to teach you."

"Teach me? What?" Keelie frowned. The last thing she wanted was more lessons. But you didn't say no to Finch.

As they left the clearing, shop owners and performers cleared the way for them. They passed Hob, who inclined his head. Finch returned the acknowledgement with a slight tilt of hers.

"How do you like your new neighbor?" she asked Keelie.

"He seems nice."

"Do you sense anything different about him?" Finch asked.

"No," Keelie said as they headed down the hill. "He's been friendly."

Finch stopped and watched Hob make his way back to his shop. Her eyebrows knitted together as if she was focusing on something.

"Why are you so curious about Hob?" Keelie asked.

"I can't read him," Finch squinted at the retreating figure of the mask shop owner.

"Read him?" Keelie hadn't heard that one.

Finch lifted her face, and her eyes were dilated like big black moons. Then her pupils contracted back to normal.

Keelie inhaled. "Are you okay?" Maybe Finch had the

hots for the handsome mask maker as well as for Vangar. What fickle games the dragon heart played.

"Yes. And you're going to try to read him too, using the To See Truly spell."

"To See Truly?" Keelie hadn't heard of that one, and she quickly rearranged her thoughts. It seemed Finch was suspicious of Hob.

"Yes." They had reached the bridge, and Finch stopped to gaze down at the flowing water rippling over the stones. Keelie wondered if the sprite would be splashing about, and if it would irritate the dragon.

"To See Truly allows you to see through layers of magic, down to a person's essence. I've been using the spell to see the faire folk and their true form, but with Hob— nothing. A blank."

"You think he's using a glamour?" Keelie toed a loose board on the bridge (oak from New Hampshire).

"I'm not seeing a glamour," Finch said. "I can see straight through a glamour."

"What do you see if he's just a human?" Keelie looked into the distance, where shop roofs peeked through the trees.

"I see their intent. But with him, I see nothing." Finch nodded. "It's possible he's human, but I have this feeling something isn't quite right, and the To See Truly spell hasn't ever failed me, which is why I want another perspective."

Keelie didn't know whether to be thrilled that Finch wanted her opinion, or to be scared. What if she failed? But since it was Finch, you had to do what she said.

"What do I do?" Keelie swallowed.

"Look at the water and concentrate. What do you see?"

Keelie gazed down. "Water flowing, stones, and green ferns growing on the embankment." A gentle breeze flowed through her hair as she inhaled the loamy scent surrounding her. She held her hands toward the water. "The minerals in the water tell me that the stream's spring isn't far away."

"Good. You're a natural. You're feeling the Earth magic of the place, and now I'm going to teach you something dragons do naturally."

"Teach me what?"

"Angle your head fifteen degrees to the right."

"Fifteen degrees?" Keelie stared at Finch. "How will I know I've angled my head fifteen degrees? What if I angle it seventeen degrees?"

"It takes practice to work with light refraction and Earth magic to allow you To See Truly. When you feel the presence of the Earth, like you did with the minerals in the stream, then you're on target. Dragons have a natural predilection for this spell." Finch's voice reflected pride. "Have you ever caught a quick glance of something in your peripheral vision? Then it was gone?"

Keelie nodded. "Yes, especially with the fairies."

"That's To See Truly. You're glimpsing through layers of magic. As you become better at using it, you'll be able to see the true form and the essence of all beings. At first, you'll see glimmers of magic, like the ripples in a pond. Next, you'll pick up on different kinds of magic, like when someone is under an enchantment. Then, when you least expect it, the spell will work, and when it does—kapow!

An overwhelming sensation of magic flows through your body, and you'll feel like you're swimming in a lake of light, but you'll see truly."

"That's powerful," Keelie said. She thought about Tavyn and Bloodroot in the Redwood Forest—if she'd been able to see through the bad elf's magic, then she would have been able to stop him sooner. "I angle my head fifteen degrees, and then what?" She was anxious to learn more.

Finch gestured toward the embankment. "Call upon Earth magic. If you're not making the connection, pick up some dirt and hold it in your hands, which usually helps. Next, concentrate on the light around the person, and then repeat these words: *Allow me to see truly*. It doesn't have to be out loud, but that'll help at first."

"Is that all you say? *Allow me to see truly*?" Keelie had recited some complicated elven spells, and this seemed so simple. As far as she was concerned, it was in the bag.

Finch arched an eyebrow and chuckled. "You think it's easy, but it takes practice. Try, now, and tell me what you see on the embankment other than ferns."

Keelie stood on the bridge, angled her head, and called upon Earth magic. She felt it zing through her, then focused on the embankment, narrowing her eyes to see something hidden within the sun light. "*Allow me to see truly*."

Nothing. No ta-da moment. Keelie was disappointed. She saw green ferns, rippling water, and granite rocks. She cleared her throat and repeated the procedure. Nothing.

"I don't see anything."

"Quit your whining." Finch touched Keelie's shoulder. A surge of power flowed through her, and suddenly the world brightened into a stark clarity she'd never experienced before. Ripples of light spread out and around the embankment, and she now clearly saw the sprite sunning herself in the ferns.

"She has the power of invisibility," Finch whispered.

"What did you do?" Keelie asked. She stared in astonishment at the little catfish-like fae sleeping peacefully on the rock. "Why couldn't I see her the first time?"

"I gave you a boost of dragon magic." Finch shot Keelie a grin. "Keep practicing. The ability to see truly will kick in."

Finch marched off the bridge. "Come on. I need to get back to the office and see what list of whiny-baby complaints I have to deal with today. You can tell me about the little tree as we walk."

"What little tree?" Keelie wondered if the aspen sapling had done something to bring attention to himself.

"I've detected the presence of goblins at the faire, and your angry treeling could form an alliance with them," Finch said.

Keelie trotted after her. As they entered the fairegrounds, some of the shopkeepers skirted away and shot angry glances in their direction, which made Keelie recall Vangar's words about being a friend to the administration. She'd studied labor relations and the rise of unions in school; it could get ugly, and here she was, now firmly stuck on the ugly side. Throw in some goblins, plus a hostile treeling?

Just what she needed.

four

"So, how did you find about out the goblin tree?" Keelie asked as they swung down King's Way toward the Admin office.

Finch's lips pressed together. "I have a reliable source."

"Ermentrude." Keelie had told the old dragon everything that had happened to her since her mother died, and Ermentrude had no doubt passed it on to her daughter. "Don't worry, the treeling won't be staying in the meadow. My dad's going to move it. It'll be over at Heartwood."

Finch pinned her with a gaze. "You swear?"

"Yes. But if you want it so much, he'll deliver it to you. Goblin blood makes very bad tree fertilizer, let me tell you."

"That's exactly why I want to see it. That was a foolish thing you did."

"Tell me about it," Keelie said glumly. "I had no idea what I was doing. I just thought I'd bring a little life back to a dead spot, and bring something of the Queen Aspen back too."

We're here, the Queen Aspen's children sang.

Yeah, I know. I wish I knew last year, Keelie told them.

"What is this about goblins? And you go seeking them without weapons and without me?" Vangar was walking behind them. They hadn't heard his footsteps. His iridescent dragon tattoos glittered in the sunlight that was filtering through the trees.

Finch frowned. "Back away, dragon breath. I was sent here to handle this situation. You can pretend all you want in front of the humans, but I know what you are."

Keelie stared. Dragon breath? Of course.

"But not why I'm here." The tall dragon regarded her coolly. "I was sent by a mutual associate of ours, to guard Keelie. Seems our two assignments should go arm in arm." His cold gaze warmed as he looked Finch up and down.

"Or claw in claw," Keelie muttered under her breath. "I already have a guardian. Who sent you?"

Vangar shook his head, his dreadlocks swinging like braided snakes. "Can't tell."

A crunching sound came from nearby and she saw that Cricket had found a trash bin and was pulling out paper plates and munching them down, a blissful smile on his shiny black face.

Vangar huffed. "Sounds like a cricket. Doesn't look dangerous, does he? But give him a couple of years and he'll turn mean."

"Not true. Some goblins are…" Keelie had been about to say good, but that wasn't strictly true. "Mean well," she finished lamely.

Finch laughed, and Vangar let out a roar of mirth. Then both shut up just as suddenly and stared at each other warily.

"Glad you two think I'm so hilarious." Keelie picked up Cricket, paper plate and all. "Come on, little guy."

He munched on the rim of the plate, chirping to himself.

"I'm glad to hear the tree will be moved," Finch said, eyes glued to Vangar's. "Keep me posted on any developments."

Keelie left the two dragons still looking at each other and headed back toward the jousting field, where Sean and his knights were exercising their horses.

Cricket clambered up onto her shoulder and perched there like a shiny black parrot.

Feminine laughter sounded from around the bend in the path, and a few steps later Keelie saw a gaggle of girls hanging on Hob's arm. Keelie didn't worry that any of them would see Cricket, but as Hob bowed his head to her in greeting as they passed, she could have sworn that his eyes flicked to the goblin on her shoulder.

Could Hob have some fae blood? Or elven? Interesting. She'd have to remember to tell Dad.

Keelie soon forgot Hob, however, as she watched the faire's merchants put the finishing touches on their shops and booths.

Cricket jumped to the ground and skittered off. He'd probably seen an interesting gum wrapper or a piece of pretzel. She didn't worry. Unlike stray kittens, little goblins could fend for themselves.

At the bottom of the hill, the faire's elf ear vendor was leveling his cart, its little roof lined with rubber elven ears dangling grotesquely from their strings. She fluffed her hair out as she passed so that he wouldn't notice that one of her ears looked just like his merchandise. She'd be mortified if he offered to even her up by putting a prosthesis on her human ear. On the other hand, it might be funny to show up at dinner with two elf ears. Dad and Sir Davey would probably laugh until they cried; they knew that she was fine with her asymmetrical ears. Janice would laugh too. She imagined how her other friends would pass the Elf Ear Challenge: Laurie, her best friend from her old life in Los Angeles, wouldn't laugh—she'd want a set for herself. Raven, on the other hand, would think it was pretty funny.

Keelie had reached the list field, as the dirt-and-sawdust jousting arena oval was sometimes called. It was also called the tourney field, depending on what movie the speaker had seen. On the long sides of the oval were wooden viewing stands, with tall poles to hold cloth sunshields that kept the audience from getting scorched by the summer sun. The poles were bare now, like skinny baseball bats sticking out of the sides of the stands.

Five of the knights were on their big horses, trotting around the inside edge of the field, but Sean was standing to one side, studying a clipboard. Sir Ian, one of the elven knights standing next to him, saw Keelie and whispered something, then turned away. Sean glanced up to see her, and came forward with a smile on his face.

He stopped when he saw Cricket, and his eyes turned down in dismay. "What is it eating?"

"A paper plate from the trash. I know, gross, but—" Keelie turned to look at Cricket and stopped. A very realistic-looking elf ear was dangling from his bottom lip. He saw her looking and pushed it all the way into his mouth with his insectile fingers, chomping rapidly.

Sean stepped backward, and Ian bent over and threw up.

"It's rubber, you guys. From the ear vendor up the hill." She turned and pointed, but the cart was covered with a tarp and the vendor was nowhere to be seen. She turned back to the two horrified elves. "Really, it was a rubber ear."

It struck her then that Sean would not think it was funny if she wore a fake elf ear over her human ear. He was always so serious. For some reason, this made her very sad.

"Well, I'm heading back up to help Dad. Hope you had a great workout," she finally said.

Sean nodded. "It was useful to have the horses in the arena again before we work out in armor."

She waited for him to ask her to dinner, or to take a walk with him, but his eyes kept returning to the baby goblin. "Those grow up fast, you know. Remember the goblins we battled in the Northwoods?"

"He's one of Herne's goblins. He won't hurt anyone." Keelie knew she'd made a mistake the minute she said Herne's name. Sean's eyes narrowed; he was jealous of the nature god, who had risked much to help them when they were attacked by Peascod's army of rogue goblins.

Keelie suddenly remembered something. "I heard a jangle by the bridge earlier. It gave me chills. I thought Peascod was around."

Sean's eyes finally left Cricket and focused on her face. "Did you see any sign of him?" The power-hungry goblin had vanished during their final battle, abandoning his army to its fate.

"No, but there's the big patch of dirt in the meadow that's tainted by the Red Cap's blood. Elianard told me once that goblin blood is useful, for those who know how to use it, when raising power with dark magic. We need to figure out how to clean the area." Too bad the EPA didn't do magical soil cleaning.

"I feel helpless—I don't know how to do that. This is an example of what I've been talking about. You're the one who can solve these things, but what can I do to keep you safe?" Sean gazed intently at her.

"Just be with me. I have fairy guardians and dragon guardians—I don't need you to keep me safe. I need you to keep me real."

The expression in his leaf-green eyes told her nothing.

If you were a tree, I'd know what you were thinking.

"As for my dangerous goblin—" She put a hand up to touch Cricket. The little goblin grabbed her fingers and nibbled at her fingernails. She pulled her hand away and reached out to Sean to show that she was unharmed. "See? He wouldn't hurt me."

"So you say. They're smart, and destructive, and evil. You can't convince me otherwise, especially after what we went through with them."

"Okay, guess I can't. See you around?" Keelie was mad now, but she still wanted to see Sean later, away from all the other elves.

He nodded, then turned to look at the field again, consulting his clipboard. No goodbye hug, no see-you-later kiss.

Keelie wanted to plant her finely crafted, medieval-style boot into his muscular, well-shaped elven backside, but instead she strode up the hill, fuming about pig-headed elves. Cricket clambered down and raced ahead.

She hadn't told the truth—she didn't have to go back to Heartwood, but she headed there anyway in case Sean was watching her. She pretended to fix her boot laces partway up the hill and glanced his way, but he was on the other side of the list field, talking to one of the mounted knights. And she was acting like a lovesick idiot.

Suddenly she was angry, but not at Sean. *Get over yourself, Keelie*, she thought. *You are independent and strong. You don't need a boyfriend hanging all over you to be important. How many tree shepherds were there?*

Thirty-two. The voice in her mind was familiar.

Dad, quit peeking in my private girl thoughts.

I'm not peeking. You are yelling. Every tree in this forest heard you. They're discussing your relationship with Sean.

Whoops. *Need some help at the shop, Daddy dearest?*

As a matter of fact, yes. I'll fix us some tea if you come dust and polish the counter, and I'll tell you of my adventures digging up the blasted treeling.

Deal. Keelie hurried up the path, relieved that Dad had gotten the little aspen out of the meadow without her help.

Cleaning Heartwood's counter would be a treat. It was one of the things that had drawn her into her new life when she'd first arrived and was rediscovering her power to communicate with trees. The counter was hewn out of a wide and curvy slice of tree, but what a tree. It must have been immense, and this piece of it lived on. Knots and rings showed through its polished top, and the sides had animal carvings that followed the natural curve of the tree trunk. At night, by candlelight, the carved animals appeared to move. The bottom of the counter was carved to look like roots digging deep in the floor. Whenever Keelie polished it, the wood showed her scenes of its long life.

At Heartwood, Dad was mounting caged crystals onto the back of a chair. "Cleaning supplies are in the back room." He didn't even look her way.

On her way to the storeroom, Keelie saw Cricket sitting on the stairs to her apartment, Knot at his side. The cat showed his pointy fangs in a kitty grin. The little goblin brightened and skittered toward her, climbing her jeans and perching on her shoulder as she tidied up, then gathered a pile of soft polishing cloths and a bottle of lemon oil. Knot had fallen asleep draped over the stair, snoozing. She got quickly to work, giving the counter a thin coat of oil, then rubbing it in until the wood glowed.

"That little tree has some issues," Dad remarked.

"I know. I feel a little guilty about disliking it, since it's my fault it was planted in that spot." Keelie refrained from saying "goblin blood" although no one was around to hear.

"Davey helped me dig it up. We used a wheelbarrow to haul it up here."

Keelie straightened. "Here, where?" She looked around.

Dad pointed at the front corner of the shop, where a large half whiskey barrel held a green-leafed sapling, its roots covered in a tidy brown mulch. "We tucked it in snugly. It'll sleep for a day or so."

"Thank goodness, because otherwise *we* wouldn't get any sleep."

Dad grinned. "Tell me about it."

With the tree safely out of harm's way, Keelie thought about Sean. She attacked the surface of the counter with the polishing cloth, easing her anger and confusion with work.

As she polished, she lost herself in the stories that the wood underneath her fingers was telling. No people ever starred in tree stories, but they were full of heroes and villains and misunderstood younglings.

Feeling very much like one of the defiant saplings in the counter tree's stories, she put away the polishing cloth and started to dust the merchandise.

"Are you almost ready?" a man in a bushy mustache asked as he passed by the shop, juggling balls as he walked.

"Absolutely!" Dad answered him.

The man pushed a Ping-Pong ball out of his mouth and it joined the whirling balls.

"Hello, Oswald." Janice struggled across the clearing with a basket stuffed full and covered by a cloth. The juggler bowed to her. "Hello, Heartwood," Janice continued. "You folks hungry?"

"What've you got in there?" Keelie asked, running to help carry the loaded basket.

"A little dinner for my favorite tree shepherds." Janice placed the basket on the flagstone floor, pulled the cloth back, and showed Keelie that the willow laundry basket was bursting with packages and covered plates. A heavenly aroma rose from one of the packages. "Fried chicken, broccoli, rice salad with nuts and currants, and freshly made rolls," Janice announced.

She sure knew how to answer an unspoken question. As Janice went to speak to Dad, Keelie watched the woman's face soften. She'd never have another mother, but Janice might be okay as a stepmom. And then Raven could be her sister.

Dad and Janice spoke, heads together, for a while, then Janice picked up the basket and sashayed up the wooden stairs to their apartment as if she knew he was still watching her. He was.

Oldsters and their romances, Keelie thought. But Dad was such a chick magnet. Maybe Janice would chase the rest away. He was like the elf version of ... of ... Hob. Keelie laughed at that.

As if. Hob was such an amateur when it came to anything Dad could do.

She returned to her work, absently noting when Janice came back down and returned to Dad's side again. He would be thrilled at the meal, however, and Keelie'd get to go to bed early tonight. She was exhausted, and she hoped to find a book on the shelves upstairs that would take her mind off that hurtful encounter with Sean. The importance of it was probably all in her mind, but that didn't mean she wasn't reliving his words over and over. Could Cricket really grow up to be evil? Herne's goblins had all been helpful, staying underground and not joining the goblins battling in the Northwoods.

"If you rub any harder, that counter is going to blind people with reflected light." The voice was manly and deep, but Keelie could only see the extravagantly plumed top of a cavalier hat.

"Sir Davey!" She dropped her rag and ran around to hug her teacher, who was several inches shorter than she.

"I was coming to say hello to your father, and to you too, of course," Sir Davey said. "But the old man seems to be busy."

Keelie shrugged. "You know Dad. And Janice came armed for seduction." She leaned over to whisper, "Fried chicken."

Sir Davey's bushy eyebrows rose, vanishing into his musketeer hat. "Well, in that case." He turned, arms stretched out like a zombie's and headed toward the whispering couple. "Chicken," he intoned flatly. "Fried chicken."

Dad and Janice turned to look at him, and Keelie laughed at the annoyed looks on their faces. Davey turned and aimed a wink at her.

Little Cricket hopped up onto the counter and slid halfway across its slick surface. Keelie caught him just before he flew off into space, then headed over to where the adults were, to tell them the story of the munched rubber elf ear and Sir Ian's undignified reaction. Janice would have to take her word for it—she couldn't see Cricket.

Sean would come around. He was probably overwhelmed as always with his responsibilities as head of the jousters. The show depended on him, and he'd gotten here weeks after the faire had opened. As soon as he got situated, he'd relax. Things would be back to normal soon. She could just feel it.

five

Keelie crouched down to warm her hands at the fireplace. She smiled at her mother, who was knitting in the armchair next to her. This was a dream. Knitting needles were alien to her attorney mother.

"I miss you so much. I'm glad you stopped by for a visit, but you need to go." Mom's voice was gentle but firm.

Keelie stood up. "I don't want to go. I miss you, too." Dream or not, Mom seemed real. Keelie stretched a hand out to touch her.

"Don't. You have to wake up." Mom's eyes were still on her work, the wooden needles slipping up and down, in and

out, knotting the strands of orange yarn into a glowing pattern against the gray and black swirls.

Keelie coughed and opened her eyes, the dream fading although the misty swirls remained, whooshing overhead in choking billows.

Fire.

All sleep gone, Keelie sprang to her feet. "Dad! Dad!"

Her father's cough came from across the room, where his bedroom area faced the front windows. Then his groggy response vanished. "Get out, Keelie! Take nothing, just go!"

Take nothing? Keelie put her feet into her shoes and grabbed her roomy purse, which hung from her bedpost. The floorboards were hot, and she could see the orange glow of flame between the cracks. Her heart pounded. The shop was on fire, too. She felt her way toward the door. The smoke was impossible now, like a thick, gagging blanket.

She dropped to her knees and crawled, coughing. She couldn't breathe. She pulled her T-shirt up and held the hem over her nose as she felt her way, on her knees and one hand, toward the wall. The wall would take her to the front door.

Her shoulder banged into something hard and objects rattled above her. One struck her head, then rolled to the floor. The pain stopped her, robbing her of what little air she had, and her hand closed on the object. It was a wooden frame (yellow pine, from Alabama). Keelie couldn't see the picture, but she knew it was one of the photos of herself that Dad kept on a little chest by the front door.

"Keelie, why did you stop? Are you near the door?"

Glass exploded behind her and a wave of fire rolled over her. If she'd been standing, she would have been scorched. But the light of the fire showed Dad scuttling toward her, a towel over his face. Knot was riding his shoulders, claws dug in, his eyes wide with fear and his orange fur puffed out so that it looked like he was on fire, too.

"Keep moving," Dad commanded, and she turned and hurried toward the door. The floor was blistering hot now, and Keelie got up and walked in a crouch. The fire sounded like ten trains and a tornado were beneath and all around them.

She reached the door and touched the knob, but it wasn't hot. In her school's fire safety training, she'd learned that a hot knob meant fire was on the other side. If the stairs were on fire, there would be no way out of their apartment.

She turned the knob and pulled the door open, gulping in a great breath of fresh air. Behind her, that same air fed the flames. Suddenly, she was on her face with a big weight on top of her. Heat roared overhead.

"Are you okay?" Dad said in her ear. "I tried to warn you, but you opened the door too fast."

"Yeah." Her voice came out as a dried-out whisper. Hands reached out through the smoke that now blanketed the stairs outside, and she found herself in Tarl the mud man's gigantic grasp.

"Hold still, little girl. I'll get you out of here." He picked her up and tossed her over his shoulder. "Zeke, you behind me?"

"I am. Knot, run ahead." Her father's voice was reassuringly strong.

Keelie watched the cat dash down the stairs as she left Heartwood for the last time—upside down, over Tarl's shoulder, bobbing in time to his rushed stride down the stairs. She saw Knot pause to look up at Heartwood, then run into the woods.

"I've got to reassure the trees," Dad said. Immediately, his soothing tree speak calmed the trees around them and Keelie realized that their panic had fueled hers. She tried to add her calm to his, but found only fear within.

Tarl set her down, coughing, by the trees at the other edge of the clearing, then ran back to Heartwood. A crowd had gathered and she was surrounded by concerned voices, but she brushed away their hands and turned to watch the fire.

Hob was at the edge of the crowd, looking up in wonder, the flames dancing in his shiny eyes.

Something about his expression reminded Keelie of someone else, but she couldn't think of who, because she suddenly remembered the Compendium. The one and only, the record of all elven magic, entrusted to her so that she could learn from it. It was under her bed.

She ran back toward the steps, her lungs hurting from the smoke and the effort. Hands grabbed at her, but she twisted away and ran up the stairs. She only got halfway up before her father's arms grasped her and pulled her away.

"The Compendium," she cried. "Dad, I have to save it."

"It's too late, Keelie. It's not worth your life." His voice was rough, as though he'd smoked his way through a million packs of cigarettes.

She kicked free and turned to head back up the stairs, but the greedy fire was now leaping from tread to tread and wrapping around the handrail like a flaming garland. If she'd gotten to the top, she would not have been able to leave again. She backed away, her heart squeezed tight in her chest.

Heartwood, her father's beautiful shop, seemed like it was being eaten by a flaming monster. The fire licked up to the trees, and their cries of fear echoed once more in her head. The whole forest was roaring in alarm. Above her, the branches were trembling with the weight of the *bhata* who'd come to watch.

Water poured onto the fire from the other side of the building and, through the crowd, Keelie saw that Sean and his jousters had dragged up a portable water tank and compressor. But the water wasn't on Heartwood. They were wetting down the trees and the roofs of the other shops to protect them.

For a second she was angry; then she realized that they were right. It was too late for Heartwood.

The crowd gasped as the front of their apartment fell into itself, folding like a cardboard toy. The roof caved down so that it looked like a floppy hat resting on the ground. Keelie's knees seemed to dissolve and she found herself sitting on the ground. Legs and long skirts swayed around her, and the trees shrieked in her mind.

As if it was a nightmare revealing itself in flashes of memory, Keelie saw the fire brigade abandon its quest. The wooden roof shingles glowed like rows of coals before tongues of flames licked up around them.

Janice appeared in front of her, face made rosy by the reflected firelight. "Honey, let me tend that cut." She gestured toward Keelie's head. Something tickled Keelie's forehead and she rubbed a hand over her face, wincing as she touched a sticky, sore spot. Her hand came away wet with blood. It seemed as black as the soot that coated her skin.

Janice started to dab at her forehead with a wet washcloth. It stung, but not too badly. She felt something in her other hand—a heart-shaped wooden frame that held her second-grade school picture. She was missing her two front teeth, but her grin was still broad. She looked at it for a moment before she remembered grabbing it off the floor.

The Compendium was gone, but she had saved this. All of Dad's beautiful furniture was destroyed, including the beautiful counter carved from a single great trunk, but she had her second-grade school picture. Tears began to flow down her cheeks, dripping from her face.

"Oh honey, I'm sorry," Janice said. "I promise I'll be

done soon, and then I'll put a nice salve on it to take the pain away."

Keelie wanted to tell her that nothing could take the pain away, but she was beyond words.

six

An hour later, Keelie was wrapped in a quilt, freshly showered, in the apartment above Janice's shop.

"This tea will soothe your throat." Janice placed the steaming mug of tea next to her on a little table (mahogany, from Belize).

"Thank you," Keelie croaked, her throat raw, as she sipped from the mug in between her hands. The scent of smoke still lingered in her hair despite having shampooed it several times in Janice's shower. She wished Sean were here to hold her and tell her it would be okay. He was still with the jousters, making sure the fire at Heartwood was out.

The herbal tea soothed her frazzled nerves a little as she inhaled its earthy goodness. Knot sat in her lap, drooling and making biscuits on her legs. She was so glad to have him next to her, she didn't care—he could make all the biscuits he wanted and drool on her as much as he cared to.

"Meow." He nestled next to her in the chair and placed a paw on her leg.

"I know, buddy. I'm glad to be here, too." She scratched behind his ear. She heard the din of the crowd of faire workers outside, gathered to discuss what to do about no Heartwood. The whole faire seemed to be gathered on the road to the hilltop.

"Hey kiddo, how you feeling?" Raven made her way through the crowded little room and sat opposite her on a trunk.

Keelie dropped her head back against the rocking chair and pulled Janice's quilt tighter around her shoulders, as if it could keep the world away and make her safe.

Janice sat in the corner of the small room, the glow of the lantern casting a soft light on her. She'd wrapped her arms around herself, and her lips were pursed in worry.

Sir Davey appeared in the doorway of the apartment, a flask of coffee in his hand. "Lass, I have the thing that's going to perk you right up."

"I gave her tea with a special herbal remedy to keep her calm. The last thing the child needs is caffeine." Janice's usual good humor seemed to have vanished.

"Caffeine will settle her nerves. Everyone knows herbal tea will jack her up, and she won't be able to sleep."

Keelie almost smiled. It felt good to have them looking after her. "I think I need some herbal tea *and* some coffee," she said.

Sir Davey walked over to her, concern glinting in his chocolate-colored eyes. "Lass, you gave us all a scare."

"Meow." Knot dug his claws deeper into her leg.

Sir Davey scowled at him. "Let the girl have some peace and quiet after all she's been through."

"Where's Dad?" Keelie asked.

"He's over at the elven compound trying to calm everyone down. They've got their robes in a knot and their pointed ears stuck inside their eyeballs." Sir Davey shook his head in disgust.

"Sounds like their normal reaction." Keelie shrugged and then caught another whiff of smoke. Would she always smell like a grill? "What's their problem? The fire was far away from their buildings."

Shepherdess, where is the angry little tree? asked one of the sycamores that bordered the path. *Will the fire consume him?*

The treeling is fine, Keelie responded. *Hob the mask maker rescued it and took it to his shop.*

It is afraid, shepherdess, and we can do nothing to stop its fear that the fire will eat it. It's beginning to convince the other trees that they are in danger from the dragon.

"I've got to go." Keelie pushed aside the quilt. Dad had gone into uber tree shepherd mode, but the little aspen tree was her responsibility. Even afraid, it was a troublemaker.

Keelie closed her eyes and opened her telepathic pathway to Dad. *Dad, I need you to meet me at Hob's shop. The goblin tree is freaking out, and it's affecting the other trees. I need your help.*

I'll meet you there. She caught a glimpse of a deeply shadowed hillside forest.

Hob had been wonderful during the fire, and afterwards. He had saved the little goblin tree, and Keelie couldn't imagine why it didn't feel safe now. She'd heard that Hob appeared right when the fire started and went straight for the tree, dragging its container to safety.

Keelie disentangled herself from Knot. He hopped down to the floor and looked up at her. "Meow?" He raised his kitty eyebrows.

"I need to meet Dad at Hob's shop."

"You need to rest." Janice stepped forward.

"I agree. Keelie, you've been through too much," Sir Davey said. "I know you feel keyed up, but if you try to sleep you'll feel much better."

"There's no choice."

Keelie suddenly remembered Cricket. Waves of guilt washed over her. Was he okay? She hadn't thought of him. Her stomach knotted with sick fear as she imagined the little goblin abandoned, trapped in the fiery apartment.

"Have you seen Cricket?" she asked Sir Davey, who exchanged glances with Janice.

Janice inhaled. "No one has seen your little creature." She couldn't seem to bring herself to say the word goblin. She didn't care about a creature she couldn't see.

"I'm sorry we have no news, lass," Sir Davey said. "I

think the little goblin may be safe, though he's a darn nuisance. He's resourceful."

Keelie took comfort in Sir Davey's words. Cricket was always taking advantage of opportunities to eat. She'd probably find him safe in someone's garbage. Yet she couldn't help but worry about him. She'd check with Dad and Vangar and see if they'd seen him.

Outside, Keelie gagged at the smell of smoke and burnt wood. She swallowed back bile and lit one of the lanterns Janice kept under a table by the door, then made her way toward Wood Row, where many of the booth owners had gathered in little groups, fear clinging to them as they discussed the fire. The faire was their livelihood, and the blaze was not as scary to them as its cause.

She overheard snippets: "irresponsible blacksmith"— "Vangar was wrong"—"the new faire director is incompetent."

Keelie hurried by, hoping no one noticed her. She didn't want to talk to anybody about the tragedy of losing her home. Of losing Heartwood. Knot ran ahead, diving from tree to tree and skulking behind corners as if he was on the hunt, protecting her.

The *bhata* jumped from branch to branch as they followed her, watching. It wasn't just the humans who were upset and fearful. Beneath the layer of fear that cloaked trees and fae and people, Keelie sensed another disturbance upsetting the balance of the faire and the surrounding forest ... but she couldn't tell what it was.

The *feithid daoine* buzzed above her. All of the fae had

been rattled. Knot swatted at several of the bug fairies as they dive-bombed him.

Keelie snapped her fingers to get Knot's attention. "Come on. Dad is waiting at Hob's shop."

Knot hissed.

"Yeah, I know you don't like him," Keelie said. "Jealous."

Keelie's steps slowed as she walked up the path that led to the shop. She didn't want to see the burned ruins of her home. Something rustled in the bushes nearby, and she heard a deep, whispered, "Keelie. I need to talk to you."

Fear rushed through her and her heart pulsed super fast. "Who's there?"

"It's me." Vangar straightened and stepped out from behind the bushes.

"Why are you here?" Keelie hissed, but Knot ran up to the blacksmith and clawed his leather boots, a sign of affection.

Keelie would've liked to claw the blacksmith's eyes out. "Hob was right—your forge was dangerous." Tears welled in her eyes and she blinked, embarrassed to show weakness in front of the dragon who had destroyed Heartwood.

He shook his head in denial. "I need your help."

Keelie stopped breathing, as if afraid that smoke would fill her lungs. "What? You can't be serious."

"My forge didn't start the fire. I'd put safety spells around my shop so that the fire couldn't escape. Someone with a lot of power removed them. I've been set up, and Finch said that you would be fair-minded and help me clear my name."

"Finch told you to ask me for help? Me? I don't have a bed, or clothes, or schoolbooks, or—or—" Tears clouded her vision, again. Keelie was going to have a long discussion with the faire director.

Vangar looked forlorn and lost. "I was sent here to protect you. Do you think I would set your house and store on fire? My honor is all to me. I would not harm my charge."

Keelie shook her head, trying to make sense of what Vangar had said. "*Who* sent you to protect me?"

"He forbade me to tell you."

"So, it was a he?"

Vangar's face clouded over with confusion and anxiety.

"Whatever. My dad is waiting for me at Hob's shop."

"It was that little pissant that set me up." Vangar hissed, smoke blowing from between his clenched teeth. "He's the one behind the fire."

Aghast, Keelie stared at Vangar. "He's been nothing but kind and helpful. How dare you accuse him?"

"Think about it. He set me up. First, he was the one who convinced everyone that my forge was a fire hazard. "

"Because your forge *was* a fire hazard. It took no skill to get people to believe it."

"But I have the magical ability to stop fire," Vangar said between clenched teeth. "I'm a dragon. If I'd been home, it wouldn't have happened."

"I'll keep an open mind." Keelie forced the words out to appease the blacksmith, who seemed to be walking a bridge between reality and buggy-buggy land. "And I'll keep an eye on Hob," she said. "I need to go."

He swept his hand forward as if guiding her up the path. "Be on your way, milady, but keep this conversation between the two of us."

Keelie edged past him, then blinked as he vanished into the bushes. Finch definitely had a lot of explaining to do.

Outside Hob's shop, Dad was waiting for her. "Where have you been?"

"I ran into some people who wanted to give me their condolences on the fire." Keelie made a quick decision not to tell her father about Vangar or how he'd asked for her help in proving his innocence—not for Vangar's sake, but because Dad had enough on his mind. Vangar had given her something to think about, and his words troubled her.

Dad nodded. "It's been a shock to the entire faire. Everyone wants to help."

Now she'd lied to her father. Her home was a pile of smoldering debris. Keelie choked back tears as silvery smoke streamed up from the wreckage. She couldn't believe she'd been put in this position. Strange, how the smoldering remains of Heartwood remained confined in a circle. And that Hobknocker's, with its fragile paper masks, had been unaffected.

Hob stepped out onto the porch, cradling the potted goblin tree in his arms. "Here you go, Zeke. I admire your dedication to your plants." He lowered the tree down onto the front steps leading to his shop. "Are you sure you want to take it tonight?"

Dad motioned toward Keelie. "Since the little tree is the only thing left of Heartwood..."

"Yes, I missed it so much. I couldn't spend another night without my tree." Keelie sighed sadly, not faking, although her sadness wasn't related to the angry and ungrateful beast of a tree.

The little goblin tree sent Keelie angry red thoughts. *You lie. You don't care about me. Nobody cares about me.*

She smiled at the goblin tree, Hob, and Dad to mask what she was truly feeling, which was to toss the treeling onto the hot embers. *You're lucky to be alive. You're going with us whether you want to or not.*

Green-red anger seethed within the little tree. Keelie sensed the goblin taint flowing its sap like venom, slowly poisoning it with dark magic. She had to find a way to get it out before it got out of hand.

I know a secret that you don't know, and when you find out, you're going to die. They want you dead. All of them, for what you did.

She didn't know what the little tree meant, so she ignored its ranting.

Dad picked up the tree and waved good night to Hob. "Thank you again for your help."

"You would've done the same for me. I'm sorry about your loss, and I'm going to make sure everyone knows it was Vangar who did this."

Dad didn't look over at the smoking ruin of what had been their shop and their home. "I don't think it was Vangar who started the fire." His voice weary. "We appreciate your help, Hob, in alerting the other shopkeepers to the fire."

"Despite your generous spirit, Zeke, Vangar is the guilty

party, and the other shopkeepers have complained about his forge." Hob lifted his handsome face, and in the light glowing from within the shop defiance glinted in his eyes.

Hob definitely had it in for Vangar.

"Keelie, let's go." Dad's voice was hard and crisp. One of the little goblin tree's branches slapped Dad across the face. He didn't flinch. Anyone who wasn't familiar with trees would've assumed it was a breeze that made the branch move.

She followed Dad into the trees. She had no idea where they were going.

Once they were on the bridge, out of sight of the shops up the hill, Dad put down the pot and grabbed the goblin tree by its uppermost branches, letting the clay pot dangle over the edge of the bridge.

Shocked, Keelie opened herself to their telepathic conversation.

Give me one good reason why I shouldn't drop you now.

Go ahead and do it.

Was the little tree suicidal, pushing Dad like this? Had the fire driven Dad to the edge of sanity?

Her lantern swinging wildly, Keelie rushed over and tried to grab the tree's trunk. "Stop, Dad. What are you doing? You've got to stop."

Knot raced by and jumped on the bridge railing. "Meow!"

Dad's look stopped her. "This tree has a choice. It can live, or if it wants to destroy itself, then I'll make its wish come true. But it's not going to take anyone else with it."

Keelie didn't like seeing her father like this. She forced herself to remain calm. "You're scaring me, Dad. I don't understand what you're doing. Let's take the tree to the elves. It'll be safe, and none of them can hear it talking."

"No! It will put them in danger."

Keelie turned to the goblin tree, who pushed its face through the bark at her.

You stupid elves won't figure out what's going on, not before it's too late.

She ignored it. "Dad, what did the goblin tree do that has you so upset?"

The treeling's laughter echoed in her mind. *The acorn doesn't fall from the tree. Hey Zeke—she can't figure it out. I'll tell you what, Keliel Tree Talker. Dear old Dad thinks that your precious goblin and little ol' me started the fire.*

Keelie inhaled sharply and coughed as if smoke had filled her lungs again.

"Keelie?" Dad seemed as if he'd suddenly come back to himself.

"I'm okay." But the tree definitely wasn't. "Is it telling the truth?"

Dad nodded grimly.

The goblin tree laughed hysterically. *Go ahead and toss me down to the river. I've always wanted to know what it is like to fly.*

"Zeke, are you and Keelie okay?" A loud voice boomed from the other end of the bridge.

Keelie sighed with relief when she recognized Sir Davey.

"We're fine," Dad answered. "Stay back, Davey."

"Folks said they saw you and Keelie walk toward Water Sprite Lane. Why don't you rest at my camper?" Davey's voice had a cautious tone.

Dad slowly nodded. "I think that's a good idea."

The goblin tree narrowed its eyes and chortled. *They're coming for you. They're going to get you and your mean cat, too.*

She had to think. So much had happened tonight. Vangar had said he had been set up—could he have been telling the truth? Keelie decided to look into it. Right now, she had to defuse the situation at hand, because it felt as if she was being dragged to a place between madness and sanity. It was a fragile border.

seven

The stream burbled under the bridge. Keelie wondered if the sprite was down below listening to this conversation.

Even the *bhata* gathered in the trees had been silent as they watched the horror unfolding before them. A tree shepherd threatening a tree. She sensed their confusion.

"Dad, should we take the tree with us to the RV? No one will know it's there, and its small enough to keep inside."

The little goblin tree spat sap. *I do not wish to be among humans. They're filthy and nasty, and they're loud.*

Dad tightened his hold on the goblin tree's branches. "Davey, this tree is responsible for what happened to

Heartwood. It could've killed Keelie and destroyed the entire faire."

Despite Dad's command to stay back, Sir Davey came onto the bridge, his hand smoothing his Van Dyke beard. "There are those among the shop owners who think the blacksmith might be guilty. How can a tree have started a fire?"

"With a goblin. This tree's roots have grown in the goblin taint. Its green soul has been twisted to evil." Dad seemed more angry than sad at the transformation of the little tree. "It worked with the goblin to start the fire."

Good thing Dad hadn't worked with her in the Redwood Forest. He would have wanted to destroy all of the goblin-affected trees. A whole national park.

"Dad, let's just take the goblin tree to the RV," Keelie said. "We'll search for a calming charm in the Compendium." Her voice trailed away and a wave of loss washed over her. The Compendium had burned. She didn't know how she'd tell Elianard. He'd never get over it, and he'd blame her for its loss. There was no other record of the spells and charms the Dread Forest elves had used for centuries, and she wouldn't be able to look for a spell to counteract the evil effect of the Red Cap's blood.

"We'll figure it out," she said finally. "I'll contact Grandmother and Norzan. As tree shepherds, we can work together to find a solution."

She had a new idea, one she didn't dare tell her father. Maybe the Shining Ones—the Fairy High Court—could help her find an antidote for the goblin tree. If she could keep it alive for that long.

Dad pulled the goblin tree back over the bridge railing and lowered it onto the wooden planks. It howled as its trunk scraped the railing. "Take the cursed tree, Davey, but watch it closely." Dad straightened as if summoning strength to continue on.

"No need to worry. I'll have others to help me keep an eye on it." Davey eyed the little tree warily, as if it might sprout bat wings and fangs. "Doesn't look menacing. Just a skinny little tree."

Knot trotted onto the bridge and sniffed around the tree's container. "Meow."

Keelie used to think understanding "cat" was hard, but once you really listened to the vowel arrangements and tonal inflection, it was easy.

"Later," she whispered.

Knot crooked his tail. It was a sign he wasn't happy, but she didn't need the added stress of dealing with Vangar.

She'd search around Heartwood for clues. There had to be evidence of how the fire started, and she'd start with a talk with Finch. Although they'd put the fire out themselves, without help from a fire department, the resident dragon and fire expert probably could tell Keelie something about its cause.

"Keelie, come with me. We've been summoned by the elves," Dad said.

"About what?" Keelie asked. "If they're offering a group hug, I'll pass."

"Not a hug at all. They're concerned about the forest, and because we're tree shepherds, we must hear them, no matter that we have pressing problems of our own, like being homeless." Dad's voice was laced with bitterness.

Davey lifted the tree and it began smacking him with its branches, but he simply tilted his head back, out of reach. He walked around the side of the bridge, where he'd left a handcart, and plunked the beastly tree into it. The goblin tree rocked back and forth as if attempting an escape. Keelie wouldn't have been surprised to see it push its roots out of the confines of the container and take off running into the woods on spindly root-feet.

If you crash and break your pot, then I'll replant you in Knot's litter box. Think about it—cat poo on your roots. So calm down and go with Sir Davey.

Knot swiveled his head around and meowed angrily.

The tree quit thrashing. *I hate that cat. It sprayed me with urine.*

Knot washed his tail, declaring his innocence, or at least his lack of concern.

Will you water me? I'm feeling a little dry after that attack. The tree was acting normal now. Seems there was a fate worse than being dumped into the stream—Knot's litter box was treemageddon. Who knew?

Dad shook his head in disbelief. "Miraculous," he said, bowing to Keelie.

Keelie dropped a curtsey in return.

Sir Davey seemed shocked at the tree's sudden cooperation, since of course he hadn't heard the conversation in tree speak.

Keelie smiled and explained. "I threatened to plant it in Knot's litter box. Keep us posted."

"I will," Sir Davey said. "Or I'll take *you* to the dragon," he mumbled to the goblin tree. Keelie caught the tree's last thoughts as it was wheeled out of the way.

Dragon? Don't take me to the dragon.

Keelie wondered if Sir Davey and Finch had something up their sleeves to get the goblin tree to cooperate. She'd offer to deliver Knot's litter box later to use as a threat, but it, too, was a pile of ashes.

They stopped at Janice's shop to borrow another lantern before heading to the elven village, which meant that Dad thought the meeting might last long into the night. Dad was silent, and Keelie thought about what Heart-wood's loss meant to him. The fine furniture he had built was gone, all his time and craftsmanship vanished in a single night. And though the apartment above wasn't his permanent home, he'd lived there every summer for years.

She put her hand on his arm, and he tucked it into the crook of his elbow. She'd lost a lot, but she had her father, and last year, after her mother's death, she'd thought she'd be alone forever.

Now she had Dad, and Knot, and Cricket. The little goblin was still missing, but Keelie kept her eyes peeled for any sign of him.

She glanced at Dad. Maybe if she said something, it would help alleviate the dreadful tension flowing from him. She didn't know what the elves wanted, but a summons was always bad news, and, in Keelie's experience, it usually involved some threat or a reminder that she wasn't one of them.

Knot slipped ahead, dancing through the ferns.

"Dad, have you seen Cricket?"

He glanced at her. "In the vast pile of problems we've accumulated over the past few hours, a missing goblin does not register."

"He's just a baby." Keelie was stunned by Dad's reaction. Although she knew he blamed Cricket for the fire, Dad could have offered a word of comfort to her rather than a scolding.

Her silence must have given him a clue to her thoughts. "It's a goblin," he repeated. "It can take care of itself. It's probably off in a garbage can, eating something vile. It'll be back. Come on. We don't want to keep our brethren waiting."

The forest path turned to crushed stone, then flat stones set into the ground. They passed the first of the gray stone cottages where the elves lived while at this faire, a sign of how old the faire was. She remembered the first time she'd come here. She hadn't been welcome then either, but now she knew more about her so-called brethren.

Sean stepped off a porch and onto the cobbled path. He greeted them, but kept his eyes on Dad with only a glance at Keelie. Her heart dropped. What was awaiting them?

"Follow me." He turned and walked briskly to the communal stone building that stood in a square of lawn. Candles in a chandelier flickered above, throwing a honey-soft light on the wooden table in the middle of the cold and austere room. Several elves had gathered around the table including Elianard and, surprisingly, Lady Etilafael, the head of the Elven Council in the Dread Forest. What was she doing here?

Keelie had been right. It *was* a Council meeting, and she didn't have a good feeling about this one. Not that her prior experiences with elves had been a picnic, but tonight's meeting seemed extra somber. Couldn't this wait until tomorrow or the next day, when they'd recovered a little from the fire?

"Good evening, Zekeliel." Elianard motioned toward an empty chair. "Please sit. It seems this couldn't wait, although I encouraged all to have this meeting take place during daylight hours."

The jousters had lined up against the back wall. They all wore stoic expressions. Keelie knew these guys—when they weren't jousting they liked to clown around with Sean, but here, under their steely and hard gaze, she felt as if she was standing accused of something. It reminded her of when she'd been taken before the Council on suspicion of using dark magic. She shivered.

"Evidence has been found that goblins are on the move, and that they are here hiding in and around the human town of Fort Collins," said a voice from the shadows.

Chills danced up Keelie's spine as she recognized the speaker. As if sensing her awareness, Lord Niriel stepped forward. What was he doing here? He'd been exiled, last fall, for his role in the assault on the Wildewood unicorn in a misguided attempt to protect the Dread Forest. Even though Niriel was Sean's dad, Keelie couldn't forgive the handsome elf.

Dad stiffened beside her, and he reached down to squeeze her hand.

Tonight Niriel was dressed in jewel-toned robes; it certainly didn't look as if he had been roughing it on the road. Of course, he'd been living in Germany, where he'd been sent on a swordsmith exchange, so he probably had plenty of cash for nice garb.

He looked around the table, then spoke in grave tones. "Recently, I sought an audience with Terciel, the leader of the Northwoods elves, and he spoke of many disturbing things." Niriel paused. "One is that a goblin army is on the move, and I have come to warn you that they are here."

Etilafael looked around at the assembled elves. "Although Niriel was sent away from his home forest, he still strives to help his elven brethren. This grave news, on the heels of the attack in the Northwoods, tells us that we need all the help we can assemble. His diligence and his need to protect all elves have enlightened the Council. Therefore, we have decided to abolish his exile, reinstating him to his former status within our clan."

Murmurs of approval circulated among the elves.

Keelie nearly swallowed her tongue. Furious, she couldn't believe what she had just heard. Niriel had been slapped on the hand, told he was a bad elf, and asked to behave nicely.

"What evidence have you found?" Dad asked, very calmly. His eyes were glued on Niriel, waiting to hear what words he would spout to worm his way back into the good graces of all the elves.

"During the months I've had to endure without my son, my home forest, and my tribe"—Niriel swept his hands around in a dramatic gesture—"I traveled to Portland, the human city, where rumors hold that goblins roam in large numbers. The diabolical creatures live in the sewers and exist on garbage, and now I have evidence they have spread, and are here."

A sinking feeling hit Keelie in the pit of her stomach when one of the jousters brought a silver cage into the room. Cricket sat in the middle of it, chewing on a plastic bottle, oblivious to his surroundings. They placed him in the center of the table. All of the elves scooted back, expressions of horror flashing across their faces.

Keelie was about to run and snatch up the cage in her arms, but Dad blocked her with an outstretched arm. She cut her eyes over to him, and he shook his head.

"This creature does not seem threatening," Dad declared. "Do you base your fear-mongering on this pathetic insect?" His voice was suddenly in her thoughts. *Don't react, whatever happens, Keelie. I'm afraid that if they destroy your pet, you will be next.* His hand squeezed hers again.

Even knowing that Dad was just trying to calm the

elves' fears, Keelie felt a twinge of outrage. Cricket was not an insect.

Niriel walked around the table until he was directly across from them. "Lord Zekeliel, you have lost much because of the goblins. Your home here, your business—I would think that you would be the first to call for their destruction."

"What is your interest in this, Lord Niriel? Or do you have unconcluded business from our last encounter in the Dread Forest?" Dad ignored the gasps around the table.

Keelie saw Sean wince, then carefully school his features. Why hadn't he warned her that his father was here?

"At the risk of sounding callous, Lord Zekeliel, where there is smoke, there is fire." Niriel gestured toward Cricket. "The presence of this small specimen is a sign that there are more, and we have seen the damage that goblins can do. We must act swiftly."

"There are no other goblins," Keelie cried. She couldn't believe the elves were accusing Cricket. "He's a baby! How could he have started a fire?"

"How do you know this?" Niriel barked.

"Because I brought him here. He was with me."

Dad groaned.

"So, you don't deny bringing this creature?" Niriel's eyes were bright with a mix of hatred and madness. "You are only confirming what we already knew."

"He followed me from the Northwoods. He's harmless."

Etilafael cleared her throat. "Mayhaps the child has

misguided intentions, but I don't think she would purposefully ally herself with the goblins."

"Our brave warriors fought against these creatures, who followed a being most foul—Peascod, a goblin in the service of the hunter god, Herne," Niriel snapped in reply. "Keelie was seen with Herne, and it has been reported to me that the god coveted her and named her consort before the Grey Mantle Council. Of course she will defend the goblin spawn. And"—Niriel leaned forward—"she knows the location of the goblin stronghold."

Stunned, Keelie glared at Sean, who shook his head. What had he been saying to his father? Were they speaking of the goblin stronghold in the Northwoods?

"I don't know anything about a goblin stronghold," Keelie said, hoping they could see the truth in her eyes. She knew that the dark fae lived Under-the-Hill, but she wasn't about to reveal the existence of this realm to Niriel, or to the other elves.

"My daughter has said all she will say tonight. She knows nothing of a goblin stronghold. Can we adjourn this meeting and reconvene another time? I lost my shop in a fire tonight." Dad's eyes flashed. "I have much to do."

"Yes, we all know of your loss. The humans accuse the one named Vangar, but the Council and the elves do not think he is behind the fire. Humans do not have the magical means to find the real arsonist."

Did the elves truly know something about who was behind the fire? Keelie yawned. Fatigue was settling into her body but she forced herself to listen to every word.

"And this cannot wait until morning?" Dad's voice was weary.

Niriel bowed his head. "I understand your fatigue and the sadness of your loss. We all sympathize. But we need to address the loss of the Compendium, too."

Dad sighed and his shoulders slumped with exhaustion. "Get on with it then, Niriel."

"Lord Elianard, if you will." Niriel gestured, and the Lore Master rose from his chair and placed a torn square of thick paper in the middle of the table. The candlelight acted as a spotlight, making the shred of paper glow.

Keelie forced herself not to react. She recognized the parchment from the Compendium. She lifted her face to find Niriel staring directly at her.

"I see you recognize it."

Keelie refused to answer, biting down on her lip as she turned to her father for guidance.

"Where did you get it?" Dad asked. "Did the Compendium not burn in the fire?"

"We found it with this creature!" Niriel flourished his hand over Cricket. "He was eating it."

Keelie winced.

The little goblin threw the remains of his soft drink bottle at Niriel. The elven lord stepped back and raised his hand as if he was going to strike the goblin, despite the bars that enclosed the creature. At the last moment he clenched his hand, probably remembering that he had an audience, and pointed his index finger accusingly at Keelie. "Do you know where the goblins have hidden our Compendium?"

Chaos erupted in the room as all the elves started to argue at once. Cricket panicked, throwing himself against the bars of his cage with frenzied squeaks, and Keelie dashed forward and flung open the cage. The goblin skittered across the table like a spider, then wove his way between feet, up the wall, and out the door, adding to the confusion in the room.

Her joy at his escape was cut off abruptly as she saw Niriel's triumphant expression. She had just given him more evidence, and in front of all the elves. Could he be using a charm, or some other form of magic? Keelie angled her head fifteen degrees and Earth magic zinged through her body. She focused on Niriel and silently recited the words Finch had taught her: *Allow me to see truly.*

She caught a tiny flash, then nothing, as Niriel turned from her.

"Keelie, it is time to go," Dad said.

He escorted Keelie out of the communal building, lecturing her on proper protocol and common sense. As he turned toward the bridge, Keelie stopped.

"I thought we were going to Davy's RV?"

"I'm taking you back to Janice's shop. Stay there until the meeting is done."

"But Dad—"

"You stay there. Speak to no one. Do not try to find the goblin."

She only nodded, numb at the events of the night.

Janice met her with a cup of tea and a hug, then handed

her pajama pants and a sweatshirt. "No need to wake up early. It's almost morning now, and you're done in."

Keelie put on the borrowed pajamas and crawled into bed next to Raven. How could the elves think she would give the Compendium to the goblins? She'd been planning to post it online, so that there wasn't only one copy.

The worst thing was, she didn't know what to do about Dad's anger. He had defended her, and then she had released the goblin, pretty much proving herself guilty. She hoped he didn't do anything foolish back at the elven village. Her face burned at the position she'd put him in.

And why hadn't Sean defended her? Was it because his father was back? She'd never expected to see Niriel again. Or maybe in a hundred years or so. The only being worse than Niriel was Peascod, and at least he hadn't shown his masked face here.

When the first rays of morning light filtered through Janice's homemade curtains, Keelie felt as if she'd barely slept—although Raven was no longer next to her, so she must have been asleep for a little while. She yanked the covers over her head. All night long she'd wondered how she could find out what had happened to the Compendium, and who had started the fire at Heartwood. She'd thought about trying to contact Herne; however, with the elves upset about the goblins, it didn't seem like that would be a good idea.

Neither Cricket nor Knot had returned home. No, this was not home. This was Janice's shop. This was Raven's home. Keelie's had burned and all was lost.

She sighed and rubbed her chest. Was this heartbreak? She hoped Knot and Cricket were safe.

Janice knocked softly on the door and poked her head in. "Are you up? You have a visitor."

Keelie lowered the quilt from her face. "Who is it?"

"It's Sean. Why don't you come out when you're dressed?"

Keelie sighed. "I don't want to see him."

Janice frowned. "He's very insistent. He says it's an emergency."

Keelie thought of Dad heading back to the elven village and fear pulsed through her, along with images of him hurt and alone. She flipped the covers off, grabbed her running shoes with yesterday's socks jammed into them, and ran downstairs wearing an old pair of Raven's pajama pants and Janice's *Earth Is Our Mother* sweatshirt.

Her bare feet were cold on the hardwood floors (oak from Northern California). Sean stood there alone, surrounded by displays of bottled tinctures and baskets of loose herbs. He turned to look at her, handsome in his jousting clothes, with his blond hair pulled back by a leather tie.

"Is it Dad? What's wrong?" Keelie rushed to him, dropping the shoes and placing her hands on his chest.

"Your father's safe," he said. He leaned down and kissed her softly on the lips.

Relieved, Keelie bent to put on her shoes, schooling her face as she jammed in her feet and tied the laces.

"If you were to stay in the elven village, it would be easier for me to watch over you."

"I'm happy staying with Janice and Raven."

Sean stepped closer to her, as if bridging the distance between them could make her do as he wanted. He pressed his forehead to hers. "We would be together, and the other elves would see that you're with me, not running around with fairies and goblin creatures. They will take note that you're trying to be more elf."

Before Keelie could answer, Knot pushed his way through the door, followed by Cricket, who had several *bhata* riding him like a spidery golf cart. *Feithid daoine* buzzed around the open window. Something had the fae and dark fae creatures in turmoil. Knot saw Sean and pushed Cricket back out the door, then sauntered back in, arching his back and meowing.

Sean cast a glance at Knot. "Stay here at Janice's, then. The elves are looking for the goblin." He didn't see Cricket, who was climbing out the window, probably headed for the roof with his *bhata* riders.

Tension threaded through Keelie's body. It would be hard to keep Cricket out of sight. "Let's go for a walk. It's stuffy in here."

Keelie looked back at Knot and motioned for him to stay. Knot's tail twitched angrily. "I'll be right back. Sean and I need to talk."

"Meow." He narrowed his eyes.

She didn't want to say it aloud, so she thought at Knot, hoping the telepathic connection they once had would work again: *Keep an eye on Cricket. He may know where the Compendium is, if it survived the fire.*

Knot ignored her and washed his front paw.

She didn't know if he heard her, but she knew Knot wouldn't listen to her anyway. When did he ever?

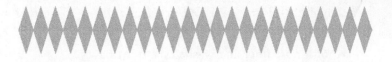

eight

Keelie and Sean started down the path. There was a different vibe to this stroll.

"As I said, your father is well. He's in talks with Elianard and my father."

"Thank you. I was worried. So, if he's okay, what's so urgent that you have to speak to me this morning?" She stopped and folded her arms across her chest.

Sean sighed. "I'm here on official business, representing the Elven Council."

Keelie fought not to roll her eyes. "Again? Another summons?"

"No, just me this time." Sean looked down at her, face sad but stern.

"You're here to represent the elves."

Sean nodded, standing stiffly. "Keelie, if only you would listen to me, then we … I wouldn't have to do this." Rubbing his chin in frustration, he watched her sadly.

"Do what?" She shivered, and it wasn't from the chilled morning air.

"They're going to question you, maybe by magical means, to discover the location of the goblins. You and I both know you're not telling them everything. I thought I'd give you a chance to speak freely, away from the others. You can tell me what you know about the goblins."

Keelie inhaled, taking in the green scent of the forest to help steel herself against her sudden anger. She should be shocked at his words, but maybe she was numb from the loss of Heartwood.

"No amount of magic can make me say what I don't know. I'm not psychic, and the goblins don't send me texts to tell me where they're headed."

Sean's eyes glinted like emeralds. "You're endangering yourself and all elves by your association with the goblins."

"I'm not endangering the elves or myself. I am a tree shepherd. I deal with the problems of the forest. In the Northwoods, that included goblins. And might I remind you that the elves sent me there?"

The muscles in Sean's face twitched, and he stepped forward to lean close. "You get yourself into situations that put your life at risk. When Herne took you

Under-the-Hill, I couldn't go. I feel like a puppet that hangs around you, unable to stop whatever threat is coming. Not this time, Keliel. You have to let us, the elves, handle the goblins. You need to stay out of it. You're putting our future children in jeopardy."

"Children?" Keelie's eyes widened in shock. She wasn't ready for a family. She was too young to think about starting a family.

"Yes, children. I want children. I want a family, but I've begun to wonder what you really want. I don't know if I'm going to have to wait a couple of hundred years before you decide you want a child, and then there's no telling how our child will turn out. Will it chase faeries and trees?"

Keelie stepped back. She realized for the first time they wanted very different things. She hadn't really accepted yet that she would live a far longer life span than a normal human. And she was sixteen. Driving was new to her. Children? Heck no.

"I haven't really thought about kids yet, but I hope my child would choose to do the right thing, and would come to the aid of whoever needed him or her—whether pureblood elf or not," Keelie said firmly. "I have done everything I can for the elves, and still you mistrust me. I restored the Dread. I saved the Redwoods, too, yet now I'm accused of being a traitor because I'm open-minded."

"You're not the only one who has made sacrifices, Keliel. I stood up to my father for you," Sean's eyes darkened. "Now he won't even speak to me, other than to give me orders."

"Your father has been plotting his return to the elves.

He must have scurried up to meet with Terciel right after we left the Northwoods. Notice how he didn't meet with Norzan. Terciel hates me. Heck, he doesn't even like Elia, his own kin, because she married Uncle Dariel after he became a unicorn. Not elf enough for him."

"My father's heart was in the right place. He wanted to save the elves, but chose the wrong way to do it, and he's paying for it." Sean stopped walking and looked at her earnestly. "Father thought one unicorn horn would save all the elves of the Dread Forest. But you want to sacrifice the elves to help the goblins."

"Goblins are part of the Other Realm. They serve a purpose. Didn't the rift in the Earth, the crack in Gaia's dome, prove that we must keep a balance in magic, in nature, and with the Earth? We can't exterminate goblins as if they were bugs."

Sean shook his head. "We'd be doing the world a favor if we did. You need to get your priorities straight. You've already lost one of our greatest treasures to the goblins, and I will not lose you as well." Sean's ear tips grew red.

Outraged and indignant, Keelie had to try twice before she could form words. "The Compendium was lost in the fire. The fire that destroyed everything I owned. I tried to go back for it..." Anguish rolled over her as she recalled the acrid smoke, the screaming trees, and the blistering heat. "My priorities? Didn't you learn anything at the High Court?"

He pointed his finger at her. "I learned to protect my own."

"Well, you don't have to protect me. I'm not yours."

"You never were, and now I think you never will be." Bitterness and sadness filled Sean's green eyes.

"You want me to be the good traditional elven girl, and that's not me." Stunned, Keelie realized her words were true. "Is this it?" she asked.

They stared at one another, at an impasse. Who was supposed to say the next word? Make the next move?

At last, Sean nodded. He reached out and touched her cheek. "We're too different, you and I."

Keelie blinked back tears. First, Heartwood, and now she was losing Sean. Maybe she'd already lost him on the plane ride from the Northwoods.

He took a deep breath and straightened, his austere elven expression replacing the sweet Sean she had thought she loved. "You say you don't know where the goblins are, but you have ways of finding out. Your pet goblin, for instance."

"He's a baby. Tell the elves to figure it out for themselves. I don't know." Heat crept up her body and into her face as anger flowed through her.

"Keelie, before this is finished, you will come to me for protection." Sean turned and strode away, leaving her alone on the path.

She watched him march toward Water Sprite Lane, his back stiff with hurt elven pride.

Keelie tried to examine her feelings, but her heart and mind were in a confused jumble. She turned her steps back toward the Green Lady Herb shop. She heard Sir Davey's deep voice in conversation inside, but she wasn't ready to speak to him or to anyone else. She hadn't had time yet to mourn the loss of Heartwood, and now of Sean. And she couldn't answer the elves' questions—she just didn't know.

Keelie felt her dry cheeks. She wondered if it was her dark fae blood that was keeping her from falling apart even though her heart felt like a shattered mirror, all the brightness broken forever.

When she'd been in school at Baywood Academy in California, she'd gone running whenever she needed to shake off bad feelings. Before she knew it, she was racing down Ironmonger's Way. She didn't even look toward the jousting field. The very thought turned her stomach. Freedom. She wanted the sweet freedom that running gave her.

She wondered what Sean would tell the elves.

Did they think she'd armor up and join this goblin army that she supposedly knew the location of? But what if it wasn't an army? Peascod had recruited his fighters from urban streets—hungry, solo goblins. Alone, they were no threat to anyone. If she ran into a few goblins making their way through the faire's trash bins, she wouldn't tell, not even Dad.

If they were armored, like Peascod's fighters, then she would tell her father and let him make the decision. Dad would take her information to the Council, and it would come under debate—or would it? The elves would more than likely go immediately into defensive mode. The goblins could even be killed.

The elves still didn't trust her, and she didn't trust them, either.

Thomas the Glass Blower waved as she sprinted by his smoking kiln. She lifted a hand in return. Humans were friendlier than elves, and right now she preferred their company. The mud men pretended to jump out of her way, with exaggerated movements, as she passed them on King's Way. "Make way for the lady in a hurry!"

Keelie noticed the flickers of sympathy in their sun-wrinkled, mud-encrusted faces.

At least humans, or most humans, were more accepting of each other. Differences were celebrated. Elves—it was their way or nothing. You were shunned for being different.

The Birds of Prey show wasn't too far ahead. She thought fondly of Ariel, the Cooper's Hawk who had once been part of the show and was now free in the Dread Forest.

She slowed a little, her muscles fatigued more quickly than she'd anticipated. She hadn't run in a while. She'd let her workouts slide because she'd been so busy with her tree shepherding duties.

The Birds of Prey area was open, but Keelie didn't recognize the costumed workers. Cameron was probably cleaning cages in the back. She should stop by and visit with her soon. With Heartwood gone, she might have time to help feed the birds.

She ran past the candle shop, where Trixie, the round, sixtyish owner, waved as her daughter, Karen, as spindly as her mom was robust, smiled. She returned the friendly gestures but didn't stop. The Horne Shoppe's owner, Elizabeth Hawkins, smiled at her as she stocked her displays of faux devil horns, unicorn horns, and fairy wings. Her cat

Luci was asleep in the shop's gutter, paws dangling. He was probably recovering from a Knot-induced bender.

Ahead, Keelie saw the tall front entrance of the faire, which looked like a castle wall, and the tarot shop in its shadow. The shop was little more than a deck with a roof over it, the sides hung with colorful draperies and twinkling glass ornaments that twirled with every breeze that billowed out the silky cloths. It looked as if Sally had a client, and Keelie would recognize that mane of red hair anywhere. Finch.

She needed to ask the faire director why she'd encouraged Vangar to ask her for help clearing his name. Maybe the answer would anger her, which might numb the hurt of her breakup with Sean. And she needed something to do since Heartwood was no more. Finch might give her a job.

Keelie pushed aside a vermilion curtain covered in tiny embroidered mirrors and stepped up onto the wide-planked floor of the booth.

"Busy?"

Finch lifted her upper lip in a snarl. "What does it look like?"

"It looks like you're having your cards read." Keelie sat down on the fat purple velvet cushion that covered the wooden bench and the faire director scooted over to give her room.

"Yeah, this is all new to me."

"What? Dealing with angry crowds?"

Finch motioned nonchalantly with her hand. "Them, I can handle. This other thing I can't."

"I'm lost. But I do need to talk to you." Keelie flicked her eyes over at Sally. She wore a scarf around her curly blond hair, and she was shuffling her cards while humming softly to herself.

"Please be quiet as I try to tune myself to the Earth's vibration," she said. She picked up her humming again.

Finch looked directly at Keelie. "You can trust Sally. We've been friends for a long time."

Sally raised one eyebrow. "A long time, kid. You aren't going to say anything that's going to surprise me."

She kept shuffling her cards expertly, the little cardboard rectangles flashing and fanning out, then sliding together with a snap. If tarot reading didn't work out for her, she could take up card dealing in Vegas.

"This is about Vangar," Keelie said.

Finch's cheeks burned bright red. "Yeah, tell me about it. Pretty intuitive of you to figure out why I'm here." Then Finch narrowed her eyes and studied Keelie as if she were a milk carton that had reached its expiration date but still might be okay to drink. "You're not right. Something's wrong."

"I'm upset about Heartwood," Keelie quickly replied.

Sally lowered her cards and pointed her finger at Keelie's chest. "Your heart chakra is clogged with dark energy."

Finch arched a red eyebrow. "Spill, kid."

Keelie inhaled to hold back a sob.

Sally reached underneath her table and handed Keelie a tissue. "Tell us. Maybe we can help."

"Sean and I broke up," Keelie said.

Finch nodded. "I know you don't want to hear this right now, because the pain is raw and fresh, but in the long run, I think you two weren't meant for each other."

"What?" Keelie blew her nose.

"He was all wrong. He's always been bound to the jousters, who are also elven warriors, you know. I give Sean credit for stretching himself and trying to expand his mind, but I've known him for many more years than you have been alive, my dear."

Finch's words hit home. She'd known Sean since before Keelie was born. Sean was eighty-six years old, and Keelie was going on seventeen. Their age difference was something else that had contributed to their problems—he had already experienced so much in life, and she was at the beginning of her journey.

Sally pointed her finger. "Let me read your cards and give you some love advice."

"That's okay." Keelie waved away the invitation.

"That's why Finch is here. Vangar stokes her fires unlike any dra—"

Finch cleared her throat. "I find Vangar rather handsome, and he's very manly."

Sally rolled her eyes.

"You mean he's very dragony." Keelie couldn't help smiling. She liked seeing Finch discombobulated.

"Well, yeah."

"Vangar said that he put protection spells on his forge, and that someone very powerful lifted them," Keelie said.

Finch nodded. "He told me about putting fire spells

on the forge. It's why I allowed it to remain so close to the trees and the other shops. He's a very powerful dragon. It would take great magic to break the spells." Finch watched Sally place three cards down on the stars-and-crescent-moon-printed tablecloth.

"Wouldn't there be a trace of such a powerful magic?" Keelie asked.

"If whoever removed them used a cover spell, and layered it with another one, then it would be hard to detect," Finch answered. She turned to Keelie. "Pick a card."

"But I don't need a reading on my love life."

"This isn't about your love life. This reading is going to help us discover the identity of the arsonist."

"The elves said that they think Vangar is innocent," Keelie said.

"For once they're right about something," Finch said, smoke drifting out of her ears.

Knot leapt into the tarot shop and hopped up beside Sally.

"Where have you been?" Keelie asked.

Knot placed a paw on the table, which didn't answer Keelie's question.

"Have you seen Cricket?"

He gave a slight shake of his head as his tail twitched agitatedly.

"Glad to see you," Finch said. "How have your investigations gone?"

Knot looked toward the curtained side of the shop, where a railing served as traffic control for customers.

Keelie heard a familiar discordant jangle. She jumped to her feet, anticipating Peascod, but he didn't materialize.

Knot nodded and the curtain twitched aside. A *bhata* hopped onto the railing, holding a round brass jingle bell the size of a cherry tomato. The bell dropped and rolled to Keelie's feet, its discordant jangling making her sick to her stomach.

"I know the owner of that bell," she whispered. "He could have started the fire." Peascod could very well be at the faire. She stared at the bell as if it were about to explode.

"What?" Finch's voice was sharp.

Keelie told her about Peascod and about the elves' suspicions of a goblin army, feeling no duty to keep their dealings secret. Not anymore. Slowly, she reached down and picked up the bell. It felt warm and normal, and when clasped in her hand, its noise was muted to a dull rattle.

Finch growled. "We're going to find him." A flicker of flames appeared in her eyes, and there was a hint of eau de charcoal in the air.

Sally reached out and took Keelie's other hand. "You're not alone. We're here for you. The people in this faire have you and your father's backs."

Keelie tightened her hand around Sally's. It felt good to have friends who cared, really cared. And she could count Raven, Janice, Sir Davey, the mud men, and several others as more than friends—they were part of her faire family. "Thank you."

Finch pointed to the three cards, and a shimmery haze grew around her.

Keelie didn't know if the dragon was using magic, but she wasn't going to argue. She leaned forward to study the cards and felt compelled to touch the middle one. She glanced up and found that Sally was staring at her. Sally flipped the card over and Keelie was surprised to see a red dragon with fire-emblazoned scales accompanying an armed, cloaked woman, both facing a dancing jester with a skeletal mask.

"Queen of Swords. I like how the artist captured the dragon's scales. Hard to do with a natural red." Finch rubbed her hands gleefully.

"What does this mean?" Keelie looked from Sally to Finch.

"It suggests a stubborn but powerful feminine presence. See, in the background, the jester is dancing, and you will need the assistance of others to stop him."

If Keelie had to face Peascod, then she was glad she had Finch's help.

"May I suggest a plan?" Finch said.

"Sure." Keelie was glad to be asked instead of told. Surprising, coming from a dragon.

"I think we need to investigate Hob. And I think I have the perfect cover." The faire administrator's eyes gleamed brightly.

"But Hob has been very nice to us. He got there right away when the fire started." Keelie stared at Finch.

"Yes, and that's what is driving me crazy. It doesn't add

up. Hob supposedly smelled the smoke, and then saw the flames when he looked out of his shop. He rushed to your shop and saved the tree. Why save the goblin tree? Then, remember, I can't detect his essence."

Keelie shivered as the bell jangled on the table, untouched. She grabbed a tissue from the box that Sally kept for weepers and stuffed it into the bell. That should do it.

"I have a witness who saw him leaving the meadow at the same time he said he was in his mask shop." Tendrils of smoke coiled from her ears and nostrils.

"What? It doesn't make sense. Who was your witness?" Keelie asked. "'If it was Vangar ... " She still doubted the blacksmith's credibility.

"It was, and yes, I believe him. And the *bhata* and the *feithid daoine*. They tried to tell you, but you were never alone."

Keelie inhaled sharply. "Then what's your plan?"

"You're going to get a job at Hobknocker's. Use the To See Truly spell on him. If he lets his guard down, you may be able to read him, see his true self."

"Hey, I thought you said I was banned from working at the faire."

"Things have changed. Desperate times call for desperate plans." Finch tapped the tarot card with the red dragon and the cloaked girl facing down the dancing jester.

Keelie felt a tiny surge of hope. She wasn't thrilled to be working next to Heartwood's smoldering ruins, but she liked Hob. He'd saved the goblin tree, and she was sure there was a good explanation for Finch's suspicions other than something magical. In the meantime, it would give her something to do other than mope around about Sean and mourn the loss of Heartwood. She would be able to do her own investigation into the fire.

"When would I start?" Keelie asked.

"I think now would be a good time," Finch said as she held up the tarot card. "And you'll need some garb." Her eyes flicked down to Keelie's outfit and she realized she'd been running in Raven's PJ bottoms and Janice's sweatshirt.

nine

"I do need garb. I need a toothbrush, too." Keelie hadn't anticipated working at Hobknocker's *today*. She tried to keep up with Finch as they walked past Sir Davey's Dragon Hoard shop. Rocks and shiny crystals glimmered from inside the window display.

They stopped at Galadriel's Closet. Finch nodded to the proprietor, Mara, as Keelie gave her friend an enthusiastic hug. "Let the kid pick out something and charge it to the faire," Finch announced. She looked at Keelie. "Choose an outfit for working at the shop. Nothing fancy."

"Nothing fancy" described all the rental garb; these

clothes were made to last a long time. Keelie picked out a drab, basic Ren Faire wench outfit: dingy white peasant top, stained flounced skirt, and corduroy vest that laced up the front.

Finch noticed her glum face and winked. "Consider it therapy. You know what they say about getting back into the saddle after you've fallen off a unicorn, oops, I mean a horse. This is preview day for faire folk family and friends, so it's a perfect day to begin. No big crowds, but plenty of people in costume."

The faire director stomped ahead on Ironmonger's Way, her boots leaving huge prints in her wake. Keelie wouldn't have been surprised to see claw impressions in the dirt.

"Your kindness and thoughtfulness overwhelm me," she called as she ran after her. "Let me guess—Ermentrude never gave you sensitivity training, did she? And by the way, what am I supposed to do? Dust the creepy masks?"

The scent of herbal soaps and aromatherapy oil wafted from Janice's herbal shop. Keelie longed to return to bed for a nap to soothe her aching muscles, but they kept moving.

"You'll do whatever he needs you to do." Finch cut her eyes over at Keelie.

All of the booth owners waved at Finch as she marched by their shops. Maybe they sensed, on a subconscious level, "here be dragon." Or maybe her faire admin personae was scary enough.

The girls hired to be fairies were working on their costumes outside Betty's Books and Baubles, cackling like hens laying eggs. Keelie recognized Marcia, Tracy, and Lily, now dressed as Shimmerlight the gold fairy, Lavender Lollipop the purple fairy, and Lily Limerton the green fairy.

Finch motioned for Keelie to stop. Keelie rolled her eyes. Why were they stopping here? The last thing Keelie wanted to do was eavesdrop on a bunch of fake fairies talking. She'd met the real deal at the High Court and was not impressed with imitations.

At least the bell the *bhata* had given her wouldn't jangle again—it was still stuffed with tissue from Sally's shop. She needed to get rid of the thing.

Finch elbowed Keelie and whispered, "Try the To See Truly spell on them."

"Did you hear that the Equus Island guys aren't letting people near the horses?" Shimmerlight sprinkled more glitter on her wings.

"They've always been snooty. Really cut, but not like Hob," Lily added.

Keelie tilted her head fifteen degrees (or so she assumed), tapped into Earth magic, and focused on the light around Lily. "*Allow me to see truly*," she softly said.

She didn't see anything around Lily, Tracy, or Marcia regarding their "intent." This seeing truly spell didn't work, and it would be the same with Hob.

Impatient to move on, Keelie tapped Finch on the shoulder. "Why are we here?"

"Listen," Finch hissed softly.

Lily Limerton was sewing some jingly bells on her tulle skirt from a bowl next to her. Keelie had really come to dislike the sound of bells.

"Hob told everyone down at the Poacher's Inn pub that Vangar is a suspect in the fire." Shimmerlight grinned, then whispered, "He's paying us to direct all the children to his shop. Isn't that awesome?"

Lily Limerton squealed. "It's our secret!" They made a silly show of shushing each other, fingers to lips.

Shimmerlight stood and held the blinged-out skirt up for the other fairy girls to see. "Is it sparkly enough?"

Lily Limerton and Lavender Lollipop both nodded.

Keelie looked away to keep from rolling her eyes. She watched Finch stride forward and smiled as the three fairies moved close together, almost into a huddle, to protect one another.

"Good morning, ladies," Finch growled.

"Good morning, Madame Faire Director," Shimmerlight said as her face burned tomato red.

"I hope you ladies will make sure the children attending the faire today, or any other faire day, have lovely dreams of gossamer wings and hummingbird happy thoughts. Make sure they see not only the masks at Hobknocker's, but also all of our fine establishments here at the High Mountain Faire. Am I making myself perfectly clear, like the ringing of a crystal bell high above the mountains of Norway?"

What did Norway have to do with anything?

"Yes!" All three fairy girls drew together even more closely, as if they could sense they had angered the inner dragon of the faire director.

"I will not hear of any side deals with shop owners, or tales that my fairies have been bad. Right?"

All three girls nodded their heads simultaneously.

"Keelie has seen bad fairies. What happens to bad fairies?"

"They get turned into brownies," Keelie said with a straight face. "Fairy servants who are all wrinkly and wear ugly clothes."

The fairy girls' eyes widened.

"What a horrible fate." Finch was very nonchalant and uber cool, so unlike her usual self. "You ladies have a great day, and don't forget what I said."

"Yes ma'am," they answered in unison.

Finch walked away, with Keelie keeping pace. She could only imagine the conversations that would circulate around the faire: *Keelie is in cahoots with the faire director.*

"What did you learn back there?" Finch asked. "Did you use the To See Truly spell?"

"I learned not to wear lime green fairy wings," Keelie answered. "And no, the seeing clearly spell didn't work."

"Keep practicing. It takes time to master the spell, so I'm not surprised at your outcome. Those three share one brain cell, and they may have misplaced it. What did you learn from overhearing them talk?"

"I learned that Hob has supposedly been spreading rumors, and you heard how he paid the fairy girls to recommend his shop over the others."

Finch rubbed her hands together gleefully. "Yes! He's sneaky. So, when you're in Hobknocker's, I want you to listen and observe. I know there is more to his story. We have to put the random pieces together to get the whole picture."

"I'll do what I can," Keelie said. Sure, the fairies were gossiping, but Keelie didn't think it was that awful for Hob to pay them to favor his shop—it was just business. She still couldn't picture him as a bad guy.

As they strode up the hill, past the familiar rooftops and colorful signs, Keelie's heart squeezed tightly in her chest at the thought of what she and Dad had lost. The sight of the skeletal and smoking remains of Heartwood saddened her to the very core of her soul. She mourned the loss of the apartment above the shop that had been home, and her refuge after Mom's death.

She steeled herself and trudged forward, keeping her gaze on Hobknocker's. Her mission was to discover more about Handsome Hob with his charming and wily ways. He kind of reminded her of a snake with glistening scales, but that didn't mean he was evil.

Despite her best intentions, Keelie glanced left, at the bustling activity where Heartwood had been. A work crew was clearing the debris. Keelie recognized a couple of Sean's jousters. Elianard stood nearby, watching them. What did he expect they'd turn up? The Compendium had been upstairs, under her bed and surely was burned to ashes by now. Her heartbeat sped up as she thought of the possibility that it might be somewhere else at the faire.

The Lore Master arched an inquisitive eyebrow as Finch and Keelie walked past. At least the jousters were helping out, though their shovels and picks stopped as they walked by. Some openly pointed and whispered. Keelie held her head high and marched forward.

It would only be a matter of time before Sean knew about the recent development in Keelie's employment status, and there would be a Council Meeting to discuss it. She hadn't had a chance to tell Dad about Finch's idea, but he was so preoccupied anyway, and she could always just explain that she accepted the job because she was after the truth about the fire and had agree to uncover more information about Hob for Finch. Not to mention the fact that Finch was right—Keelie needed something to do besides grieve for Heartwood, pine for Sean, and wait for Dad while he attended the never-ending Council sessions.

The scent of roasting turkey legs floated up the hill from the food merchants near the jousting arena. Her stomach rumbled. She'd eat later.

She cast a quick glance through her lashes to see if there was a familiar blond head among the elves, but Sean wasn't there.

She was disappointed, but on the other hand, she wouldn't have to look at him while she worked at Hobknocker's today.

"Heartwood, move it," Finch bellowed.

Suddenly, Keelie felt queasy. There was a huge jester's mask painted on the side of the shop. She hadn't noticed it before, since Dad's shop was on the other side and the wall would have been shadowed at night. She felt silly for being afraid, but she didn't want to go in.

"I don't know if I can do this," Keelie said, stopping.

Finch placed her hand on Keelie's shoulder. "Yes, you can. You're strong, and you're not going to let one guy stop you from doing what you have to do. You're Keliel Katharine Heartwood, and you have saved many a forest. Are you going to let one elf's opinion stop you?"

Keelie shook her head. "You've got it all wrong. It's that thing—" She waved a hand at the leering clown face on the wall.

"It's a picture, Heartwood. An image. Paint on wood. Art, and not a very good example of it, either. Don't worry, this'll be a picnic. Just don't break anything."

The dragon was right; Keelie couldn't let the memory of Peascod's mask keep her from getting this job done. There was no danger here, anyway. She'd have fun with Hob.

A crowd of women had gathered around Hob's shop. Raven was right—women were flocking to the hill. Keelie sniffed, trying to detect the smell of cinnamon, the scent of elven magic. It usually accompanied the "charm" spell elves used to persuade humans to do as they wanted. There was no sign of it here—Dad could charm women this way if he chose, but he didn't have to rely on a spell since women liked him for his good looks (those Heartwood cheekbones and green eyes sold a lot of chairs).

But the bellydancers, kissing wenches, and Hot Tub wenches hanging around on Hobknocker's front porch didn't make for a very charming sight, if you asked Keelie.

Twisty copper wind chimes had been added to the low-slung roof of the shop. Entwined in the wire were semi-precious jewels, which glittered and tinkled loudly as a gentle breeze blew through them. The sound was enchanting but sometimes oddly off key, like one of Peascod's jester hat bells.

Keelie checked in with the trees and discovered that the jangly noise irritated them, too.

Hob sat in the midst of his groupies, a hand puppet on each hand, making funny voices for them. The women laughed and clapped, though it seemed odd to Keelie that grown women were hanging around watching a puppet show.

Removing a witch puppet from one hand, Hob replaced it with a jester puppet that wore a red and gold costume with green rickrack trim on the cuffs of the sleeves and pants. Its little triangular hat was missing a bell.

Keelie rubbed her arms to dispel the sudden chill the sight brought on.

The bell in her pocket vibrated as if it sensed familiar magic, or its owner. But the bell couldn't belong to the puppet, since it was almost as large as the puppet's head.

"That is all, sweetings. Shop for masks and add mystery to your glance." Hob stood up and swept his hands apart as he bowed low from the waist, then turned to Keelie and Finch. "Good day, my lovely ladies. What may I do for you?"

He smiled, his white teeth sparkling like headlights. Keelie decided she would need to wear sunglasses while working for him.

Finch flashed him a dazzling grin of her own. "Hello, Hob. Hello, Toshi."

The jester puppet imitated Hob's earlier bow, then

motioned a tiny wooden hand toward Keelie. Hob turned the puppet around to him. "You would like to know who she is?"

Weird, having a grown man talk to a puppet about her. When did the act end? "He wants to know about me?" Keelie asked.

The puppet nodded.

Keelie turned to Finch. "Seriously?" she implored. "Talk to a puppet?" Hob had seemed so cool before.

Finch grinned, seeming to enjoy Keelie's discomfort.

"That's Keelie Heartwood," Hob told the piece of cloth and wood covering his right hand. "And sadly, she lost her shop to a terrible and tragic fire started by a negligent blacksmith."

Keelie waited for Finch to explode. She didn't.

"Hob, I have hired you a shop assistant," Finch said calmly. Oscar performance here.

"What?" Hob flinched. "Why?"

The puppet placed its hands over its mouth in surprise.

"Word is you're going to be very busy." Finch flashed him a knowing grin.

Hob blushed. "I don't know what you mean."

"According to our projections, your sales are going to be off the chart," Finch said. She turned her gaze to encompass the crowd of ladies busily trying on masks. Some appeared put out that Finch had interrupted their gathering. "As faire administrator, I took it upon myself to get you the help you'll need." She glared at the women, who were listening in. "Seems like some of you should get back to work."

"We came to see the puppet show," one of the Hot Tub wenches said in a plaintive whine. Her breasts were so tightly corseted in her bodice that they looked like round flotation devices popping out of the top.

"I suggest you return to your shops and to your jobs before I decide you don't have one." Finch shot the woman a blazing glare, and the crowd dispersed as if a stick of dynamite had been thrown at them.

The puppet waved goodbye to the departing groupies.

"You're an amazing and talented faire director, Finch. I didn't realize you had taken such an interest in my shop. Who do you have in mind as my new shop assistant?"

"Keelie, of course." Finch gestured toward her as if she were a new appliance in a department store.

Keelie stepped forward and produced what she hoped was a convincing smile. "Me again, neighbor."

Hob's whole demeanor changed, from reluctance to surprise to elation. "Keelie! I would love to have her. Her experience at Heartwood makes her invaluable to me."

Finch beamed at Hob. "That's what I thought."

In the trees above, the *bhata* had gathered, and Knot sat on the edge of the mask shop roof watching her, his tail twitching. He pointed it toward the meadow. What was he trying to tell her?

"I'll leave you two alone, and if you have any problems with her, Hob, let me know. I'm going to check on the armor shop." Finch turned around and walked away, leaving Keelie alone with Hob. Keelie swallowed.

"Why would she say that, I wonder?" Hob stepped down from the front porch, and for a fleeting moment, Keelie thought she saw a shimmery outline around his body. That was new.

"I'm glad you're here to help me, and so is Toshi," he added. The puppet extended a wooden hand.

"Hello, Toshi," Keelie shook the puppet's hand. Yes, she was being introduced to a puppet.

"Would you like to come inside?" The mask maker motioned toward the door.

Keelie wasn't so sure she wanted to be alone with Hob. Quirky didn't begin to describe him, and that shimmer concerned her. Was it magic? Maybe he was under a spell.

A cloud of orange cat hair drifted down onto Hob. He sneezed.

Keelie looked up at Knot, who jumped down from the roof onto the porch. Hob stepped back.

"Why is that cat here?" Another sneeze.

"He followed me. Is it okay if he comes inside the shop with us? He misses Heartwood so much. There's nothing like having a shop kitty. People love to pet him, and it relaxes the customers."

Hob sneezed again. Toshi the puppet covered its nose with its hands.

"He can stay, but I'm allergic to cats. Knot has to stay outside." Hob sneezed again.

"Strange. I thought Knot had visited you before," Keelie said.

Knot rubbed his head up and down Hob's leg and purred happily. Lots of cat fur floated around him.

"He likes you," Keelie said cheerily.

Hob blew his nose into a multicolored handkerchief. "Come back Saturday morning, and I'll give you a tour before we open. Right now, I've got someplace I need to be."

"What about preview day today?"

Hob's eyes darkened. He turned toward the meadow, then whirled around to face Keelie. Sweat beaded on his upper lip and he shook his head. "I must go." He ran inside the shop and closed the door. She heard the clicks of locks as Hob barricaded himself inside with Toshi and his masks.

Keelie was relieved she didn't have to spend time alone with Hob and his creepy puppet.

Knot pointed his tail to the south. "Meow."

"There's something you want me to see in the meadow?"

Knot nodded.

What now? She hadn't had time to catch her breath since she'd arrived back at the High Mountain Faire. It had been one crisis after another. Following Knot down Wood Row and Water Sprite Lane, Keelie avoided eye contact and tuned her senses in to the trees.

Something was definitely up, but she couldn't tell what.

ten

The meadow seemed undisturbed. Keelie glared at Knot. "You brought me all the way down here, for what?"

Knot raced up to Hrok and Keelie followed.

Well met, Hrok. Everything okay here?

Hrok's face pushed through the bark. *Most certainly, Tree Shepherdess. How goes your faire? Have you met goblins there? We've seen them in their metal skin. The bhata have seen them too.*

Keelie's blood chilled at the words "goblin" and "metal skin." Armored goblins? Finch and the elves had been right. Yet Hrok didn't seem concerned.

Where have you seen these goblins? she asked.

They came from Under-the-Hill. The bhata will show you.

Keelie looked around nervously. The meadow seemed like an obvious location for an entrance to Under-the-Hill, but Keelie knew that the dark fae were wily.

Several *bhata* appeared from their nearby hiding places. The dry sound of sticks rubbing together, along with the crackling whir of wings, surrounded her. She felt a tug on her hair and put her hand up carefully to feel for the creature. She'd become used to the *bhata*, but it was still strange to feel one in her hair.

Her fingers touched something long and slender, shorter than a chopstick, followed by a fuzzy softness that she knew to be moss, which the *bhata* used to bind together their stick-and-berry bodies. She lowered her hand, not surprised to see the little *bhata* riding on it as if it were a fairy elevator.

"Hello, little guy. Any chance you can show me where Under-the-Hill is?"

The *bhata*'s hands, made of grass seedheads, flew up to cover purple berry eyes. It chattered and backed away on her hand.

"I'm sorry. I didn't mean to upset you. I've been there before, you know. Just not here at the High Mountain Faire."

One berry eye peeked out from behind the improvised hands. The *bhata* seemed to consider her for a moment, then chirped and flew straight up. Others joined it, until the air was filled with the clicking sticks.

The little creatures hopped from branch to branch,

flew, and skittered over the ground. Keelie followed them, stepping carefully to avoid crunching one underfoot. Not that it would hurt them—the sticks and moss were just what the *bhata* assembled for a physical presence, and Knot loved to chase them down and trash them. Apparently they didn't mind, since it gave them an excuse to chase Knot down and try to disassemble *him.* So far, he was still in one piece.

The *bhata* moved faster, and Keelie and Knot hurried after them. They were heading through the woods that edged the faire and circling around to the performer's campground.

She closed her mind to the trees so that word wouldn't get back to Dad about where she was going. He would never let her go Under-the-Hill again, not after the goblin battle in the Northwoods.

The *bhata* whirred and clacked around her, and she realized that they were circling now, a buzzing vortex that was pushing her forward.

Ahead of her was the raw rock face of the mountain that towered over the faire. Keelie stopped. She was not going to go rock climbing. Not in her job description.

The *bhata* clung to the jagged rocks. A spindly pine grew from a patch of dirt about twenty feet up. Maybe it had some answers.

Hail, hill climber, Keelie greeted it. Trees liked to be given names.

Well met, Tree Shepherdess, the tree answered politely.

Behind the tree's soft words, Keelie heard a chorus of tree voices also greeting her. She considered ignoring them, but she might need their help to find Under-the-Hill and keep watch over the forests. Trees saw everything.

You honor me.

Be careful, the *bhata* whispered to her. *Do not go in.*

A large granite rock at the base of the mountain soared from the dense carpet of grass like a lone Egyptian obelisk guarding a temple.

It couldn't be so obvious. Keelie glanced at the accumulated *bhata* and down at Knot. He ran to the edge of the rock, but the *bhata* stayed back. Why were they afraid?

Knot pressed his paw on a small depression in the side of the obelisk. A loud click and the stone levered back, revealing a dirt staircase cut into the earth.

A dark feeling of fear overpowered Keelie, but she reached for her rose quartz, tugging on a thin stream of magic to light it. Not too much—she didn't want to alert whatever might live in this place. A slightly dank odor, like overgrown mold in a shower stall, grew stronger as she descended downward. The light grew dimmer. Keelie held the quartz aloft, and its soft pink shimmer illuminated the walls.

Mica glittered in the light. She touched the walls with her fingertips. Smooth. This area had not been carved by chisel. Knot wandered ahead.

When she'd lived at the High Mountain Faire last summer, Keelie hadn't known about the existence of Under-the-Hill, or that she had fae blood. The elves didn't know about Under-the-Hill at all, though they had lived above it in various locations for centuries. They either couldn't see, or ignored, the dark fae.

She passed huge doorways as she continued down the tunnel, doorways big enough to drive a school bus through. A clink of metal on metal sounded ahead; she pulled back and flattened against the wall, trying to make herself as tiny as possible. Something or someone was nearby. Then the staggering scent of unwashed body nearly knocked her over. She'd smelled this before.

A goblin, taller than she was and wearing leather and metal armor, stomped past, never looking her way. He vanished into the darkness of a side tunnel.

Keelie's heart was hammering in her chest. This goblin was huge—much bigger than any she'd seen in the Northwoods. Where had he come from?

She moved slowly down the tunnel again, her back to the rock wall. She kept glancing around, trying to make sure nothing was sneaking up on her. Soon a breeze tickled her face, signaling a large space ahead. Keelie moved toward it, promising the scared part of her mind that she would only look to see what was there, and then she would get out of here.

Knot rubbed reassuringly up against her leg. He meowed softly.

A boom vibrated through the rocks, followed by another one. Earthquake? Keelie knew she could get trapped down here. Her heart couldn't beat any faster. Better to get this over with. She hurried forward, toward a muted roar that sounded like an underground waterfall.

She heard sharp clinking on rock, and knew that sound. She'd made it herself when she was at Baywood Academy, running across the parking lot in cleats. The metal striking the pavement made that exact sound just before she'd slipped and fallen. Cleats were made for firm footing on mushy ground.

This was the same sound, multiplied many times over. The roar built as she moved closer. Her lungs burning, Keelie stopped at the mouth of the dark side tunnel, then turned her head slowly and looked into the cavern beyond.

Goblins. The cavern was shiny with torchlight reflecting off slick, fungus-like skin where it wasn't covered by armor. It looked like a war party of demons. A few of the goblins were like Cricket—glossy, black, and insect-like— but they were almost man-tall. And there was no waterfall. It was the goblins who roared, arms raised in celebration.

It suddenly occurred to Keelie that she'd done such a good job of blocking herself from the trees, so that Dad wouldn't know where she was, that she'd also blocked her magical senses.

She felt the magic now, waves of it prickling against her skin. She had to notify Dad, but if she tried to use magic, the goblins might notice it. Or maybe her use of it would be hidden from them? Keelie suddenly craved fresh air. Her chest burned and ached as if it was being squeezed.

Panic attack. She needed to get out of here now. What if they captured her and tortured her?

Knot placed his paw on her foot, and the waves of anxiety crashing in on her began to ease.

"Meow this way."

Keelie fought the fear, taking deep breaths to calm herself. She was okay. They hadn't sensed her yet, and if she could back out as quietly as she'd entered, they would never know she'd been here. In the cavern, the goblins were starting to bob and shuffle. Now was her chance to back out, while they were busy doing whatever they were about to do.

A familiar jangle made her freeze before she'd taken a step—the sound of a belled hat, somehow audible over the roar of the goblins. Peascod. It had to be. She edged back to the cavern opening and leaned forward to peek in.

The goblins were dancing now. Their squatting and jumping and shuffling would get them kicked out of any L.A. club, but it was definitely dancing. Were they celebrating?

Standing on a stone ledge, on the opposite side of the cavern, was a slender figure who seemed to be leading the dance. It was definitely male, or at least Keelie thought so, given the broad shoulders and slender waist—and mask. Keelie's breath caught. The figure was dancing maniacally, and then he started to bang a big kettle drum that stood waist-high on the floor. The goblins bounced to his beat and banged their boots on the stone floor. The figure reached down, snatched something from the floor, and jammed it on his head. A jester's hat.

Torches blazed into light around the cavern and the goblins roared their approval. The light reflected off the shiny mask on Peascod's face. He began to pull it off, to cheers and cries of approval.

As Keelie leaned in, not breathing as she waited to see what Peascod hid behind his mask, a steel-covered hand grabbed her shoulder and pulled her around. The goblin stared at her for a second, face tilted; then his lips skimmed back to reveal jagged yellow fangs.

Keelie wrenched free and leaped down the corridor, dropping her rose quartz. The next tunnel junction had to be ahead. Metal rang on stone as the goblin gave chase. Keelie's knees were like jelly and her fingertips scrapped against the stone wall as she tried to keep her bearings. A guttural cry sounded behind her and she ran even faster, banging painfully into the walls in the darkness.

Words from the Compendium floated behind her eyes. Her breath came in harsh gasps as she tried to remember what they meant. It couldn't be a coincidence that they'd come to her now. She started to say the words aloud, then paused. What if it was a get-your-socks-clean charm? Or one to keep mice out of your knitting? She recognized the elven word for "red," but that meant nothing. It could be a charm to make tree leaves brighter in the autumn.

Hot pain shredded across her left thigh and she leaped in reaction, startling a grunt out of her attacker. Furious and panicked, Keelie yelled the words of the charm. A wave of heat pushed her forward, propelling her up into the air and smacking her sideways into the stone wall. Her right shoulder went numb, and her belly curled up in fear.

She fell to the floor, shaking and in pain. When she could breathe normally again, she realized that the fear she felt was the Dread—she must be close to the part of the forest where the elves lived, their protective spell somehow penetrating the soil beneath them and carrying down into Under-the-Hill. This place was scary enough without adding the Dread.

Since she no longer had her rose quartz, Keelie summoned Earth magic and wrapped its protection around her. The Dread's grip diminished. The rock walls still thumped to the beat of the drum, but she didn't sense any living creature nearby. She reached out with her tree sense.

Hrok? Are you there?

Immediately, Hrok's comforting presence flooded her mind. *I'm here.*

Goblins. Lots of them. Need to warn Dad. She sat up, rubbing her shoulder, then paused. She could see, dimly; her connection to Hrok must be allowing her to see in the darkness.

Milady, you shouldn't be afraid of the goblins. They are our friends.

Keelie couldn't believe what she was hearing. Knot slid in between her and the wall. His soft warmth comforted her.

A movement to her left caught her eye, and she froze.

It was the goblin who'd chased her, passed out on the floor. He looked a little scorched, having been on the receiving end of whatever that charm had been. He moved again.

"Meow follow me." Knot head-butted her, encouraging her to keep moving.

A chirp sounded from above her and she looked up to see a pair of inquisitive eyes looking down at her.

"Cricket!"

The little goblin jumped down and poked her sore arm. She batted his sharp-pointed fingers away. "Stop. It hurts."

Cricket chirped again, then stopped and looked behind her, his expression somber. He'd spotted the big goblin. Did he realize that he was one, too? He dropped to the ground and went to explore his unconscious relative, then he turned and looked at her arm, his eyes troubled.

Keelie glanced down and gasped, feeling queasy. Her arm had two gouges on it, and her sleeve was stained with blood. She'd thought her arm just ached from hitting the wall.

"Come on, Cricket. Let's go."

She crawled around the goblin's body and followed Knot up the tunnel. She flexed her fingers. They still seemed to work, which was good. They finally reached the dirt staircase and she eased up it, bit by shaky bit. There was a long moment when Keelie thought she would be climbing forever, but then she smelled the green of the grass near the obelisk rock.

She was already out in the open before she realized that her journey was over. It was dark outside now, but the sound of the crickets and the faint strains of a fiddle from the players' campground finally penetrated her foggy mind.

Outside. Keelie took a deep breath and fell over, lying on the grass and watching the stars above. Knot plopped down beside her, and his purring presence filled her with relief and comfort. Cricket crunched on some rocks near her feet.

"Come on, guys, let's get going. I don't want the goblins to catch my scent."

As they came to the bridge, a warm wave surrounded Keelie. It was not just Hrok, but the other trees in the meadow. Keelie could hear them all, but one in particular caught her attention—a longleaf pine who seemed to be speaking to someone else. Keelie realized that it was talking to her father.

She interrupted, using the pine's connection to call out to Dad.

Danger, Dad. I need you. She sent mental images of what she'd seen Under-the-Hill.

Also, Dad, Hrok told me that the goblins are friends to the trees. I don't know why he would think that; he knows what goblin blood can do to a tree. If the others believe this too, we have a big problem. Maybe they're mixed up because the goblins are coming from Under-the-Hill like the bhata.

Where are you now, Keelie?

On the lane, headed toward the bridge.

A mental impression of a hug came from her father, and she sensed his worry, as well as a whiff of cinnamon.

She hurried on toward the bridge, halting when figures appeared out of the darkness on the other side of the stream. Keelie stopped, ready to run into the woods. She wondered if the goblins had come after her from another entrance to Under-the-Hill.

Moonlight filtered down through the branches and she saw that one of the advancing figures was tall, and the other came to just above his waist.

"Keelie?"

The relief that flooded her at the sound of her father's voice made Keelie realize just how scared she'd been. She broke into a run and slammed into his chest, clutching his soft shirt and inhaling his scent. Sir Davey stood quietly next to her.

Dad's big hand cradled her head and he murmured "There, there" while she sobbed, her tension eased by her father's comforting presence.

After a moment she lifted her head. "There were so many of them, Dad."

His worried eyes looked into hers and he grasped her face in his hands. "You are not to go down there again, do you understand? We'll put guards at the entrance."

Sir Davey nodded. "I'll alert Finch. She's said something about a magical shield. She and Vangar are working on combining their magic."

Sharp prickles climbed Keelie's leg and she reached down to pull Cricket from her jeans. Dad recoiled slightly at the sight of the little goblin, but he seemed to force himself to relax.

"Let's go to my RV," Davey said.

They walked back down the East Road toward the performer's campground and Davey's deluxe RV. Dad motioned to Keelie to be silent, and they said nothing as they passed the lights glimmering from tents and voices raised in song, oblivious to the danger just a few yards away.

In the RV, Davey turned on lights as Dad latched the door, then turned to Keelie.

Go away. Leave me alone, the goblin tree shouted in Keelie's mind.

She'd forgotten that Sir Davey had taken it home with him. In the clay pot, huge chunks of amethyst surrounded the tree's trunk. Sir Davey was using Earth magic to neutralize the sapling's negativity. But it pushed its irate face out of its trunk and stuck its green tongue out.

Dad scowled at the tree. He turned back to Keelie. "On second thought, I want you to go back to Janice's. You and Raven are to stay together at all times."

Keelie frowned. "No way I'm walking all the way to Janice's right now. Can't I rest a minute? The goblins were really scary, and I hurt one of them, so they might think this fight is personal."

Puny elves versus goblins. My vote is on the goblins. The tree sneered at them.

"I'm going to confer with the elves," Dad said. "This will definitely propel them to make a decision."

Davey looked up at Dad, his grim face shadowed by the lamplight. "What do you mean, 'confer'? Niriel will stir up the elves with this information. That's one elf I don't trust."

Dad shook his head. "The elves must know about the goblins. We can't keep this a secret. The goblin army is indeed here, and Keelie's found the entrance to their lair."

Davey straightened. "I will call my brothers. The dwarves must know as well."

"So do we tell the dragons too? Finch and Vangar?" Keelie asked. Ermentrude had kicked goblin butt up in the Northwoods.

"I'll tell them," Dad said. "You stay out of sight at Janice's. There are those who will say that you've known where the goblins were all this time, and only chose now to reveal them to get yourself out of trouble."

"I don't doubt it," Keelie said. "But what about the faire folk? The shopkeepers? Can we tell them? They'll fight too." Keelie imagined a scene out of an old monster movie, with angry peasants carrying torches and pitchforks as they stormed the castle.

"No humans." Dad's voice was firm—his "don't argue" tone.

Outraged, Keelie was about to launch into argument anyway when she heard the trees crying out a warning. "What's happening?"

Davey stuck his head out the RV door. "I smell wood smoke—it's more than just camp fires."

Dad lifted his head, listening. "Fire, on the other side of the hill. Davey, warn the others."

The goblin tree began to chant. His tree voice creaked with malice. *Burn. Burn. Burn.*

eleven

Davey threw himself out of the RV and disappeared into the campground, his cries of "Fire!" cutting through the merriment.

Dad leaped out of the RV after him and ran to a large, military-style lodge-tent next to them, calling out, "Fire!" He ran on to the next tent as Tarl and his friends poured out of the lodge, tankards in hand, sniffing the air.

Dad ran back to the RV. "To Janice's, Keelie," he yelled, then raced up the road as Tarl's men spread the alarm. In seconds, the spaces between the tents were full of faire workers who'd dropped their meals, guitars, and books to help.

Davey returned and grabbed a fire extinguisher from under a cabinet, which he handed to Keelie. "Take this to Janice. Not sure if she has one, and I have an extra."

Keelie stared at the fire extinguisher. If the fire wasn't controlled early, it would turn into a monster like the one that had engulfed Heartwood. No fire extinguisher could have stopped that one.

"I don't want to run away," Keelie said. "I'm part of this faire and I want to help."

"You're not running away," Davey said earnestly. "You have to warn Janice so that she can save her shop and spread the alarm to those living on the grounds."

Keelie grabbed the heavy red extinguisher and ran up the road, pushing past the blue-jean-clad faire folk who jostled past her, carrying shovels, rakes, buckets, and even more fire extinguishers as they rushed toward the blaze, visible now as an orange glow on the horizon near the jousting arena. Thomas the Glass Blower huffed his way down the path, carrying a hoe, Sam the Potter beside him.

"I wonder if this was Vangar the firebug's doing," Sam said.

"Don't know, but Finch will defend him if it is," Thomas answered as they glared at Keelie.

She was the only one headed away from danger as she turned toward Green Lady Herbs, wishing she had the Compendium.

"Hurry, Keelie!" a red-faced Raven shouted, waving Keelie to the herb shop.

Janice was hosing water onto the roof and around the

building. "Keelie, thank goodness you're here. I need your help. Go inside and cover my herbs and tinctures with cloth."

Inside the shop, the sweet, woodsy scent was now mixed with the smell of burnt wood. Keelie blinked back tears—the faire was slowly dying. Shimmerlight, Lavender Lollipop, and Lily Limerton showed up and helped cover the herbs. Then Janice ran toward the jousting arena, the girls behind her.

The stands were fully engulfed, the flames shooting high into the trees. The trees shrieked in Keelie's head, howling in terror as the flames licked at their trunks and branches.

Keelie joined a bucket brigade that scooped water from the horses' spring-fed trough and passed buckets to be flung at the fire. It was like spitting into a volcano, but it was something. Endless buckets passed her on their way to the roaring inferno, and while her body worked mechanically, her mind was trying to soothe the forest.

She sensed her father's voice as he worked on the other side of the fire, and then she felt her uncle and her grandmother joining in from their far forests. The tree shepherds were working together. Despite her fear and exhaustion, Keelie's pride lightened her heart.

Around her were signs of a similar spirit as the faire workers pitched in to help each other. The faire folk were family, maybe not by blood, but by choice and circumstance.

It wasn't until after midnight that the last remnants of the fire were under control. The jousting arena had been turned to ashes. The Silver Bough Company would have to perform its demonstrations in the parking lot until the embers cooled.

Keelie trudged back to Green Lady Herbs with Janice and Raven, thinking this was getting really old.

Dad joined them just as they neared the shop. Janice stopped walking a moment, overcome with emotion at the sight of her little cottage unharmed.

Dad was dirty and his hair was loose, his ear tips exposed. "Thank you for letting Keelie stay with you, but she'll sleep at Sir Davey's tonight."

"She helped me save my shop. I couldn't have done it without her," Janice said.

"Can't she stay with us?" Raven asked.

Dad shook his head. Keelie sensed that something was off about him. For one thing, he never showed his ear tips around humans, even Janice and Raven who knew about the elves.

"Keelie, thank you for all of your help," Janice said. Her cap was askew, and her face ashen and smudged with dirt.

Keelie wiped her hands over the forehead. Dirt and smoke came off in her hands. "I think I need a shower."

"Let's head to the RV." Dad rubbed his eyes with the palm of his sooty hands.

"Be careful, especially around Vangar." Janice hugged Keelie.

"We'll be fine," Keelie said.

Walking back to the performer's campground, exhausted and desperately wanting to feel hot water sluicing down her body, Keelie yearned for Sir Davey's RV and its expansive luxury spa bathroom.

"Keelie, I hope you didn't say anything to Janice about the goblins?" Dad asked.

"No, we didn't have time to talk." Keelie frowned. "Why don't you want her to know about the goblins? She knows you're an elf. "

"Things have changed. The battle in the Northwoods has convinced the elves that the less we interact with humans, the better. For the Ren Faires there'll be little change, but even so, the less humans know, the better."

Keelie stopped. "It's wrong, Dad. I think we should be more open, not less. Why can't humans know about elves, anyway?"

Dad shook his head. He seemed so standoffish right now.

"We'll argue about this later. Once I drop you off at Sir Davey's, I must meet with the elves."

"Again? It's the middle of the night." Keelie dropped her sarcastic tone and placed a hand on his sooty shoulder. "Dad, you need to rest too. You're getting a little loopy."

Dad hugged her. "Later." They had reached the edge of the campground, and he left her standing among the parked cars. Thomas the Glass Blower waved to Dad as he walked toward the woodland path leading to the elven camp.

Feeling abandoned, Keelie went inside the RV for her much-needed shower. She'd get some sleep and clear her head. Two fires in two nights was not a coincidence. Someone in the faire was an arsonist, and he or she had to be stopped.

Four hours later, Keelie threw her pillow at the goblin tree in the corner of the RV's living area. "Shut up."

She'd gotten two hours of sleep before the tree had started singing pub songs about wenches. Loudly.

Oh, the pretty lass was quite the wench.
But she never washed, she had a stench.

It added more verses as it went along, and it was clearly no Grammy hopeful.

Keelie sat up. "We should have known not to put that tree where it could hear Tarl and the mud men."

Knot meowed angrily, walked over to the little angry tree, and unsheathed his claws. "Meow firewood."

"Threaten me all you want, stinky cat, but you don't scare me," the goblin tree shouted out loud. It pushed its face though its bark and stuck its green tongue out at Knot.

Keelie lowered herself back onto the sofa, hoping to go back to sleep.

"I saw you naked when you showered," the tree continued. "I sent the image to all the trees around the mountain."

Keelie blushed with embarrassment. "Silly tree. There's a lot of serious stuff happening here. Besides, I don't care. What do trees care about naked people?" But it gave her pause that the tree had spoken aloud. It was growing in power.

Keelie couldn't stay in the RV another moment with the obnoxious thing. If she'd had the Compendium, she would've used a silence spell on it and then, just in case, sent out a forget-it spell to the trees so they wouldn't re-member the image of her naked.

A wave of regret washed over her as she remembered the Compendium. Cricket climbed on top of her head, as if sensing her sadness.

Keelie's tree sense kicked in. *Hrok?*

Lady Keliel, your father is still in the elven village, and he will be so for many hours. He says you need to rest.

Thank you, Hrok. She paused. *Hrok, can you sense the goblins? Are they near the entrance to Under-the-Hill?*

No, milady. They have moved, but we do not know where. We sense they are near.

Yesterday, you told me that the goblins are your friends. I find it hard to believe that a tree could say that.

Oh yes. We like them very much.

Later, Hrok.

Keelie abruptly ended the conversation. She'd have to be careful talking to trees about goblins if they thought the goblins were their friends. Something was badly wrong with them, and with Dad too. She thought about her ac-tions the past two days, but couldn't think of anything strange about herself other than bone weariness and a growing hatred for the smell of woodsmoke. Whatever was going on, it was affecting more than tree shepherds.

A knock at the door interrupted Keelie's thoughts.

"Hey, Human. Somebody is at the door. Can you ask them if they have some fertilizer? It will be an improvement over the company in this place." The goblin tree swatted a branch at Knot as he strolled past on his way to the door.

Knot hissed and smacked the air in front of the pot.

Keelie needed a shovel to bury … no, to replant the tree in some clean, nourishing soil that might help with its attitude. Maybe a personality transplant could be done too.

She opened the door of the RV, blinking in the bright daylight that streamed in. Outside, Lily Limerton was looking up at her. She wore a T-shirt and jeans, and looked like a mundane except for the fake glittery wings still on her back.

"Finch said she needs to see you in her office," Lily announced.

"When?"

"Like an hour ago," Lily Limerton said. "I got lost."

"I'll be there as soon as I can."

"Thanks. I don't want to make her mad. She scares me."

"Me too." Keelie wondered if she and the fairy girl could become friends. She seemed nice when she wasn't in character.

Lily pursed her lips and rocked back on her heels. "You know, I shouldn't ask, but I was wondering, since you and Sean aren't together right now, if it would be okay if I went out with him?"

Keelie felt as if she'd been knee-punched in the stomach. How had word gotten out so quickly? Forget the part about being friends. "Sean is a big boy," she managed to say.

"Thanks." Lily smiled. "Hob said you were scary, but I don't see it."

"Hob said that about me?" Maybe she and Finch hadn't been as discreet about their investigation as they'd thought.

"He doesn't seem to like you."

"I don't know why." Keelie felt miffed. Hob had certainly pretended to like her.

"See you later," Lily Limerton waved, spun around, and walked away, almost skipping.

Keelie slammed the door.

"Sounds like Hob and I need to have a drink together," the goblin tree said.

Tired and mad at the world, Keelie decided she might as well make her way to Finch's office. She thought she'd take the path by the elven village in hopes of maybe seeing Dad or Sean. Give both of them a piece of her mind.

Crossing the bridge over the stream, Keelie listened for the water sprite, but she wasn't revealing herself. If she'd had time, she would've tried the To See Truly spell. Cricket followed her, munching on bits of trash he found along the way. Knot kept step with her. He'd been by her side almost constantly lately. Good old Knot.

Sticks crackled in the bushes nearby. Keelie's pulse quickened, but she steadied herself.

Keep calm, she thought.

She felt the Dread when she got within several feet of the path that, hidden among the trees, led to the elven camp. She clasped a polished rose quartz tightly and felt the elves' strong aversion spell being beaten back by Earth magic. Her anxiety eased.

The bushes rustled again. Keelie's heart raced with real fear as she searched the darkly shadowed trees for any sign of goblins.

An elf stepped out in front of her. She started to relax until she saw that it was Sean's father, Niriel.

"Halt! Who goes there?" Niriel raised the sword in his right hand.

He knew who she was. Keelie lifted her hands to show she was unarmed. "It's me."

Knot hissed at Niriel.

"Identify yourself. You might be a goblin in disguise," Niriel commanded.

Keelie sighed. "Keliel Katharine Heartwood, daughter of the Lord of the Dread Forest." She needed to remember to act like the daughter of the Lord of the Forest when dealing with Niriel and other Council elves. "I was walking past the camp, and I thought I would see if Dad was out of his Council meeting."

"Keliel, you may be the daughter of our Lord of the Forest, and some of the elves may think you're special, but to me you're an abomination, a mutt. Something that should not exist in this world." Niriel narrowed his eyes. "Why you? Why were you chosen to be blessed with magic? I don't understand."

Cricket climbed up Niriel's leg, chirping in delight at the chain mail leggings, which made an easy climbing wall of metal links.

"Speaking of abomination—this creature needs to be destroyed. The fewer of them, the better." Niriel pulled Cricket off his leg. The goblin's little legs scrambled in the air, looking for purchase.

"Hey, let him go."

Niriel threw Cricket, not even turning to watch where he landed. "Take your goblin and get out of here. Your kind isn't wanted. The Council has moved to banish you until the end of the faire. If I see you or that creature skulking in this area, then I will have no choice but to turn you in." He flourished his sword at Keelie. "Or I may mete out your punishment myself."

Keelie plucked Cricket from the ground and cradled him. "Banished? When did that happen?" She wasn't upset, since hanging out at the elven village wasn't among her favorite activities.

"At a recent Council meeting, according to our laws." Anger simmered underneath Niriel's cool elven exterior, and she had to admit he was scary.

"Glad to hear you get stuff done at those endless Council meetings."

"You scoff, Keliel Heartwood, but you will find how serious a matter this truly is. It is good to see your father acting like a true elf." Niriel peered down his nose at her. "I suggest you follow his example."

"Come on, Knot. I know where we're not wanted."

"Smart move, girl. I never understood what my son saw in you."

Keelie blinked back tears as she clenched her fists. She wanted to hurl a green energy ball at Niriel, but it would be considered an attack, and Dad would experience the consequences from the Council. She didn't want him to lose his position because his mutt daughter had lost her temper and used magic against the elves.

She remembered what she'd said in the Redwoods, when confronting Bella Matera, the mother tree of the forest. She wondered if it would confuse Niriel.

"Ever heard of the karma fairy?" Keelie kept her voice calm.

He shuddered and his voice constricted. "Karma fairy?"

"She balances magic and punishes those who do wrong." Keelie projected her voice like Mom would in the courtroom, making her appear more confident and stronger. Convincing. "If I were you, I'd be careful, because you know I have fae blood—which makes me, as you put it, a mutt. But the karma fairy still sees me as one of her own."

"Then leave before you befoul me with your evil magic." Niriel's nostrils flared and his ear tips turned red as he shoved his sword back into his scabbard. "Be gone and take your creature with you."

Keelie marched away with Knot following her. She grinned down at the fairy cat.

"Meow not trust him."

"No kidding."

As Keelie traveled up the East Road, she stopped in at Mrs. Butters' and grabbed a turkey-on-whole-wheat sandwich. She just about inhaled it, she was so hungry. Shimmerlight and Lavender Lollipop were back in costume and character. They sat at a corner table along with Thomas the glassblower.

"I think we need to run Vangar out of the faire," Thomas was saying.

"Hob's got our back, but Finch doesn't. How are we

going to entertain the people when our jousting arena has been burnt?" Lavender said in a conspiratorial whisper. She caught sight of Keelie and her face flushed bright red.

"Poor Sean is beside himself," Shimmerlight said in a very loud voice. "Lost his love, and now his jousting ring."

It was time to leave before they broke out in song.

Keelie paid for her lunch. A lot of the faire folk were disgruntled, and she questioned whether the faire should open at all this weekend. But she also knew things would be worse if they were closed. If people started to put two and two together, they might think she was a jinx. But it was the goblins, and Peascod, and whoever controlled them who were making the faire a dark place.

She cut by the Muck and Mire Show stage and found herself on King's Way. It all came down to discovering the truth about Hob, she realized. He seemed to be fanning the embers of discontent among the shopkeepers and performers at the faire. Finch might know what the next step should be.

twelve

Keelie shifted uncomfortably on one of the hard plastic lawn chairs that furnished Finch's low-key office. Vangar and Finch were watching Sally as she hummed over her tarot cards, supposedly to tap into the energy field around the faire.

When Keelie had burst into the Admin building fifteen minutes earlier, she'd shared with Finch some of the conversations she'd overhead on her way through the faire. It made smoke billow out of the dragon's ears—she wasn't happy to learn that a lot of the faire folk were scared and unhappy not only because of the spontaneous nature of the fires, but also because of the way they'd been handled. There was no natural cause of the fires, yet also no arson investigation. The rumors that Vangar was responsible for the Heartwood fire were now circulating widely, and there was talk that the whole faire was cursed. The faire folk didn't realize how close to the truth this was, Keelie thought grimly. The faire *was* cursed—with goblins, hiding Under-the-Hill.

As everyone remained hushed to allow Sally to concentrate on the cards, Keelie examined the fantasy-book-cover posters of dragons that decorated the walls. She recognized many of the artists, some of whom had booths and shops at the faire. One picture, of a red dragon with golden scales, looked suspiciously like Ermentrude.

Sally stopped humming and shuffled the cards. "I need a break—too many powerful beings in this room," she muttered.

"I can't believe people said those things about me." Vangar's bronze eyes glinted with sadness. He tapped his fingers on the edge of his chair, refusing to make eye contact with anyone.

Keelie felt sorry for him. Since she'd arrived, she hadn't heard anyone say anything nice about Vangar, and if he was telling the truth, he'd done nothing to deserve it.

"While Sally ponders the card, what else can you tell me?" Finch glared at Keelie from across her desk. The pad in front of her was full of names.

"That's it." Feeling like a snitch, Keelie leaned back in her chair.

"So, Lavender and Shimmerlight think I'm doing a piss-poor job of handling the faire? Stupid fairies with their little glitter wings and tulle skirts, skipping around all happy." Finch broke her pencil in two. Today, her red hair was piled on top of her head in a messy bun and she was dressed in a black T-shirt, blue jeans, and serious steel-toed work boots with flames stitched on the sides. They looked like they could kick some fairy butt.

Knot hopped through the open office window, dragging a bedraggled puppet in his mouth. He jumped into Vangar's lap.

"What do you have there, buddy?" Vangar removed the weird little puppet from Knot's mouth. The cat swatted at it. It looked flat and lifeless without Hob to animate it. The puppet's red and gold outfit was muddy and smelled smoky. Strange. Must be because the mask store was next to Heartwood.

"Why did you take Hob's puppet, you bad kitty?" Keelie asked.

"You're right, it's Hob's poppet," Sally said.

"You mean puppet," Keelie corrected her. "He calls it Toshi."

"No, a poppet. They're used to enchant people, to make them do their will," Sally explained. "The way people act around here, I'm thinking he's got them enchanted. It's dark stuff. Most practitioners won't touch it." She waved her hands, as if wafting away the bad vibes.

Whatever it was, the puppet looked the worse for wear,

thanks to Knot. Its dark beady eyes still shone with a sinister gleam.

"Poppets can be very powerful," Sally said. "A lot of practitioners will find a spell in a grimoire and shape it to their purpose."

"What do you want me to do with it?" Vangar asked, picking it up gingerly.

If Keelie had had the Compendium, she might have been able to find a spell to take care of the poppet.

"I'll get rid of it." Sally reached for Toshi, touching its hat. The bell in Keelie's pocket rang as if in recognition. Keelie put her hand over the bell to quiet it as Sally took the puppet outside. Finch, Vangar, and Keelie followed her to the door and watched as Sally walked to the privies on the other side of the front gate. The privies were the perfect place for the horrible little poppet.

"Where are you, sweeting?" a sad and plaintive voice shouted. Keelie turned in the direction of the heart-wrenching plea. Immediately she stepped back into the safety of the office; Hob was wobbling down King's Way as if he'd had too many meads down at the Poacher's Inn. "Where are you?" he shouted outside the Magic Maze. "I need you. Sweetness, come back. Toshi. I need my Toshi."

"What's wrong with him?" Keelie asked.

"He's acting weirder than usual." Vangar arched an eyebrow. "He was in his mask shop screeching about something earlier. I'd say he's been hanging out with his masks too long. All those empty eye sockets watching him all day long probably pushed him over the edge."

Keelie could totally see that.

"Strange..." Finch mused. "He has several dozen Toshi puppets in his store, but he's going nuts looking for this one? Too late now, unless he goes searching in the privies." She wrinkled her nose. "Never mind. Let's get back to the reading."

Keelie glimpsed several large books stacked in a corner behind Finch's desk. Some of the books shimmered; but when she looked again, nothing. She wondered if these were magic books and her To See Truly abilities were kicking in.

Sally, who had remained outside, joined them and began shuffling cards. "Something is definitely wrong with Hob," she said. "I saw him dart between the Magic Maze and the candle shop, and then he bolted down the lane when Tarl asked him if he needed any help." She shook her head. "Enough distractions. Let's concentrate on the cards."

For a moment, the only sound was the ticking of the dragon clock hanging behind Finch, its pendulum tail swinging back and forth, ticking with each movement. The Timekeeper would've liked this clock, Keelie thought. Maybe Finch bought it at the Quicksilver Faire, or perhaps it was a present from Ermentrude.

Knot hopped onto the edge of Finch's desk, closed his eyes, and purred like a contented feline Porsche.

Sally studied her cards, her gaze contemplative. "I have seen great danger. The cards say that something moves this way, and we must be prepared."

"It's goblins," Keelie said. She'd seen them—she didn't need a tarot card to tell her to be prepared.

"We know it's goblins." Finch motioned toward the cards. "What do they say?"

Sally spread more cards out on the desk. She didn't blink at the mention of goblins, so Keelie figured she'd been around magic folk for a while.

The back of this tarot deck was very pretty, gold trim around a black and white checkerboard design. Sally deftly swept the cards into a deck with one smooth move. "Let's try something new, to use all the energy in the room. Tap them."

Finch did.

Vangar snorted, unimpressed.

"Each of you will draw a card," Sally said as she held out the deck. "First, Finch."

Finch pulled from the top.

Sally walked over to Vangar, who rolled his eyes. "Do I have to?" He cut a questioning glance over to Finch.

Her red brows rose to her hairline. "We talked about this."

Keelie knew who wore the pants in this relationship. She smiled.

Vangar sighed. He pulled a card from the middle of the deck.

Sally strolled over to Keelie. "Now you."

Keelie didn't know why she was nervous. She'd drawn a tarot card before, but something felt different in the room, as if there was a layer of magic filtering through the doorway and settling around Sally. Keelie removed a card from the bottom.

Sally tapped the deck again. "Reveal your cards, at the same time, on the desk."

Keelie leaned forward, as did Vangar and Finch. They laid their cards out at the same time. Finch had a red dragon—the seven of swords. Vangar's was the King of Wands, a big gold dragon with glistening scales that would have made Shimmerlight jealous with its sparkles.

And when Keelie flipped her card over … the Fool, here pictured as a jester whose stare glittered at her through a mask's eyeholes. Great. This meant one thing: Peascod.

"Now what?" Finch barked.

"Now you each study your card. Together they have a larger meaning."

The gold dragon on Vangar's card winked at Keelie, and gave her a thumbs-up. Since when did tarot cards come with animation?

"Wait a minute—I saw that dragon wink at me," Keelie said.

Vangar grinned. "Rascal."

"This is a deck brought to me from the Quicksilver Faire," Sally said. A faerie deck. Keelie knew it.

Sally pointed to the red dragon on Finch's card; it flew above a castle as a ragtag army of seven peasants gathered outside the drawbridge. "You will have to be a leader, even to those who are afraid of you," she told Finch. "But you will be able to rally the troops if you can cast aside the doubt within. You must find the inner strength to lead."

Finch sighed. "This means that we're going to have to teach the humans how to fight. Davey and I were talking about that last night."

Sally arched an eyebrow. "Right. Vangar, do you have any idea what your card might mean?"

He stared at the gold dragon as if might talk to him. "No."

Simple enough. Keelie liked that about Vangar. You got what you saw.

"It means you've led a lonely existence, by yourself, flying from one location to another." Sally pointed to the sky on the card. "Do you see that star?"

"Yeah," Vangar said.

Keelie leaned forward, and sure enough, there was a star on the horizon. That hadn't been there before, but then again, this tarot deck was from the Quicksilver Faire.

"What does it mean?" Keelie asked. Although it was Vangar's card, she wanted to know the answer.

Sally smiled knowingly at the big hulk. Vangar's face flushed bright red.

"It means he made a wish upon the dragonstar, and it was heard by the higher powers."

"Oh!"

Sally's eyes twinkled. "That old saying still holds a lot of truth—be careful what you wish for."

Finch leaned back in her chair and smiled a delightful yet evil grin. "Yes, be careful." A hint of charcoal wafted through the small office.

Keelie didn't know if this meant the two dragons'

pheromones were kicking in. She tapped her card. "I think this means I'm going to encounter Peascod."

"It's the Fool. We can read it that way, but also look for the deeper meanings in the symbolism of the images around the Fool. What do you see, Keelie?" Sally asked.

Keelie looked deeply into the card, her eyes stopping, transfixed, on the bag in the fool's hand.

"He has a small velvet patchwork bag. It would make a great purse. Very boho chic."

"It's the bag of possibilities," Sally said. "Whatever your decision is about Peascod, then it will be your choice, so gather the wisdom of your own experiences."

"What if I make the wrong decision?" Keelie asked.

"There are many paths, but we can choose only one. Once chosen, there are still infinite possibilities available to us, branching forward."

Keelie felt very confused.

"I think the cards are trying to tell us that there is danger other than the goblins," Sally said.

"What? Other than goblins?" Keelie didn't think anything could be more frightening than an angry goblin, other than Peascod, who was sort of an uber-goblin. Did it mean Niriel?

"I'll be on the lookout for any dangers." Vangar looked protectively at Finch. A mental image popped up in Keelie's mind of two dragons kissing. Would they burn each other?

"Whatever happens, I don't think we can depend on the elves," Finch said. "Your father is thinking like an elf, and he will not make choices that include all the faire folk." Seeing Keelie's expression, she added, "Want another opinion? Talk to Davey. You've always listened to him."

Keelie was reeling at the thought of excluding Dad from their plans, but the goblin situation wasn't just about the elves. It was about all the faire folk.

"I trust you, but I don't like keeping things from Dad."

"It's only for a couple of days. Vangar and I are trying to coordinate our defenses. We want to protect everyone in the faire, but with the people angry and suspicious of Vangar and me, it's hard to protect them."

"I guess you're right. I just don't feel like I'm an elf. I feel like I'm betraying them." Keelie rubbed her pointed ear. "Is this all of me that's elf? That, and I can hear trees speak?"

Finch steepled her fingers. "You're more than an elf, Keelie. Just as I'm more than a dragon. It's part of who we are, but it isn't all that we are. We have to find a way to blend in with this world. With humans."

Vangar nodded. "For centuries I've had to deal with the same thing. When I had a sheep farm out in the Old West, folks around used to say a dragon can't keep sheep. Hey, I believe in free enterprise, and that's why I'm here at the faire. Not only am I a dragon, but I like to think I'm a brilliant businessman." Vangar straightened his shoulders.

Keelie could almost imagine him as a dragon deep within his lair, counting the money he'd made from his business deals. But herding sheep? That one boggled the mind.

Finch reached out and touched Keelie's hand. "Trust me, Keelie."

Keelie was moved. The faire director wasn't known for her soft side. "I do."

"I believe Hob may be the link to the goblins, and I'm hoping we can find the connection," Finch continued. "While the goblins are gathering, we have to prepare ourselves, and one way of doing that is to keep intel on our enemy." She leaned back.

"He's always seemed like a human to me, although I did notice an odd shimmer around him once," Keelie said. "And then there's that puppet obsession, of course." She had the brief thought that maybe Hob and the Wildewood Faire's puppet shop owner, Lulu, should get together. It wouldn't work, though—Lulu was in witch rehab somewhere.

"Go to work in the mask shop as planned, and if you're right, then wonderful—Hob merely needs therapy. If I'm right, we have problems."

Keelie straightened her shoulders. She would practice the To See Truly spell and use it on Hob.

She placed the jingle bell on Finch's desk. "I want you to keep this."

Before Finch could respond, the office door slammed open and Sir Davey stood before them, clothes torn and mustache quivering with agitation. "I've been robbed!"

thirteen

Finch sat Sir Davey down in the chair Keelie had vacated and poured him a small glass of golden liquid from a dusty bottle. The musty whisky smell was strong even across the room. Sir Davey drank it in a single gulp.

"I left the Dragon Hoard for only a minute, to use the privies down the lane. The shop was almost empty, but there were guards about the place. I didn't think the shop would be in danger." His mouth tightened. "Now I know differently."

"Can you tell what's missing?" Finch was back in full faire admin mode.

"Geodes, the best of them, which were in a glass display. Smashed now," he said disgustedly. "My big brass astrolabe, too. It was there for show—it wasn't for sale. That instrument is irreplaceable."

Finch took notes, then noticed Keelie. "Heartwood, go home. We'll be here a while. Don't speak of this to the shopkeepers or you'll start a riot."

Keelie nodded, though she knew word was even now spreading faster than a summer cold. She hugged Sir Davey, then let herself out of the little building.

"Lady Keelie?" Finch's errand boy stood by nervously. "I have a message for you."

"Eric, right?"

He nodded as he handed her a rolled paper secured with a pale blue ribbon, then whipped another rolled paper out of the bag slung over his shoulder and jogged away to his next delivery.

Keelie pulled the ribbon off and unrolled the paper. It was a note from Dad, which read that he'd been delayed in the elven camp. So what else was new?

Keelie headed to Green Lady Herbs. Whatever Dad might prefer, she was not about to spend another night under the same roof as the goblin tree. She felt like a stray cat. They needed a home of their own at this faire, provided no more buildings burned down. At least Raven would be there, and maybe she could offer some insight as to what was going on.

That night was the most normal one Keelie had had in days. Janice made soup and Keelie and Raven constructed a salad. The three talked about college choices and unicorn husbands, then Keelie went to bed. Maybe the tea Janice had insisted she drink had a special ingredient in it, but Keelie slept all night, undisturbed.

The following morning she got up early, awakened by the faire noise. It was Saturday, a faire day, and Janice had laid out some of Raven's old Renaissance clothes. Keelie put on a tan and brown brocaded corset over a white poet's shirt and a full, plain green skirt that fell to her ankles. She thought about all of the garb she'd lost in the fire. Sadness overcame her, and she tried to be happy that she and Dad had walked away uninjured. It wasn't easy. She had a pity party ready to go, complete with engraved invitations. But she set those thoughts aside and concentrated on today. Today, she had an important assignment: to use the To See Truly Spell on Hob. She was also anxious to hear how Sir Davey was doing.

Raven smiled at Keelie as she strode into the kitchen area. "Brought you some tea."

"Good morning. You look so nice in those clothes," Janice said.

"Thank you, Janice. They're wonderful. They fit, too."

"You've grown, that's why. Are you ready for a day of greeting customers at Hobknocker's?" Janice asked. "I'm surprised you took the job."

"Mom." Raven wrinkled her brow in disapproval. "Keelie needs something do."

"She's right. I do need something to do. Of course, it won't be the same as working at Heartwood." Oops, pity party words. Keelie needed to change the subject, but the next thing that came to mind was the Dragon Hoard robbery, and she'd been told not to discuss that.

"Your dad came by this morning to check on you," Janice said as she blew on a cup of tea. The scent of mint wafted over to Keelie.

"Where is he now?"

"He said he had to finish the cleanup at Heartwood, and then he had a meeting with the elves," Janice smiled wanly. "He was very curt. I know he's upset, tired, and under a lot of pressure, but … "

"But?" Keelie exchanged a knowing glance with Raven. "He seems different?"

Raven cut her eyes over to her mom. "Maybe this isn't the time to talk about this."

"I think this is the perfect time. Surely Keelie's noticed the changes." Janice sipped her tea and placed her mug down on the counter top. "Zeke seems different now that he's taken over the leadership of the Dread Forest. More standoffish. Even with the fires."

"More elven," Keelie said.

"Exactly." Janice looked out the small window. Hurt reflected in her eyes.

"I know. He's got a lot on his mind right now." Keelie rubbed her ears. "I need to get moving. Hob will be waiting for me."

"Do you want some breakfast?" Janice asked.

"No, I'll grab a muffin at Mrs. Butters'. I'm meeting Finch there."

"You've become quite friendly with the faire director." Janice's voice held a disapproving note.

"Mom." Raven rolled her eyes. "Keelie, Mom is just tense after the fires."

"I worked with Finch at the Wildewood Faire, and we sort of forged a bond," Keelie explained weakly. "She may be gruff, but she comes through in a tight spot."

"She does take getting used to." Janice shook her head.

Although Raven's magical sensibilities had become stronger since marrying Einhorn, Keelie couldn't exactly tell either Raven or her mother about the goblins or the robbery. She was starting to run out of conversation. And she didn't want to frighten Janice, who had always been so kind to her.

Janice broke the awkward silence that fell between them. "I need to prepare some herbal tea packets for a special client, and when I finish that, I'll open the shop." She poured the remainder of her tea down the drain. "So I'll see you later."

"I hope you have a great day," Keelie said.

"You too."

"I may see you later at Hobknocker's. I've been wanting to check out the masks," Raven said.

At Mrs. Butters' shop, some of the jousters were hanging out with Marcia, Tracy, and Lily, who were dressed as their alter egos Shimmerlight, Lavender Lollipop, and Lily Limerton. They were laughing and joking with one another. When Keelie stepped up to the order counter, they stopped their conversation and stared rudely at her. It was as if she was wearing a scarlet "E" for "enemy" on her chest. Sean wasn't with them. These guys had been her friends, and now they looked at her as if she was a traitor.

Keelie touched her rounded ear and then her pointed one. She was part elf, she reminded herself.

"I want a crystalberry muffin," she told Mrs. Butters, although she'd suddenly lost her appetite. She'd take it with her, and maybe eat it on her way to Hobknocker's.

"Yes, dear." Mrs. Butters moved very slowly as she reached into the display counter and removed a muffin for Keelie.

Bromliel, one of the jousters, stood up from the table and walked over to her. "We wanted you to know that we're sorry about you and your Dad's loss, and not everyone agrees with the Council's decision to ban you from the village."

Moved, Keelie blinked several times to keep back the tears. "Thanks."

He leaned closer to her as Mrs. Butters gave Keelie her muffin. "But there are others who want you to be banished forever and seek to turn your father against you. Be careful around Niriel. He's using his power of persuasion to poison the other elves against you."

He straightened quickly and returned to his fellow elves. He clapped his hands, then rubbed them together. "Okay, boys, it's a good day to do battle."

Keelie forced a smile at Mrs. Butters and paid for her muffin.

"Have a great day, dear," Mrs. Butters said, and ambled to her next customer.

As Keelie got to the top of the hill and saw where Heartwood had once stood, she stopped. Her mouth dropped open as if she'd suddenly developed cast-iron hinges in her jaw. The elves had worked miracles.

Where Heartwood had been forty-eight hours before, five-foot-tall cedar trees were now planted. A fountain flowed in the center, surrounded by pine-bark mulch paths and container plantings with benches. A cart, adorned with painted dancing corn cobs, stood at the edge of the impromptu garden, guarded by a girl wearing a hat with ears of corn sticking out like donkey ears.

Keelie walked up to her. "When did this happen?"

"Oh, the former owner and his gardening crew came out here and created this beautiful evergreen oasis overnight."

The cedars greeted her in unison—*Hello!*

Hello, trees, she answered politely.

It's very nice to meet you. They sounded fresh and young.

When were you planted? Not that she didn't trust the corn seller, but she wanted to be sure.

Last night. We were planted by the elves. Are you an elf? Elves don't talk to us, except for the Tree Shepherd, but you're different.

Keelie reeled inwardly. These new trees didn't recognize her as a tree shepherd. The ground didn't show any signs of the fire, and the area smelled like a Christmas tree farm. It was as if someone had taken a big eraser and wiped out any traces of the existence of Heartwood.

"Would you like to buy a hot buttered ear of corn? The faire gates aren't open yet, so you get dibs." The corn girl held out a buttery ear wrapped in aluminum foil.

"I might," Keelie said numbly. She would never buy corn from the spot where her father's shop had once stood, but the corn smelled yummy, and as she imagined hot butter dripping down the golden kernels, her stomach growled.

"I like your outfit." She could say this honestly. The gathered skirt and billowy shirt with the corn cob hat were much cuter than the ridiculous Steak-on-a-Stake mock-cowhide dress she'd worn at the Wildewood Faire, or the green pants of her Pickle Girl days. Maybe Finch had relaxed her standards.

A howl interrupted their transaction, as breaking glass from Hobknocker's was followed by a Santa Claus mask that flew out the door and landed on the porch. "I hate Christmas," someone inside screamed. "Where is he? Where's Toshi?"

Keelie recognized Hob's voice. It was going to be an exciting day for her at the mask shop if he was already having a temper tantrum. Unfortunately, Keelie knew that Toshi had met an unpleasant end.

She turned back to the cedar trees.

What do you know of the mask maker?

He's a strange fellow. He's been upset about something called his Toshi, and he's been screaming for it all night long.

The elves who planted us laughed at the mask maker, and that made him even angrier.

Hob stormed out onto the porch of his shop and paced back and forth, weaving like a drunkard, clenching his fists tightly and mumbling to himself.

No, it wasn't going to be a good day. Keelie reached for some loose soil on the ground and placed it in her pocket before strolling up to the mask shop. "Good morrow," she said, in a Ren-Faire-standard faux English accent.

Hob stopped, startled to see Keelie. She cocked her head fifteen degrees. Earth magic flowed through her, and she focused on Hob.

Allow me to see truly. Thick slow ripples of true sight radiated from her in all directions; bright light expanded like a sunny pond, surrounding her. Keelie closed her eyes, then opened them. A shimmer glowed around Hob's body, and then disappeared. She was getting the hang of this spell. But what did that shimmer mean?

Startled, she suddenly realized she was seeing everything truly. The Hot Tub wenches, despite all their makeup, looked like plain little girls. In the trees, balls of energy hung suspended like holiday lights. She realized she was seeing the *bhata* as they really were.

The spell had unintentional side effects that Finch should have mentioned. Keelie shivered, then turned to see that Hob was staring at her.

"Is everything okay?" Keelie asked, placing a foot on

the first step to the porch of the mask shop. She ran into a skin-prickling wall of magic, which quickly faded.

Knot hopped onto the porch ahead of her and rubbed up against Hob's leg.

Hob recoiled. "A cat! I hate cats!" His eyes turned bleary and his skin blotchy, as if just saying the word "cat" made him break out in an allergic reaction.

The illumination around Hob became brighter as Keelie felt Earth magic flow through her. He bent down, and she saw shadowy tendrils of magic twisting and turning like storm clouds around his face.

She bit down on her tongue to keep from gasping.

"I don't think I'm going to be able to open the shop today." Hob peered about the porch, wringing his hands together. "I need to find something."

Keelie's heart drummed against her rib cage, but she steadied herself, focusing on the magic. "What can I do?"

"There's nothing you can do." Hob turned toward her. The weak muscles in Keelie's legs almost gave way when she saw Peascod's contorted and wrinkled goblin face underneath the glamour that masked him as Hob.

Hob was Peascod. Peascod was Hob. Keelie's first instinct was to run, but she remained calm. She had to act like she didn't know. She would be in danger if he discovered that she knew his real identity. Just wait until Finch found out! Imagining the dragon flaming the wayward and murderous jester steeled Keelie's resolve to see the morning through until she could think up an excuse to report back to the dragon.

"Look, Mommy. There's a mask store," a little boy yelled. "I bet there's puppets!" He grinned at Keelie as he stomped up the steps to the porch and ran right through the front door.

"I guess the show must go on," Hob muttered. "Shall we entertain our faire guests?" He lifted his mouth in a snarl, revealing jagged teeth.

"Sure." A cold sensation wrapped itself around Keelie.

When Keelie entered the shop, she felt another ripple of magic that set her on edge. The shop had a warped Willy-Wonka-meets-the-circus vibe, and the unique atmosphere was given a creepy twist by the puppets that hung from the walls between the hundreds of masks. It was as if eyeless faces and little men were staring at her.

Keelie walked behind the wooden counter (alder, from Colorado) and touched the brass register; cold metal, hard to the touch. It was very different from Heartwood's wooden register. Her heart seized with sadness as she peeked through the shop window, between shelves loaded with papier-mâché carnival masks, and saw the newly planted cedars, and the corn-on-the-cob vendor talking happily with a group that had paused by her cart.

Keelie strolled over to look at the puppets and was struck by their sameness. As Finch had mentioned, each one was identical to the Toshi puppet; the only difference was that they wore different-colored versions of the jester's costume. Hob's special friend wasn't so special if there were hundreds of him... *why* was he so upset? He could have grabbed one of these.

Their little faces leered at her. Keelie shivered.

"What do you want me to do?" Keelie asked, backing away from the disturbing Toshi display.

Before Hob could answer, families started streaming into the shop. Everyone seemed to love the creepy masks and puppets. After they had been working for two hours, Hob—or rather, Peascod—came to stand at her side. Keelie fought to act normally.

"I no longer need your services." He eyed the door as if eager to leave.

"What about the afternoon? Your customers?" Keelie had to find out where he was headed.

"I have other plans. I'll just close up."

Once they were out of the shop, Hob closed the door and locked it.

"Do you want me to come back later?" Keelie asked. "Tomorrow?"

"Things have changed." He fumbled with the keys.

At least this time, Finch wouldn't go ballistic about Keelie tanking at a job in under a day. Of course, Keelie hadn't messed this one up.

"I'll leave your wages with Finch. I'll pay you for a full day." Hob stared at her, as if about to say something else, but instead turned the corner around Hobknocker's and was gone.

He'd vanished.

Keelie wondered if she should try to track him through the trees, but Knot sat down on her foot.

"Meow. No. Not safe. Meow will go."

"Fine. I'll go and tell Finch."

fourteen

The Admin office was empty, and Keelie let herself in and waited. The thin walls did little to mute the noise of the happy throngs outside. The dragon clock ticked loudly. What was Peascod up to? Why had he disguised himself as a shop owner? She wondered what Knot would discover by following Peascod. She hoped the fairy cat kept a low profile.

Tick. Tick. Tick. The minutes passed slowly. Tapping her foot anxiously on the floor, Keelie didn't know if she should search for Finch or keep waiting.

Goblins. Peascod. Keelie didn't have any magical solutions. It was like she had used up all her luck in the Northwoods.

A lump of orange fur jumped through the open office window and landed on Finch's desk.

"Knot!" Keelie ran to him, then stopped, aghast. Blood streaked the cat's nose and slack skin flapped over one eye, loose from a deep cut.

"What happened to you?" Keelie asked, wondering if she should bundle him up and rush him to a vet.

"Meow, bad news."

"What is it?"

"Meow, need to come."

A sickening wave of Something Wrong welled up within Keelie. "Tell me."

"I tried meow to save meow Cricket."

Keelie inhaled sharply. "Save Cricket? Where is he?"

"Meow fought against Peascod, but he was angry, meow, he threw Cricket against the wall," Knot said. He wiped his paw across his face, and he sniffed. "Meow dead."

Peascod! Cricket! Keelie placed her trembling hand against her mouth at the dark and horrible image of Peascod tossing Cricket aside like trash. She could almost imagine the horrible smack his little body made on impact. Tears trailed down her face and a sob escaped from her lips as she sat down in the hard plastic lawn chair.

"Meow, Cricket Under-the-Hill." Knot hopped onto Finch's desk and reached out with his paw and placed it on Keelie's hand. It was a tender gesture for the fairy cat, and Keelie felt comforted by his presence.

"At least you were there, trying to save him." Keelie patted Knot on the head.

"Meow needs to get body. So goblin spirit can travel to Sylvus."

Keelie felt sadness seep into her bones. She wouldn't see the little goblin again. Just like she wouldn't see Mom. If she needed to retrieve Cricket's body so his little spirit could travel on to its next destination, she would do it.

Peascod had done many terrible things to humans and fae, but she hadn't thought that he would turn on one of his own kind, especially a young goblin.

"Cricket was like one of Peascod's own," Keelie said. "I don't understand how he could've done this. I mean, is this what goblins do to one another?"

"Meow, cruel heart in *some* goblins. Cruel heart can be in human, elf, and fairy. Doesn't matter the fur or skin if meow evil flows in meow's blood." Knot licked his paw and rubbed it over his injured ear.

"Keelie, what are you doing here?" She turned around and wiped her face with the back of her hand. Dad stood in the doorway, then stepped into the office. "I knocked, but Finch didn't answer. Then I heard your voice."

He seemed regal in his elven robes, but Keelie detected something different about him even without using the To See Truly spell. He was definitely more elven than he was even a few days ago.

"Knot's hurt. And he says that Cricket is dead." She started to cry again.

Dad took two large steps toward her and pulled her

into his arms. For a moment, Keelie let herself cry into his shoulder, comforted by her father's arms around her. She sniffed. "Thanks, Dad."

He let go of her when she pulled away a little.

"Why are you here?" She wanted to go find Cricket's body and bury him, but she didn't want to tell Dad about her plans.

"I had to speak to Finch. I'm sorry about your little creature, but I must say that I'm disappointed to see you here. I was hoping you'd be staying indoors with Janice, where you would be safe." He turned to Knot. "Janice can stitch you up." He seemed so cold.

Keelie closed her eyes and sighed. When she looked at Dad again, he was all blurry—but she caught a glimpse of something shimmering around the outline of his body. That was not normal for elves.

She was about to look again when Dad spoke. "I'm sorry for the loss of your pet. I know you were fond of him." His green eyes gleamed hard and bright. "But Keelie, I've come to believe that I've been too indulgent with you, and as a result, your reckless decisions have endangered you and many others. Your little friend was a goblin, a dangerous creature that would have betrayed you eventually."

"Dangerous? Cricket?" Keelie managed to choke out the words as indignation rose in her. "Cricket showed me affection, no matter what you thought about him. I cared about him." She tried to keep her voice steady. "He would never have turned evil, or done anything to hurt me."

"Hard-headed child. Mourn your pet, but you must

prepare yourself to leave the faire. All the elves will be leaving. You must keep your focus on the Dread Forest, where you will stay and be protected."

Keelie shook her head. "Elves leaving?"

He nodded. "It was decided at the last Council meeting."

"Dad, I don't want to argue. I can't deal with elves and Council decisions right now." Keelie stood up as Knot jumped down from the desk. The cat hissed as he strolled past Dad. "I need to go and find Cricket's body." Keelie reached for some tissues on Finch's desk.

"The trees will not accept the body of a goblin buried in their soil," Dad said. "Remember what happened with that nasty goblin tree. We can't risk another infection."

"Cricket wasn't a bad goblin," Keelie retorted. Dad's cold-hearted attitude made her inwardly wince, but she would stand her ground.

"Doesn't matter. Cricket"—it seemed Dad struggled just to say the name of her little companion—"was a goblin. The elves will disagree with a burial too. Leave the goblin, and allow nature to take his remains. It is the elven way."

Lately, everything was the elven way.

"I can't leave Cricket. I need to bury his remains according to the traditions of the dark fae." Keelie glowered at Dad.

"Where is the body?" he asked.

She didn't dare tell him it was in Under-the-Hill, so she altered her story. "It's in the meadow, close to the performers' campground."

He studied her intently, as if trying to determine whether she was telling the truth.

"Too dangerous," he finally said. "And we have preparations to make for our trip back to the Dread Forest."

At that moment, Finch walked into her office, rifling through papers she carried as if Keelie and Dad weren't standing there. She wore cat frame glasses perched on her nose, and when she saw Dad and Keelie, she blinked. "Did I miss an important meeting?"

Keelie could tell she'd overheard every word.

"No, we were just leaving." Dad gestured, indicating he wanted Keelie to follow him.

"Zeke, Keelie has been a big help to me," Finch said. "We need her here. The humans need her."

Dad held Finch's intent gaze. "You're driving a wedge between us, Rose."

Finch certainly didn't look like a Rose.

The faire director scowled at Dad. "Zekeliel, you can't blame me for the situation at the faire."

Keelie forced her full attention on Finch and breathed deeply, summoning up her inner strength. "I came here to tell you that your suspicions were right. Hob is Peascod."

"What? Peascod is at the faire?" Dad's face became chalky white. He whipped around to face Keelie. "And you knew?"

"Not until this morning." Keelie winced. She wondered what she could have done differently so that Cricket would still be alive.

Oh Cricket!

"I knew it," Finch growled, walking over to her desk and tossing her papers onto it. She sighed in frustration, then removed her glasses and flung them onto the desk too. They clattered loudly as they landed. Smoke drifted from her ears. "If the goblins storm the faire, they could expose our world. And with Peascod in the mix, I'm sure they're going for a full-blown attack."

Dad glared at Finch. "That is not my problem. You will have to deal with Peascod. The elves wish for Keelie and me to return to the Dread Forest, where we will be able to protect our home forest. My daughter's powers will aid her kind."

Keelie stared at her father. Who was this elf? This didn't sound like Dad. Had he been brainwashed from listening to Niriel and the other elves advise him on how to take care of his mutt daughter? She could hear them now: *Reel her in, Zekeliel, before she goes totally human. Or worse, totally fae.*

"Your daughter is more than an elf—she is a glorious combination of all that is good in this world," Finch snapped. "What you're doing to her, by expecting her to be one way, is breaking her heart, and she will follow her own path. Trailblazers always do."

Keelie stared at Finch, who blushed under her admiring gaze. Or maybe she was turning red from anger.

"Don't tell me how to raise my daughter." Dad's voice rose. When had he started to yell so much?

"Zeke, I'm not telling you how to raise your daughter,

I'm advising you to *listen* to your daughter," Finch said. Draconic scales formed around her hairline, popping up through her skin.

Keelie decided it was time to stop this interchange before Finch became a full-on dragon and flamed her father. "Dad, we need to go." She touched him on the shoulder, avoiding eye contact with Finch.

He nodded. "This is how a daughter listens to her father."

Keelie recoiled. "Who are you? You sound like an old-school feudal lord who demands total obedience from his daughter. That's not me!" Her face flushed with anger and embarrassment.

Dad sighed. "Keelie."

"I need to go find Cricket," Keelie moved toward the door.

Knot placed his paw on Keelie's leg. "Meow."

"Where is that little goblin? I was going to put him on garbage detail," Finch said.

"He's dead." Keelie choked the words out.

"I'm sorry, Keelie." Finch's voice was soft. She seemed to really mean it. "He was a good little fellow, and he would've made a hell of a good detail worker. I've never seen anyone recycle trash the way he did."

"Keelie, we must go." Dad's tone was insistent. He sounded more like Niriel every minute.

Keelie's resolve to go and find Cricket deepened. "I'm going to find my little friend's body!"

She pushed past her father and ran, Knot at her side, toward the meadow.

fifteen

She followed Knot down the West Road to the woodland area behind the privies. Along the way, she overheard bits of conversation about the fires and angry opinions about Vangar and Finch among the performers and shopkeepers. Everyone seemed to be unhappy, and more people had noticed Hob's strange behavior. Nobody had seen him since he'd closed his shop. Keelie kept quiet about Hob's whereabouts and what he had done—murdered one of his own kind.

Thirty minutes later Knot and Keelie were at the entrance to a small cavern, standing under a huge sandstone rock that overhung the entrance like a porch roof. "Are you sure there aren't any bears in there?" Keelie asked. Dragons in Colorado were surprising, but black bears were native to these mountains.

"No. Meow."

Keelie breathed deeply of the fresh mountain air. She would need it in the stale underground. The stench of goblin reeked through the small opening, and it would probably be much worse inside; hygiene wasn't part of a goblin's daily routine. It hadn't smelled this bad earlier. There must be more goblins now.

She coughed. "How far in is he?"

"Meow close." Knot wrinkled his nose, but he pushed his way into the opening and Keelie followed him down the wet slope, slippery beneath her borrowed shoes. She wished for the dry dirt stairs of the other entrance, or at least for decent boots.

Light from the opening illuminated the tunnel. Water dripped from the cave roof, part of a freshet that trickled down from the rocks above. Keelie walked cautiously toward a dark passageway that stretched to one side, careful not to alert any goblins who may have strayed this far.

Twelve steps in, she discovered Cricket's broken body lying against the wall. His little legs were sprawled carelessly, and his eyes were open wide, glazed with fear and frozen in death.

A sob escaped from deep within her chest. She reached out and picked him up, cradling him against her chest. "Poor little guy. You didn't deserve this."

"Halt." The growled command came from behind.

Keelie's heart boomed loudly as she slowly turned around, fearing it was a goblin. She hoped it would understand why she was here and would let her go do what she must.

"Help me. I just wanted to get his body and bury it with the respect and dignity that he deserves," she said without looking up. She held Cricket in the palms of her hands and extended them so the goblin could see the body. The little creature's sharp-taloned hands dangled.

"Your kindness to others always amazes me. I think it is one of your better qualities." The voice transformed, becoming warm and smooth.

"Dad! What are you doing here?" she asked.

He didn't acknowledge her question, looking around the cavern instead. "Interesting place. Made by dragons— can you tell?"

"Dragons, really?" What was up with her father?

Dad seemed more relaxed and less rigid, less the angry elf, here in the goblins' lair than he'd been up in Finch's office.

"Yes, and since Peascod has invoked the anger of two dragons, in the end he will be dispatched to the Goddess of Death. One does not make a dragon angry without facing the consequences." Dad's voice was calm.

"The Goddess of Death. I thought it was the Grim Reaper," Keelie said.

"The Grim Reaper is an image, sort of like Santa Claus. The Goddess of Death has her minions dress in black robes, and she carries a scythe, the whole scary thing, but she's the one who runs the spirit world."

Keelie blinked and looked once more down at Cricket's body.

"Come, Keelie. Bring your companion and let us take him where his body can rise forth and meet the Great Sylvus," Dad said gently. "Do not worry, daughter. Your friend will be put safely to rest."

Keelie nodded and blinked. She would not cry. "Dad, what happened to you?"

"Why?" His eyes widened as if he realized something was different about him. "I feel more my old self now. I've felt odd since arriving at the faire." He touched the smooth rock wall.

And acted odd, too. Touching the dirt in her pocket, Keelie tilted her head fifteen degrees, called upon Earth magic, and focused on Dad. *Allow me to see truly.*

Fading green tendrils surrounded Dad. It looked like nature magic, the kind used by elves.

"I think you've been enchanted," Keelie said.

Dad narrowed his eyes. He lifted his hands and looked at them as if he could see the spell. "Enchanted. That would explain why I cast my vote at the Council meeting for the elves to leave. My vote was the deciding factor. Niriel was pleased."

"He said you'd been acting more like a proper elf," Keelie said.

"So he did." Dad grimaced. "Niriel enchanted me. Yet despite that, I followed you here. I remember thinking that

I needed to go to the elven village, but still, my feet stayed on the path behind you."

"The magic doesn't seem to work at all in this cavern," Keelie said. "You're shielded from its influence."

"I need a strong talisman to shield me from Niriel's magic above ground, and I think I know who can help." Dad gestured toward the entrance. "We need to return to the surface before we meet up with any goblins."

"Dad, I can draw on Earth magic directly to shield myself from the Dread, so I can spare this." Keelie put the rose quartz in his hand and closed his fingers around it. "I hope it helps."

He smiled tenderly. "Thank you." Putting a hand on her shoulder, he followed as she headed out, holding Cricket's body tightly.

When they reached the surface, Keelie gulped in the fresh air. Relief flowed through her at having her dad back. "Who can help find a permanent talisman to protect you?" she asked. "That rose quartz isn't meant to defend against heavy-duty magic."

"Sir Davey, who else? But first, let us put your little friend to rest." Dad's voice was gentle as he looked at Cricket.

"Where?" Keelie asked.

"We're going to ask for a little help from the trees to find the proper resting place." *Hrok,* Dad telepathically called.

Yes, Tree Shepherd. Green filled Keelie's mind.

We need your assistance.

Images of herself holding Cricket spun through her

mind like a zoetrope, and then circulated through all the trees in the surrounding forests and mountaintops.

We hear your call, Tree Shepherd.

Dad's presence and voice encompassed the trees as he instructed them to find a resting place for the little goblin. Green magic enfolded Keelie; she felt a sense of peace, and a oneness with the trees and their energy. She hadn't known that Dad wielded quite this much power.

Feeling lighter, she opened her eyes to see herself floating above the ground. Then a sickening wave of nausea overcame her as she experienced the familiar sensation of a whoosh.

sixteen

The vertigo faded as soon as Keelie's feet touched the ground, Dad beside her. They'd landed in a valley tucked between two large Rocky Mountains, which rose like granite teeth on either side. Red, yellow, and orange wildflowers carpeted the meadow where they stood.

The afternoon sun was low on the horizon, its light golden and soft. Fresh air brushed against Keelie's face and she inhaled deeply. She turned to look at Dad. "I didn't know you could transport to another location."

Dad staggered, pale. "I didn't know, either. Ever since we've returned from the Northwoods, my powers have surged, and I don't know how or why. I don't even know if it's permanent or just the result of the wild magic we were exposed to."

"I'm impressed. But where are we, and how do we get back?" Keelie asked.

"Trust." Dad pointed to the right. "Why don't you ask them where we are?"

Three Colorado Spruce trees greeted her, their green voices blended as one. *Hello, Tree Shepherdess.*

Keelie reached out with her tree sense. *Hello.*

Your father has become strong, and he is favored by the Great Sylvus.

Pride coursed through her.

What are your names? Keelie asked. She sensed that these trees were very nice. This could be a wonderful place for Cricket.

The first, round tree answered. *I am Bruce.* He had a jolly tone.

The second, skinny tree waved his branches. *You can call me Deuce.* His voice was nasally.

You have the privilege of addressing me as Zeus. The third, very tall spruce had a deep baritone echo to his tree speak.

Keelie bowed her head to hide her smile. She didn't want to offend these trees. *Very nice to meet you. I wish it was under better circumstances.*

Dad walked up to the trees and bowed his head respectfully.

It is time, Bruce said.

You know why we're here? Keelie asked. She wasn't sure

yet if they would bury Cricket here, but if they did, she had to know why these trees were allowing a goblin to be buried among their roots. She shuddered, remembering her recent experience in the Redwood Forest with a goblin-infected tree.

A shower of green left Deuce's branches, laying a trail across the ground that led to a rocky outcrop. *The Great Sylvus has asked us to help the little one to carry on his journey.*

This wasn't the first time Keelie had had indirect contact with the elven deity.

Several *bhata* climbed through the branches of the spruce trees. *Feithid daoine* buzzed near the top of each tree like a crown of insects. Pixies, the little light fairies, danced in the meadow, and hundreds of butterflies waltzed in midair with them.

It was a peaceful place, and Keelie felt better knowing that this was where Cricket would rest.

The pixies flew to Keelie, and Cricket's body was surrounded by light. The little goblin floated out of her arms to the spruces, and each took a turn holding him in their branches.

The pixies lowered Cricket to the ground, their bodies creating a glowing pillow upon which he rested. Keelie gathered wildflowers and placed them around him.

The trees watched in reverent silence.

Keelie remembered the Tree Lorem last summer for the Aspen Queen, and felt the need to speak.

"May your spirit rest in peace, my little friend," she said as she sniffed. A little sparkle shot out of the grave and joined the glittering pixies. They winked out once Cricket's bright light had joined them.

The spruce trees sighed in unison.

Do not worry, Tree Shepherdess. All will be well. Bruce waved his branches.

Thank you. Keelie smiled through tears.

Dad reached out his hand and she accepted it. "All will be well," he said.

With a green whoosh, they traveled back to the faire, landing outside the elven village on the path hidden by the trees. Keelie heard the sound of jingling harnesses and chain mail. Sean, Bromliel, and some of the other jousters rode by on horseback, and she and Dad had to jump out of their way.

Keelie and Dad's sudden arrival startled the horses, and the elves had to rein in their frightened animals.

"Whoa!" Sean shouted. "Lord Zekeliel."

"Pardon me, gentlemen, my timing is off." Dad bowed gracefully.

"What are you doing here?" Sean asked. "You're supposed to be helping my father."

Above the elven village, helicopter rotors beat the air.

So soon?

Sean straightened in his saddle, haughty and handsome. He met his elven companions' eyes, as if they all shared a secret.

"You can't leave yet." Keelie whirled around and grabbed the reins of Sean's bay gelding. The horse stepped sideways, but, well-trained, didn't startle.

"If you're an elf, then you will return to the Dread Forest with the rest of us," Sean said. "Where do you stand in this world, Keliel?"

"You're really and truly abandoning the faire?" She'd hoped maybe Sean would stay.

"If the threat was a human one, or a natural one, we would stay. But goblins—they're after *us*, Keelie. We have our own lands to protect. Our own forest." He held out his hand. "Come with me, and you and I will defend our Dread Forest."

A sharp pain lanced through her chest as she realized how far apart she and Sean had grown in only a few days.

His expression softened. "Keelie, I will speak to the Council on your behalf and tell them that the fae magic in your blood contaminates your decisions. They will forgive you."

Saddened, Keelie saw that he truly thought he was being kind.

"It isn't too late. For us." Sean's eyes pleaded with her to say yes.

Releasing the horse's reins, Keelie shook her head. "I have to stay."

Dad came to Keelie's side. "Stand beside us, Sean, and persuade the other elves to join us against the goblins. Let's put a stop to Peascod once and for all."

Sean frowned. "Lord Zekeliel, you helped form our escape plan. You yourself said that humans are in no danger. Humans can't even see goblins, remember? I cannot join your foolish venture. Our forest needs us." Sean turned his horse, as did all the other elves.

Before he galloped away, Bromliel turned around and bowed his head. "Good luck to you, Daughter of the Forest. Lord of the Forest." He clicked his heels against his horse's side and cantered away after Sean and the others.

"They're really leaving." Keelie looked up at Dad. Another helicopter circled above. "Dad, what you said before, about goblins not hurting humans, might not be true."

Dad watched the helicopter fly off, then shook his head. "Humans have never seen goblins, and some goblins live side by side with them, thriving on their refuse. Why would they hurt them?"

"Because it's an army?" Keelie sighed. "I think things are very different now. Peascod is leading them, for one thing."

"If we had a large number of magical warriors, then the goblins might be swayed not to attack," Dad said thoughtfully. "We could turn them against Peascod."

"Where are we going to find magical warriors?" Keelie asked.

"I don't know." Dad frowned. "I still believe that humans are in no danger here."

"Except that if Peascod wins, the whole world will suffer." Keelie looked closely at her father. "We need to get you a stronger talisman soon." She bit her lip. "The only other option is ... "

"What are you thinking?" Dad cast a worried look in her direction.

"I'm thinking that in order to keep the humans safe

here, they need to know what they're up against. They need to know about the goblins because no one else is willing to protect them. They need to know about the magic, so that they can defend themselves."

Dad's mouth dropped open, and then he closed it quickly. "Why would they believe you? How would they defend against a foe they can't see, who might not even want to harm them?" His shoulders slumped. "I need to rest now. In the morning, let's talk to the dragons, after we stop at Sir Davey's RV to find a talisman. I do not want to come under another of Niriel's enchantments."

seventeen

The next morning, Keelie slipped out early to grab tea and muffins from Mrs. Butters' shop. The place was practically deserted without the early rising jousters.

"Your father's gone to see Sir Davey," Janice said when Keelie returned. "He doesn't look well."

"Alone?" Keelie set out a couple of muffins and abandoned the tea on the table. "I brought breakfast. Gotta go."

She raced through the faire's lanes. She spotted Dad at last leaning against Sir Davey's RV. His face was pale, with sickly green undertones.

"What's wrong?" she asked, forcing the panic of out her voice.

"I feel the enchantment becoming stronger, trying to take over—I feel the need to leave with the elves. It's as if I've been infected with something."

"We need to get that talisman," Keelie said. She helped Dad inside.

It seemed very quiet, considering the goblin tree was there.

"Davey?" Dad called from the doorway.

No answer.

Dad dropped into one of the recliners by the door.

Keelie heard a moan from the bedroom and walked silently toward the back, apprehension slowing her steps.

Sir Davey lay on the floor, unconscious, blood pooling around his head. Was he dead?

Keelie ran to kneel at his side. "Dad, over here! Sir Davey?" She touched his arm. *Please be alive.*

Dad staggered in and yanked off one of Sir Davey's boots. He grabbed the foot, in its sparkly amethyst-colored sock.

Keelie raised her eyebrows.

"I need to check his vitals, and a dwarf's pulse beats strongest in the soles of his feet."

Sir Davey moaned and Keelie let out the breath she'd been holding, relieved when Sir Davey moved his hand and tried to sit up.

"What happened to you?" she asked.

Dad propped Sir Davey up against the wall. The dwarf

opened his eyes, then moaned and closed them again, pressing a hand against the wound on his forehead. "I didn't see them—they hit me upside the head with a heavy object and took that tree before I could stop them."

"The goblin tree has been stolen?" Keelie scanned the interior of the RV, although she didn't know what she was searching for. A trail of potting soil?

"Who'd want it?" Dad shook his head. "We'll find it later. We need to treat your wounds."

Keelie wet a clean washcloth in the bathroom and found bandages and some of Janice's herbal healing salve in the cabinet.

Once she'd bandaged his head, Dad helping out, Sir Davey sat down in the diner-style booth in the kitchen.

"I'll make coffee," Keelie said.

"Please." Davey shook his head as if to clear it.

"Make me some tea." Dad lowered himself across from Sir Davey.

As she prepared the coffee, Keelie reached out telepathically to Hrok. He might be able to sense the goblin tree.

Hrok?

Yes, milady.

Someone has injured Sir Davey and stolen the aspen sapling.

Oh dear. Whoever has that tree doesn't know what they're in for. Hrok seemed amused.

We have to find it. Alert the trees.

I will, Daughter of the Forest.

Once the coffee had finished brewing, Keelie poured Sir Davey a cup and brought it to him. "Thanks, lass."

She placed a cup of chamomile tea in front of Dad, and he nodded his thanks. She poured coffee and sat down with them in the circular booth.

"I alerted Hrok about the missing goblin tree," Keelie said.

"It will be interesting to discover who has taken it." Dad grasped the cup in his thin fingers. "Davey, I need some sort of talisman. I've been enchanted, and we think it's Niriel's doing."

Davey scowled. "I've always known that elf was a bad seed."

Dad sipped his tea, then lowered the mug. "The first group of elves have already left, and the others are awaiting the return of the helicopters."

Sir Davey looked up. "So much for waiting several days before making a decision."

"I cast the deciding vote to leave, under magical influence. It seems my vote carries more sway than those of other Council members," Dad said.

"Sean hasn't left yet. The trailers just arrived for the horses." Keelie chewed on her lip.

A frantic and rapid-fire knock at the door interrupted their conversation. Keelie's heart thumped against her rib cage.

Sir Davey rose cautiously, his hand pressed against his bandaged head.

"Expecting company?" Keelie asked.

"No." Sir Davey opened the door, and to Keelie's surprise, Knot rushed inside the RV followed by Sally the tarot reader. Her face was rosy red, as if she had jogged all the way from Equus Island. She looked like she was already having a bad day.

"I've read the cards seven times, and they reveal the same thing each time. It's scaring me," she gasped. Her wild eyes flickered over toward Sir Davey, taking in his bandaged head. "The cards have shown me what is coming."

"We can stop the goblins, but everyone is going to have to work together." Dad used the same soothing tone of voice he used on the trees.

Sally arched an eyebrow. "You really believe that?"

"We have to. Tell us what the cards have shown." Dad motioned toward the table.

It was good to have good ol' Dad back where he belonged. Keelie vowed to make sure he had a protective talisman shielding him at all times.

Knot hopped onto the table and lapped some of Sir Davey's coffee, as if it would calm him. Sir Davey ignored the cat. Sally sat down in the booth across from Keelie.

Knot walked over to Keelie, leaving paw prints on the table. "Meow tell her what you told me."

"You're talking to Sally?" Keelie asked, shocked.

"Meow." He nodded.

Sally laughed. "I talk to faire cats all the time, though not like with your fairy cat here. It's the horses you need to worry about. Total airheads." With a quick movement, she removed a purple bag embroidered with dragons from inside the deep, pocketed vest she wore. She carefully placed the bag on the table, then opened it to reveal her tarot deck from the Quicksilver Faire.

Earlier, there had been dragons on this deck, and some had resembled Finch and Vangar, but now the deck had goblins and wizards. Sally shuffled the cards like a Las Vegas card dealer.

Keelie gazed at the cards curiously as Sally spread them out, face up. "Did you get a new deck?" she asked. The images of goblins on the cards looked like the ones she'd seen Under-the-Hill. Dad's eyes met hers, reflecting worry. He studied the cards.

"I didn't." Sally placed three cards face down. "Turn them over."

Chills skipped down Keelie's back as she flipped over the first card.

The first card was the Fool card—it was a jester, but not just any jester. This one was Peascod, with Toshi on his hand.

Sally nodded encouragingly. "The second one."

It was the nine of swords—a battle scene with goblins attacking a festival that appeared to be the High Mountain Renaissance Faire. People were running for their lives in the background. Keelie felt sick to her stomach. This was what could potentially happen at this faire if the goblins attacked. She'd warned Dad that the humans were in danger, and this card showed that her fear was well-founded.

She didn't want to turn over the third card. But she did, with trembling fingers. It showed a goblin dressed in armor, magic flowing from his hands toward a cowering, masked jester begging for his life. This was almost encouraging.

The jester was Peascod. But who was the armored goblin?

"What does this mean?" Keelie asked. All of the images scared her.

Sally turned the tarot deck over, and now all of the cards contained the armored goblin, in the same scene, over and over.

"This has never happened before, yet it is something I've seen many times this morning." Sally frowned. "Something so powerful lurks among the goblins that it is transforming the images on my tarot deck."

"Why? What? Who could do this?" Keelie asked. She tapped the image of the magical goblin.

Knot hissed.

Dad leaned down and picked up one of the cards. "Something about this goblin looks familiar."

"Is he sending us a message about the faire? Will he attack?" Keelie leaned forward.

"That's just it. I don't know if the cards are being manipulated by the goblins, or if they're reacting to a goblin's magic." Sally threw her hands up.

Sir Davey had been silent the entire time, but finally spoke. "This is strange indeed. I'm not one to put much stock in the fate cards, but this frightens me." He picked up the five of cups and the two of swords, each containing the same image of the powerful goblin wizard and a dying Peascod.

Keelie placed her hands flat on the table. "We need to show this to Finch and Vangar."

"I think we need to contact the fairy court and Herne as well," Dad said. "This is bigger than goblins, elves, and dragons. My gut instinct tells me this is a play for power. Leftover business from the Northwoods."

Sally's jaw dropped open, and then she quickly closed it as if regaining her senses. "Are we talking about Herne, *the* Nature god?"

Keelie nodded.

"Holy cow!" Sally gulped down Sir Davey's coffee and Knot meowed in protest. "I need this more than you do," she muttered to the cat. "Tell me more."

Keelie quickly told Sally about the events in the North-woods—the widening rift in the Earth and the crack in Gaia's dome.

Sally listened, wide-eyed and excited. "I knew it! On the day you sealed the rift, I did a tarot reading, and the cards showed that world changes were on the way. Things would never be the same."

If there was a goblin wizard leading the wild goblins, then he must be the one in charge. Or was Peascod in charge? Keelie remembered Peascod mentioning that he had a new master after he broke with Herne, but she'd fig-ured he'd meant Avenir, the dragon lord who died in the rift's fires. But was *this* his new master? She picked a card up and studied it.

"I say we're going to need all the help we can muster," Sir Davey said. "If Herne and the High Court will join with us, then I'm all for it. If the cards show truly, we're going to need their aid."

Dad nodded.

"Sir Davey, about that talisman for Dad. What do you recommend?" Keelie asked.

"Dwarfstone." Davey held up a dark stone, then tossed it to Dad, who snatched it out of the air and examined it curiously.

"Of course, I'll have to show you how to use it." Sir Davey winked at Keelie. "Not so hard, if your daughter learned how."

"Hey!" Keelie protested, but she felt better with Dad protected from Niriel's magic.

◆ ◆ ◆

Later, Keelie leaned against the wall of Finch's office as Dad and Sir Davey brought the red-faced faire director up to speed. Keelie waited for the draconic transformation that was sure to come as soon as Finch discovered how dire their situation was.

Sally displayed her cards on Finch's desk. Once more they showed all the same image—the one of the goblin wizard, his eyes red and rimmed in darkness.

Smoke drifted from Finch's ears, and an outdoor grill scent filled the room as she perused the entire tarot deck. "And this is the deck from Quicksilver?"

Sally nodded. "They seem to be aligned with some external magic right now.

"Interesting." Finch lifted one card up and studied it. "Did you notice something different about this goblin?" She turned the card around so everyone could see it.

Keelie leaned closer. "No. He has green skin, like they all do."

"But he has ears like an elf." Finch directed everyone's attention to the goblin's head.

"What?" The word escaped Keelie's mouth, and then she snapped her mouth closed as she remembered. "It couldn't be him."

"Who?" Finch asked.

"In the Redwoods, there was an elf—or half-elf, since his other half was goblin—who had a lot of magic. His name was Tavyn. He overpowered and possessed Blood-root, a redwood tree."

"Half elf, half goblin," Finch said. "An interesting combination. Almost as unique as yours, Keelie."

The statement hit Keelie like a lightning bolt. She did not appreciate this comparison to Tavyn. Her cheeks flushed with heat. Dad patted her on the shoulder, as if to reassure her everything would be okay.

But she did have things in common with Tavyn. And if he was the one behind the goblins and Peascod, she might be the only one who could stop him.

eighteen

"Do you think that if we find Peascod, we'll find this goblin wizard?" Sir Davey asked, his eyes locked on Finch.

"I don't know. Damn goblins!" The faire director shook her head. She reached into a cup full of pencils and snapped one of them in two, as if she imagined she was snapping a goblin neck.

"Last sighting of Peascod was when Knot tried to save Cricket." Keelie's breath hitched at the memory of finding the goblin's little body, but she forced herself to concentrate on the conversation at hand.

Finch leaned forward on her elbows. "Vangar is out

scouting for goblin activity and possible entrance points into Under-the-Hill, looking for a way to prevent a secret attack. We don't know if they're watching us. We just can't find them. We must let Vangar know about this powerful goblin with the pointed ears, and that he may be their leader." Finch stared at the tarot deck. "If the fate cards are affected by this goblin wizard's magic, it means we're dealing with a powerful foe."

"King Gneiss and his army were supposed to be here by now." Sir Davey's voice was weighed down with worry. "I'll need to contact them again and tell them to hurry."

Finch nodded. "Good idea."

"Anyway, can we persuade the elves not to leave?" Finch asked Dad.

He shook his head. "Believe me, I tried. Niriel's influence has spread far and wide among my kind."

"Elves!" Finch reached for another pencil and snapped it in two. "I've sent a message to Ermentrude. She'll fly to the High Court, and she hopes to find Herne."

Sir Davey ran a hand down his face. "If the elves aren't going to help us, and we have to wait for Herne and possibly members of the High Court, what are we going to do in the meantime? I'm sure the goblins are waiting for a weak moment to attack. What if they're just waiting for the elves to leave?"

Keelie listened, remembering how in Under-the-Hill she had seen the tendrils of elven magic on Dad. But what if it *hadn't* been Niriel who'd cast the spell on Dad? A disturbing thought was forming in her mind, and she cringed inwardly. Tavyn could be hiding among the elves. He had a cold side to him, and he was bitter toward the elves, blaming them for not accepting him or his mixed blood. Keelie tried to remember each of her encounters with Tavyn. In the Redwoods, he had first appeared to be a pureblood and charming elf; he hid his dark side beneath an illusion of elven-ness, much like Peascod had disguised himself as Hob.

"We're going to ramp up our patrols," Finch announced. "We'll ask some of the humans to join us, telling them we've had problems with vandals. Maybe that'll keep the questions at bay."

Sally clenched her hands. "Rumors are circulating around the faire about the jousters leaving. The shop owners say the faire is cursed with bad luck. So they'll believe anything at this point."

With the elves gone from the faire, Keelie felt sure there would be panic among the humans. They'd be distracted and fearful, and Tavyn would take advantage of it as part of his strategic plan.

"I know. I know. Until I have some intel, I don't have a better plan," Finch said. "Zeke, can you talk to the trees, find out if they've seen anything?"

"What do you want to know?" Dad asked.

"I want to know if they can sense any difference in Under-the-Hill."

"Tavyn can disguise himself as a pureblood elf," Keelie blurted out.

"What?" Finch stared at her.

Keelie tapped the goblin picture. "He can look like an elf. He did it in the Redwood Forest. He fooled me."

"You're right—and he could've been the one to put an enchantment on me. Maybe it wasn't Niriel." Dad scratched his chin in worried contemplation.

Sir Davey stood up. "Come with me, Zeke. We'll need to get you a better specimen of dwarfstone from my shop while we have time."

"I'll enhance its protective qualities with my magic," Finch said.

"We need to warn the trees about the goblin wizard," Dad said. "Hrok in the meadow would be the best one to spread the message."

"I'll do it. You need that dwarfstone," Keelie said. And Hrok thought goblins were friends.

Dad was about to protest, but Sir Davey intervened. "Keelie is right. She can talk to the trees. First things first—you need that dwarfstone, then you can meet her in the meadow."

"Keelie, I'll be back as soon as possible." Dad's troubled eyes couldn't conceal his worry.

"I'll be careful."

Finch tossed a communications radio toward her, the kind the faire workers used to talk to one another. Keelie caught it.

"Keep in contact. I want a report every fifteen minutes," Finch bellowed. "Cat, go with her."

Knot saluted with his tail. "Meow on the job."

Once Keelie and Knot were outside the Admin building,

Keelie inhaled the dry summer air. It was hotter than usual today. As they made their way through the faire to the East Road, a greenness filled Keelie's mind. One of the trees was about to contact her, and she closed her eyes and opened her mind.

She recognized Hrok's energy. She wondered if he had any updates on the whereabouts of the goblin tree.

Hrok. I need to know…

Hold on, Tree Shepherdess. I have someone else who wishes to speak to me.

Hrok had never put her on hold before. Who else was speaking to Hrok?

An icy darkness skated through her mind, and vertigo overcame her. Keelie stumbled and fell to the ground. Knot rushed to her and pressed his paw against her forehead.

She'd never experienced this particular type of dark, strange dizziness during tree speak, but she had sensed this magic before. She lay with her body pressed to the moist dirt, enjoying its coolness against her back, watching the clouds drift past in the sky until the spinning feeling eased. She didn't bother to stand. Tapping back into the greenness, she again reached out to Hrok.

Who is this other person you're speaking to?

Melankin.

Melankin? She'd never heard the name before.

Yes, Keelie. He is a friend, and he is like you. He can talk to trees.

Do you mean there is another elf in the forest? Another tree shepherd?

No, Melankin is a goblin. We trees found it very strange at first, but he is like you, his magic is like yours and he speaks to us. He has reassured us that the goblins will not harm the forest. They only want to restore a balance to this magical area and allow us to live in a sanctuary of peace.

A goblin tree shepherd? It sounded like this Melankin was trying to bamboozle the trees into thinking he was there on a peaceful mission.

Shocked, Keelie tried to think clearly. Maybe there were things the goblins could do that she wasn't aware of. The whole concept of a goblin tree shepherd seemed like something from an upside-down universe.

Would you like to speak to Melankin?

Keelie didn't know if she should have contact with a goblin tree shepherd without knowing more about him first. Opening yourself telepathically to someone could be dangerous. Her palms were all sweaty.

Hrok, does Melankin know about me?

Oh, yes. All the trees have told him about your magic, and what you've done for all the trees since we discovered you. He finds the stories very interesting.

Keelie quelled the panic flooding through her.

Does Melankin tell you about the goblins?

No, we talk about trees, and the land, and the magic of the forest, and like I said, you're a topic of conversation. He seems particularly interested in your father's growing power as Lord of the Forest.

Keelie did not have a good feeling about this. Not at all. How could you muzzle a tree? Duct tape their bark?

How long has Melankin known about me?

Since you arrived. He sensed a change in the magic when we first spoke, and he asked about you, so we told him. We had no reason not to, Forest Daughter. The goblins wish us no harm.

How do they feel about the humans here at the faire? The elves?

If you have a conflict with the goblins, then you must resolve it. We trees stand with our roots deep in the soil, strong in the nurture of Mother Earth.

These goblins don't encourage nurturing Mother Earth.

How do you know?

I met an army of them that had power and control on their agenda.

Oh, Melankin had to go. Too bad you didn't take the time to speak to him. He seems as alarmed that you know about him as you do that he knows of you. I explained to him, like I did to you, that elves are friends to trees, as are goblins. Humans and other species are so strange.

Keelie wanted to bang Hrok's branches against a wall to knock some sense into him. However, she closed off the image as it appeared in her mind. She didn't want to startle the tree. Hrok was a gentle soul.

Keelie, are you feeling well? Your sap is boiling. Not good—your leaves will die off.

Don't worry about me, Hrok. I'm not feeling well, so I'm going to rest. I'll talk to Melankin another time. Maybe you can arrange a meeting?

I would be delighted.

Before I go, any word on the missing aspen sapling?

No, milady Keliel, but a lot of the trees in the forest are glad it is gone. It was a mean tree.

Keep searching for him.

Keelie wondered if the mysterious Melankin could be in league with Tavyn, or maybe Peascod.

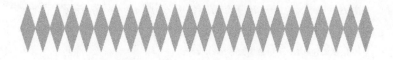

nineteen

Clutching the radio in her hand, Keelie suddenly realized that she'd blacked out. She shook her head as a headache throbbed behind her eyes. How long had she been in telepathic contact with Hrok? She was near the woods bordering the East Road. She could hear people talking as they passed by her, not seeing her.

Knot rubbed up against her legs. "Yeow call Finch."

Keelie was supposed to have contacted the faire director every fifteen minutes on the radio. Judging from the sun's position in the sky, she figured she was over an hour late. Finch would be furious, and Dad would be worried. Keelie picked up the radio, but dropped it in her lap when she heard a snap of twigs behind her.

Goblins?

"Excuse me, miss?" someone said.

Keelie rose to her feet and looked around at the speaker, and her body relaxed when she realized she wasn't dealing with an attacking goblin. A woman in jeans, a short-sleeved T-shirt, and sensible shoes was watching her, accompanied by a stringy-haired man who had a camera with a huge telephoto lens—the kind professional photographers use—strung around his neck.

Keelie didn't recognize them. They weren't performers or shopkeepers.

"Yes?" Keelie said cautiously.

"I was wondering if you knew why all the helicopters are flying into the faire? Is there some sort of emergency?" The woman pointed in the direction of the elven camp. She pulled out a small pad and paper, ready to record Keelie's answers.

"Who are you?" Keelie asked.

"My name is Blakely Kilpatrick. I'm a reporter for the *Fort Collins Daily*, and you are?" The reporter smiled, expecting an answer.

A reporter?

"Why are you here?" Keelie asked.

"There've been a lot of wild rumors about this faire. I'm here to check them out, and look into the reason why the faire has been plagued by so many fires. Do you work here?" Blakely still held her pencil poised.

"My dad owns one of the shops." Keelie looked up as more helicopters flew overhead. Where had the elves gotten so many? They were probably taking the entire remaining elven folk out in one group.

Blakely followed her gaze. "Strange to see these big transport choppers. Something's up." She motioned toward the photographer. "Come on, Ralph, let's follow them."

"You're not supposed to be back here," Keelie said. The reporter and photographer would be whammied with the Dread any second.

"I smell a story, kid." Blakely and Ralph bounded off toward the woods before Keelie had a chance to stop them.

Knot lifted his head up toward her. "Meow not good. Snoopy human will meow trouble."

"I'll need to let Finch know we not only have rogue goblins, we have rogue reporters. She's going to explode when she finds out." Keelie pressed the radio switch, but it was dead. She tried again.

"Meow wrong?" Knot asked.

"I think the battery is dead." She pressed the "on" switch again. Nothing but silence. "Weird."

The sound of stomping footfalls and the rustling of leaves caught Keelie's attention. It was coming from the woods across the meadow from the faire. Then loud screams erupted from the woods as the sound of war bugles echoed through the trees. It was the battle cry of the goblins.

Knot grew to his human size, looking like an orange tabby leopard. "Yeow go to faire. Tell Finch."

Blakely and Ralph crashed through the bushes and

came running back toward them, rushing right past Keelie. "Run! Monsters are attacking!"

They'd seen the goblins. Keelie's worst fear had come true. Dad had to know this right away.

The reporter and photographer had stopped to stare at the abnormally huge cat. Ralph lifted his camera and got some shots.

"Meow will take care of them." Knot flicked his tail and bounded into the woods.

"Be careful," Keelie shouted out after him. Then she gestured toward the parking lot in the performers' campground; it would be better to get Blakely and Ralph out of here for their own safety. "You should go that way."

"That cat talked," Blakely Kilpatrick said, looking dazed.

Keelie ignored her statement and jogged ahead. "Follow me."

They ran down the path. When an arrow zinged past them and struck a tree, Keelie came to a complete stop. The alder screamed in pain, its cries rippling through her head.

"We need to go back." She would have to lead the reporter and the photographer into the faire itself. "Run."

She moved as fast as her legs would take her. She heard the huffing and puffing of the winded duo from the *Fort Collins Daily*, but they were still talking as they made their way after Keelie.

"Did you see that thing back there?" Blakely asked.

"Yeah, and I got great photos," the camera dude answered.

So they had proof—they had seen the goblins. Keelie wondered what the photos would show.

As they came around the Griffin jousting ride, Keelie saw Vangar walking quickly toward Wood Row. He stopped when he saw her with her bedraggled companions.

"Keelie, I was about to go and search for you. Finch is beside herself with worry," he called.

"Goblins," she said breathless. "They're coming in from the woods side of the faire."

Vangar's face reddened as his shoulders hunched and his hands clenched. He was about to transform. Keelie held up her hand. "These are reporters."

He shook away the transformation, relaxing his shoulders, then smiled and nodded. "Hello, folks." He turned to Keelie. "I'll gather the others," he said softly.

"There are monsters in the woods," Blakely said, her voice shrill. "Don't go down that road." She pointed to the East Road.

Vangar nodded. "Thanks, I won't."

Before Keelie could stop her, Blakely was yelling into phone. "I need the editor, now. I'm sending some photos from my phone. I have the scoop. Those sightings of green men at the faire—I have proof they're real. No, not makeup. We're talking some kind of green monsters, with axes, wearing armor. This is big."

Keelie didn't think Finch was going to like this latest development. If the world discovered that goblins were real, what would happen to those with real magic? Would they be subject to government testing? Would they be socially ostracized? She hadn't thought that far ahead.

"I think you need to meet our faire director," she said.

"Does she know what's going on here?" Blakely asked.

"Um, yes." Keelie ran toward the Admin office by the main gate, the reporters huffing and puffing behind her.

In Finch's office, the dragon-woman broke several pencils as Blakely explained how she'd run into goblins and sent the pictures into the newspaper.

Then the reporter's phone rang. "No, that's awesome news—I'll let them know," she said into her phone. She beamed at Keelie. "CNN, the Associated Press, all the news stations picked up my story, and they're on their way with cameras. In twenty-four hours this place is going to be covered with reporters." She did a little dance step, beaming with excitement.

Finch's pile of broken pencils was getting scary.

Keelie needed to find Dad and make sure he was safe. He was probably thinking the same thing about her.

Finch's radio crackled on her desk. Vangar's voice was garbled, but clear enough to make out his warning. "Goblins have been seen near the elven camp. I'm sealing the shields around the faire."

Finch paled.

"What does he mean, seal the shields around the faire? Do you have soldiers guarding a secret compound?" Blakely asked.

"It means you're not leaving."

"What?" The reporter reeled back from Finch's booming voice.

Once again, Keelie wished she had the Compendium—she could've cast a forgetful spell on the reporters.

"Keelie, contact the trees. Find out the situation with the elves."

"Elves. Contact trees?" Blakely looked like she was about to wet her pants. "If I hadn't seen those slimy, greeny-gray guys myself, I'd think this was a LARP."

"LARP?" Finch frowned.

"Live Action Role Playing—it's a game," Keelie explained.

"What kind of games do humans play?" Finch asked, not expecting an answer. She pressed a button on a remote control and a wall panel slid to the left, exposing swords, spears, and maces. It was a fully stocked medieval armory.

"Quite the collection," Keelie said as Finch removed a short blade from the wall.

Blakely stood, open-mouthed, while her photographer got busy snapping pictures.

"Can you handle a sword?" Finch asked the reporter.

"I took fencing in school, but I did foil. These are all edged weapons," she said.

"I'm impressed that you called it an edged weapon. So, close enough." Finch handed the hilt of the short blade to the reporter. "We're at war, sweetheart, so you're going to have to slice and dice if you're attacked. Otherwise, you're dead. Keelie, what do you want?" Finch held out a selection.

Keelie had wielded a sword before. She chose a rapier with an emerald in the pommel. "This one."

Finch nodded her approval. "Good choice."

"This is for real." Blakely's voice was serious.

"It's for real," Keelie replied. "I'm going to contact the trees." Plus, she wanted to make sure Dad was safe. She took comfort in knowing that the elves, at least, were on their way home.

Stepping outside, Keelie took a deep breath and sought out the greenness.

Hrok.

The tree didn't answer. What did reply to Keelie's summons wasn't Hrok.

Do you seek counsel with your tree friend?

An orange and red light filtered through Keelie's mind. The fieriness reminded her of a goblin's eyes.

Who are you?

Surely you can guess?

Melankin?

Perceptive. That is one of my names.

Elven lore doesn't tell of a goblin tree shepherd. I'm not sure it's possible. Goblinkind are linked to rocks and crystals, not living things.

The elves think they're the only species who can live in harmony with nature. My kind lives in close association with the humans in the cities, nature of a different sort. It is our way of preserving our independence, but still being part of this world.

Keelie couldn't argue with this point. The elves had withdrawn into their forests and isolated themselves.

Why are you attacking the faire? These are innocent people here. If you're a friend of trees, then you wouldn't put them in harm's way. You would leave the faire. And you say goblins live closely with humans, so why hurt them?

I am indeed a friend of trees, but I'm not an elf friend, nor a human friend.

Why this faire?

Why, Keelie, I thought the reason would be obvious.

I'm clueless. Enlighten me.

Laughter erupted in her mind, making it pound with red and yellow bursts. She inhaled. Could it be Tavyn? He had talked to the Redwoods, but those ancient trees could be seen and heard by all if they wished to reveal themselves.

Getting closer. In fact, you're red hot.

The trees may know you by the name Melankin, but the goblins and elves call you Tavyn.

Ah, Keliel, you're a smart one. What else do you know?

You're here at this faire because you want to get your revenge against me for foiling your plans in California.

One of the reasons. But you have something in your possession that I want.

Keelie had no idea what he could want. She had nothing of value. Could it be her magical cat? *You mean Knot?*

She felt a wave of disbelief trickle through her mind. *As if. That cat is a curse to anyone who owns him. You two are a well-matched pair. I'll make a bargain with you, Keliel. We'll save the trees, we'll save the humans and their little faire, and no one gets hurt if you make a trade with me.*

Keelie's heart started to thud faster. What could he

want that was worth disrupting and destroying so much? *What do you wish to trade?*

You give me the Compendium, and I'll call off my goblins, and your humans will be safe. You have until sunset today.

It was already mid-afternoon. Keelie felt sick to her stomach. She couldn't possibly comply. The Compendium was a pile of ashes.

twenty

Once Keelie emerged from her telepathic communication link with Tavyn, she dropped onto a nearby bench to steady herself. Her head ached even more than from her earlier contact with Hrok. She glanced up at the position of the sun. She had about four hours before Tavyn's threat would come to pass.

It was eerily quiet. There were no birds singing, and the trees were silent. The hairs on the back of her neck rose. Could goblins be lurking and watching her every move and reporting back to Tavyn? She fought the urge to flee back into the Admin office.

Something warm and hairy rubbed up against her leg. Keelie jumped up from the rock.

Knot, back to normal-cat size, rubbed his face against her leg as the familiar tree greenness formed in her mind. She recognized the essence: Hrok.

Daughter of the Forest. You seemed distressed. Melankin's request seems reasonable. He explained to me he merely wants to read this book. Yet fear flows through you. Why are you so afraid of him?

How did she explain this to Hrok?

I don't think Melankin is as nice as he's making himself out to be. I think he has a shadowy-bark side.

He seems very nice to us.

Keelie didn't have time to debate the situation with Hrok. She had to report to Finch.

Be careful around Melankin. He's not what he seems. His rings are stained with treachery and betrayal. Hrok, can you sense my father?

This conversation puzzles me, Daughter of the Forest. As to sensing your father, I do not. In fact, I think he has left the area.

I need to see him. It's an emergency.

I am sorry. Still, I do not sense his presence. Let me ask the trees within the elven camp.

Their connection thinned and became a wispy green thread as he consulted the rest of the forest. Then it flared back to life.

The little cedars at Heartwood would like for me to tell you that they saw your friend Hob. It looked as if he was making magic with a book.

Keelie's heart raced. *A big green book?*

Yes, milady.

Keelie's knees felt rubbery and she leaned against a fence post (cedar, from Washington State). The Compendium wasn't lost after all. But Hob was Peascod, and he had the Compendium. Perhaps he'd set the fire so he could steal it, but why? Her head reeled. Was he going to give it to Tavyn?

"Meow what's wrong?" Knot swished his tail as he waited patiently down at her feet. He hadn't left her side.

"The Compendium didn't burn, but Peascod has it."

Knot placed his paw on her leg. "Meow will help you get it back, meow."

Love for the fairy cat flowed through her, but she wouldn't ruin their relationship by telling him.

"Whatever happens, thank you, Knot."

He lifted his head, eyes dilated. "Meow why thank meow?"

"Because you're a good guardian."

Knot turned his head. His ears tilted forward. Keelie thought she heard a sniff, sniff. But she didn't push the cat. Sentimentalism wasn't his style.

What should she do next? She tried reaching out to Dad but she couldn't reach him; her head was all fuzzy with green energy.

She had to get the Compendium back. Maybe Elianard would help her once he found out it hadn't been destroyed. He might already have left for the Dread Forest, but she could use one of the elven cell phones that used tree magic to call him. Dad had his, but maybe one was left behind in the elven village.

"Knot, go tell Finch what we've learned. I'm going to the elven village."

The cat meowed agreement and dashed up the Admin building's steps as Keelie clutched her rose quartz and ran down the path toward Water Sprite Lane, keeping an eye out for any remaining elves. The strong wallop of Dread hit her as she approached the woods, but she breathed in and pushed on, breaking through the Dread spell as she entered the village.

The streets were empty, but she heard the whinny of horses. A huge pickup truck and horse trailer were parked by the meeting hall, the trailer marked with the logo of the Silver Bough Jousting Company. Keelie almost gasped with relief that the village wasn't totally empty.

Two jousters appeared, leading their tall, muscular horses. Then her heart raced as she heard Sean's voice shouting out orders.

He appeared from behind the trailer. "Bromliel, do we have enough hay in the back?"

Keelie stepped toward him. Did she still love him, or was this just her body reacting out of memory?

Sean noticed her and stared disbelievingly. "Keelie?" He rushed toward her. "You're going with us." A statement—not a command, nor a request. His voice was happy, reminding her of the old Sean, the one who loved her. "You can ride with me in the truck."

Part of Keelie wished she could hop into that truck and be the girl he wanted her to be, but she knew she couldn't.

"Sean, I didn't come to see you. I need to speak to Elianard. It's urgent. Do you have an elven cell phone I can use?"

"And why would you need to speak with the Lore Master, if not to make travel arrangements?" a familiar voice grated.

"Lord Niriel." Keelie bowed her head to him. She was the daughter of the Lord of the Dread Forest and she would act accordingly. She would be respectful to Niriel for her father's sake, although she wanted to throw a mud-ball at the haughty, pinched-faced elf traitor.

He bowed his head in return. Dressed in the richly embroidered robes that reflected his high-ranking Council position, he seemed like a character from a fairy tale. The evil vizier, perhaps.

"I need to speak to Elianard about the Compendium," Keelie said curtly. Time was growing short.

"It's too late for apologies. Didn't you destroy our most valued treasure? Have you come to grovel for forgiveness?" A puzzled expression crossed Niriel's face, as if he was pondering a riddle. The horses in the trailer stomped their hooves on the metal floor. They were growing impatient, as if they sensed danger looming near.

"I thought I heard my name," Elianard said as he walked up to them. He wore a green linen tunic with long flowing sleeves, the edges appliquéd with silver oak leaves.

"You're still here!" Keelie rushed to him, leaving Lord Niriel open-mouthed at her lack of manners.

"Keelie, why are you here?" Elianard frowned. "You are still forbidden to enter the village."

"I need your help in finding the Compendium. It wasn't destroyed—Peascod has it."

"We have proof that it was destroyed. You cannot delay us with your human tactics," Niriel huffed, raising his eyebrows at Elianard as if in warning.

Keelie didn't want to reveal too much in front of Niriel, but she didn't have a choice. "The Compendium contains goblin magic as well as elven charms."

Elianard's face paled. "Impossible."

"I think it has hidden layers that it's revealing for the first time. Peascod took it, but I'm sure he learned about it from another." She quickly told them about Tavyn the half-elf/half-goblin and his power grab. "Tavyn can use the power in the Compendium, and he said if I didn't bring it to him, then he would attack the faire."

"Even if we had the Compendium, why would we give it to you to trade to this abomination?" Niriel's scalding gaze made it clear that he included her in that category.

Elianard was frowning, deep in thought.

"Because I don't think Tavyn is going to stop at the faire. I've seen the goblins in Oregon and in California. They're everywhere, and in every city. Tavyn can rally them, form an army, and attack humans as well as elves. You won't be safe hiding in the Dread Forest for long."

"Let him attack. We'll be ready," Niriel said. "Enough of this foolishness. If your father won't rein you in, then I will.

You are to return to the Dread Forest, where you will reinforce the defenses of your home forest with your magic."

He grabbed her upper arm. "Sean, take charge of her. You wanted her, now you can have her."

"Dad, this is wrong." Sean's face flushed red.

Keelie turned to Sean, pleading with her eyes for him to help her. He wouldn't look at her, but his hands fisted and his eyebrows slammed together in a mighty frown.

"What?" Niriel asked, seemingly amused by his son's anger. "Do you question me?"

"Yes, I do," Sean cried. "You may not approve of Keelie, but I think she's right. I fought Tavyn, and I know what he is capable of. He could attack the Dread Forest, and if he has a huge army of goblins, we don't stand a chance against them."

Keelie raised her fist, ready to punch Niriel to free herself, but Elianard stepped forward, hands outstretched. "Niriel, release Keliel. This is no way to treat a tree shepherdess. She is the daughter of the Lord of the Dread Forest."

Niriel looked shocked that Elianard had come to her defense. Keelie was a little surprised, too.

Elianard folded his arms and looked down his nose at Niriel.

Niriel glowered. "You would follow Zekeliel."

Elianard nodded. "He is the Lord of the Forest. Our chosen leader. And Keliel is right—if the Compendium still exists, we cannot leave it in goblin hands."

Niriel scowled and shoved Keelie toward Elianard. "Do with her as you wish. She's nothing but a curse upon the elves with her mixed blood." A landing helicopter distracted him. "I must see to the evacuation."

Keelie didn't appreciate being tossed around like a misdelivered package, but she was glad to be free of Niriel's clutches. She had to get the Compendium. She looked up in the sky. Time was running out.

She turned to Elianard, ready to plead for his help.

Elianard placed his index finger against his lip. "Walk with me to the edge of the village, and from there you can make your way back to Finch and the others."

"But—"

Elianard began to walk quickly, silvery hair drifting behind him in the breeze.

Behind them, she heard Bromliel's voice. "That's the last one. Let's move out."

She turned to see Sean walking toward the open cab of the big pickup truck. He turned to look at her, and their eyes met. For a moment she felt like rushing to him, but then a horse kicked from inside the trailer, rocking it, and Sean glanced toward it, breaking their contact. The moment was over.

Keelie knew she had grown past the girl who would have been happy living out her days in the Dread Forest and going from faire to faire, year after year. There was more to her, and there was more to the world. She wanted to see it before she settled down.

She turned and hurried to catch up with Elianard. She took a deep breath to swallow the sob that wanted to burst from her chest. Later.

As they neared the edge of the village, Elianard glanced at her. "You know, Keelie, you may be able to find the Compendium because it likes you."

Keelie stopped walking. "It's a book. How can it like me?"

Elianard waved his arm for Keelie to catch up. She had to fast-walk to keep up with his pace. It was as if he was trying to get her out of the village as quickly as possible but be subtle about it.

"You said that the Compendium was revealing hidden layers. I knew this could happen, but for it to reveal goblin secrets? Amazing. When magical objects are exposed to additional magic, they sometimes develop a consciousness, and that must be what happened to the Compendium when it was with you. It is rare for a magic book to change and adapt like this."

Shocked, Keelie didn't know what to say. But she did feel a personal attachment to the Compendium. She'd even written additions for it, chronicling the information she'd learned in the Northwoods about dragons and dark fae.

"If the book has grown a consciousness, then the book can be like a familiar. It can assist you in your magical needs. But the book has to choose you." Elianard stopped at the edge of the woods.

Keelie turned to him. "Peascod has the Compendium and Tavyn wants the magic for himself. First the rift, now the Compendium. I don't understand."

"You will have to figure out the answer," Elianard said.

Chills danced up Keelie's body as she realized what the

jester wanted with the Compendium. "I think Peascod wants to use the magic in the Compendium to break free of Tavyn."

"What hold does Tavyn have over Peascod? And how are they both so powerful, in any case?"

"Peascod absorbed the wild magic of the rift, and if he was in thrall to Tavyn, he could have fed that power to him." Keelie shrugged. "It's a theory. And if Tavyn gets his hands on the Compendium, he'll be even more powerful. He'll be able to use the magic of the elves and goblins, and he would probably challenge Herne, who was once Peascod's master."

Tavyn's goblins were already imbued with wild magic. Once he reached his goal, would Tavyn become King of the Dark Fae?

"Herne the Hunter." Elianard sighed. "Elia told me the tale of your journey north. If I had known it was so dangerous, I would have gone in her stead. But your thoughts about the strength of the Compendium and its use to these rogue goblins is sound. The Compendium knows you. Maybe it will try and reach out to *you*." Elianard pointed at her.

Keelie thought of Sally and the prophecy of her magical cards. Her stomach knotted with tension. If those images gave her anxiety attacks, how was she going to react when she saw Tavyn face-to-face again?

"Can the Compendium warn me through a magical tarot deck?"

"It's definitely in the realm of possibility." Elianard tilted his head. "Have you seen such?"

"The tarot reader, Sally. Her deck started showing the same image of Tavyn, over and over."

"Then you must find the Compendium quickly," Elianard said grimly.

"If I find Peascod, I'll find the Compendium," Keelie stated. It sounded easy, like finding the clues to a mystery game. She knew the truth would be very different.

Overhead, a helicopter lowered to the ground, sending debris flying around. Elianard held his robes close as the wind whipped them. A door opened on its side and a green-clad figure jumped out and ran toward them.

"In your studies, did you notice a section that dealt with finding missing household items?" Elianard shouted, his eyes twinkling.

"Of course!" Keelie had used it to find her father's car keys when he'd hidden them right after she'd learned to drive. "It starts with a tree branch, freely given," she yelled over the noise of the rotors. She recalled the rest of it, too.

"Exactly," Elianard replied. "I have the utmost confidence in you."

"Lord Elianard, we must depart," the elf called as he reached them. "Lord Niriel says that if you and Lady Keliel are leaving, then it must be now or never." The elf turned his face when she looked at him. Guess he was a Niriel follower.

"I must go, Keliel. Good luck and may the Great Sylvus watch over you in your quest to vanquish the goblins."

Elianard kissed her on her forehead. "You have been one of my most promising pupils."

Keelie choked back tears. That sounded like a goodbye forever.

Elianard hurried to the helicopter in a swirl of robes and dust.

It was up to her. First, she had to find Hrok, because she needed a branch. Then she'd find her book.

She watched as the helicopter lifted and passed low overhead. She waved to Elianard. She felt his gaze on her, and wondered if Niriel was glaring down.

The walk back down Water Sprite Lane was spooky. With no elves, the woods behind her seemed menacing, even though it held the same trees she'd become friendly with last year. Now they thought that goblins were their friends, and she couldn't help but think that the forest might be spying on her.

Keelie trudged through the meadow. Dad had hammered into her the importance of education, and he'd been right. Although he could never have foreseen this—a situation where the fate of many depended on how well she'd done her homework.

twenty-one

The meadow was quiet. Keelie glanced uneasily toward the place where the goblin tree grew, but it was still just bare earth. She marched up to the aspen tree.

Hrok, I need your help.

Hrok's face formed in the bark. *Milady, I am surprised to see you. How may I help you?*

I need a freely given branch.

Hrok's eyes widened in surprise. *Of course.* A large branch lowered so that she could reach it. *What is this for, milady?*

It will help me find something I have lost. Will it hurt you?

Hrok grimaced. *A little. Do it quickly.*

Keelie snapped the branch, twisting to make the thin green bark release, then pulled it free from the big branch. *Sorry.*

She ran through the directions of the spell in her mind. One must turn in all cardinal directions, and then visualize the lost item, and the branch would direct her. She hoped it would work.

Hrok's face vanished into the bark, then quickly returned, eyes darting wildly. *Milady, I sense goblins firing at trees with flaming arrows. They carry weapons. They're close, milady. They're coming in from Equus Island.*

Flaming arrows? Panic filled Keelie. She sent reassuring waves to Hrok. *I must go into the campground and rally everyone to fight.*

You were right, milady, the goblins mean to burn us. What will we do?

Green shrieks pierced Keelie's mind. Rampant fear spread through the forest as the trees discovered the goblins meant to burn them down. Keelie nearly fell over from her telepathic connection to the traumatized trees.

Knot bounded up to her, his eyes dilated with alarm. He kept looking over his left shoulder. "Meow must go now."

Keelie hated leaving Hrok and the other trees vulnerable to a goblin attack, but their only hope was for her to get back to the faire, rally everyone, and find the Compendium. She wasn't about to hand it over to a goblin, though. If it had chosen her, as Elianard said, then she would use it to defend the faire and chase away the goblins.

I will return with help.

Keelie ran. Not far away she could hear the clanking of armor and the goblins horn of battle being blown loud and clearly, its strong deep sounds ringing up against the Rocky Mountains. The sun was almost touching the mountaintops to her left—the four hours had passed. Propelled by the need to warn everyone, Keelie forced herself to keep running. She remembered the image on the tarot card of the goblins attacking the village.

Ahead, she saw the Ren Faire buildings peeking through the tree line. Cars were lined up at the performers' entrance.

What were the fools doing outside the faire?

"Get inside! We're being attacked."

Thomas the Glass Blower gawked at her. "What say you?"

"Goblins! Need to find Finch."

Thomas guffawed. "You've been living too long at the faire—the real and the fantasy are intermingling in your mind, girl."

"No. Goblins. Get inside the faire," Keelie shouted.

He wrinkled his forehead. "What games are you playing?"

Keelie didn't have time to argue with him. "You must get inside. Goblins are on the march."

Inside the faire, shopkeepers including Sam the Potter had pulled their vehicles up to their shops, and many were loading up their merchandise and other personal belongings. Mrs. Butters was serving cold drinks outside of the tea shop.

"What are you all doing?" Keelie asked Mara.

"We're getting the hell out of Dodge. It's been one bad thing after another. This place is cursed." Mara was holding her two-year old daughter, Ava. "We can't stay, Keelie. It's not safe. I've been having visions of creatures with swords. They're here, and I'm afraid."

Could the Compendium have been reaching out to everyone in the faire to warn them about the goblins, because that is what *she* wanted to do? Keelie wondered. She tightened her grip on the branch.

"My grandmama said I had the sight, that I could see fairies, but these aren't fairies—these are monsters that are going to attack us." Mara hugged little Ava.

Keelie didn't know what to tell her. Some goblins, like Peascod, had the hearts and souls of monsters because they wanted power. They would kill and hurt and destroy whomever and whatever to achieve their goals—but not all goblins were like that. She blinked back tears as the image of Cricket formed in her mind. She was starting to understand how goblins were a lot like people. Some good, some rotten.

Keelie made a decision. She had to tell everyone about the goblins. Their lives could depend on that knowledge.

"I have to go find Finch. You need to stay inside the faire. These visions you've been having are real. Those monsters are goblins, and they're on their way right now."

Mara's face grew chalky white as she clasped her daughter closer to her.

"I don't blame you for wanting to leave, but it would help if you stayed. We're going to need all the help we can get in the battle," Keelie said.

"What do you mean, goblins?" Mara backed away from Keelie. The expression on the young mother's face said *you've lost your mind.*

Keelie hadn't considered the possibility that people wouldn't believe her. Without visible proof, most humans wouldn't believe the truth. Not until it was too late.

Keelie took off before Mara could say anything else. If the goblins were coming in from the west, then it would be better to face them head on. Keelie turned the corner on the West Road and jumped back as a motorcycle came tearing down the lane.

Riding like a bat out of hell on his chrome beast was none other than Vangar, Finch clinging to him as if she were his biker babe. Talk about major attitude turnaround. Love can make you do crazy things. The bike slowed, then turned around and came back to where Keelie stood.

Finch dismounted. "Why didn't you contact me over the radio?"

Vangar wiped his forehead with his sleeve. His face was red and his dreadlocks were tangled and wild.

"The trees say the goblins are marching in from Equus Island. The elves have left, and the goblin wizard is in fact Tavyn, and I have to get the Compendium from Peascod if we want to have any hope of defeating the goblins." Keelie rushed the words out, so she could say everything she needed to before Finch could bellow at her.

The shop owners and performers had gathered in a big crowd, watching and listening to Finch and Keelie.

Thomas pushed his way through. "This girl says we're being attacked by goblins."

Mara stepped forward with her daughter in her arms. "Is it true?" Her voice on the brink of hysteria.

Finch's gaze held Keelie's. "You told."

"Tavyn's attacking. He wants the Compendium. I didn't know what else to do." Keelie looked at little Ava. She didn't want this little girl to die at the hands of goblins.

Finch grinned wickedly. "Time to make a battle plan."

"What?" Thomas asked loudly.

Blakely the reporter stood in the background writing furiously on her pad. Her photographer now had a camcorder and was filming the action. Finch was too busy to notice.

"Everyone, I want you to go back to your businesses. We're under attack, and you'll be safe as long as you stay inside the faire."

Thomas confronted Finch. "What in the hell are you talking about?"

"I'm saying it's too dangerous for you to be out in the open unless you can wield a sword or some other weapon against an ugly beast that looks like an orc," Finch snarled back at him.

"That's why we're getting out of here. You have no business telling us what to do," Thomas yelled. "And if we're going to be afraid of someone, how about that firebug?" He pointed at Vangar.

"Vangar is innocent. It was Hob who set the fires," Keelie said. "Hob was just a disguise for a dangerous creature who wants to destroy us."

Marcia, Tracy, and Lily arrived, dressed in jeans and T-shirts. They looked like ordinary girls except for the swords they wielded. They stood in front of Finch like a human shield.

"You heard Finch, Thomas," Marcia shouted. "Get back in your shop, or get out here and fight and help defend our faire."

Keelie's opinion of these three fairy-wing wearers went up several notches.

"You're wrong, Marcia. Hob tried to help us all. He warned us about Finch and Vangar," Sam the Potter said.

Lily snorted. "He lied and cheated. He's nothing but a fraud."

Tracy scowled. "He was nuts, too. He started going around talking to his puppet, which was weird." She carried her broad sword with an air of expertise.

Finch smiled and cut her eyes over to Keelie.

"You fools need to listen to Finch and Keelie." Sir Davey's eyes flashed. He shouldered his axe. In full dwarven armor, he was a formidable sight.

Then a loud roar split through the air. Spinning around, Keelie couldn't see if something or someone had transformed, or appeared out of thin air.

"It's too late to run. Now is the time to fight," Finch said as her eyes narrowed to slits and flame blazed within the irises. "They're on Equus Island, but the shield holds for now."

In the distance, Keelie heard a loud booming of a drum and the familiar blare of battle horns.

Marcia, Tracy, and Lily joined up, shoulders together, ready to take on whatever came their way.

Dad! Keelie heart's thumped hard against her chest as everyone looked toward the sound of the horns. She made her way to Sir Davey. "Where is Dad?"

"Once he had the dwarfstone, he said he needed to speak to a friend named Bruce." Sir Davey scowled. "He said if he was late, not to worry—he will be here with re-inforcements."

Not to worry. Keelie planned to give Dad a good talking to when he arrived. Until then, she would help Finch and Vangar. Wait ... the only Bruce she knew was a tree. She shrugged; she didn't know everybody.

With a cry of horror, Thomas pointed at a charging throng of armored goblins wielding swords and battle axes. "Keelie was right," he squealed. "The goblins are real."

"It isn't real. They're probably making a movie," the turkey-leg vendor said, but her eyes were wide.

"You fool, those goblins are the first wave of an attack, and if you had any sense about you, you'd get inside and protect your family. All of you," Sir Davey bellowed to the assembled shopkeepers and performers. "Stay within the faire. You're protected by a magical force field."

Keelie turned to Finch. Sometimes people needed a

demonstration to change their minds and convince them that something was real.

"Finch, show them what you are."

The dragon smiled her wicked grin as smoke drifted from her nose and ears. "Yes, I think it's time."

A tornado of fire swirled around Finch, and Keelie shielded her face with her hands as the intense heat blasted toward her. Small beads of light twirled, then sucked inwards as if Finch were magnetic. Bright light exploded, then collapsed, too bright to endure. Keelie closed her eyes.

When she opened them again, Finch was gone. In her place, a red dragon with glistening scales reared up on powerful back legs, her wing tips soaring in an arc over their heads.

"Wicked cool," Marcia said.

"Can you teach me how to do that?" Lily's eyes blinked several times, as if she couldn't believe what was before her.

Tracy just stared, jaw dropped open.

"Consider me impressed," Keelie said to Sir Davey, who was dusting dirt off of his hat. "The woman has a flare for theatrics, just like her mother."

"I agree." A bronze dragon lowered his head in between Keelie and Sir Davey. Keelie saw her reflection in a yellow-gold eye with an iris slit like a goat's.

"Vangar?"

"Yes," he answered, his voice a deep, rich bass that conjured up warm evenings by a fire as soft music played in the background. If Vangar ever became a lounge singer, he'd have women throwing their underwear at him. The dragon body might be a PR problem, but his voice was like smoky velvet.

"I knew all along we had dragons amongst us," Thomas declared, oblivious to the skeptical looks that others threw his way. He pointed at Vangar. "I said there was a firebug, and there he is."

Vangar turned his massive bronze head toward Thomas, then lowered it until he could look the glassblower in the eye. "I thought we had established the fact that Hob was the firebug, not me."

Keelie's opinion of Thomas had dropped fifty points in her personal opinion poll. Was he crazy? You didn't call a dragon a firebug.

Finch turned to Vangar. "I think it's time to nip this rebellion in the bud and show these interlopers who's the boss around here."

Vangar stretched out his wings. "After you, my dear."

Keelie motioned for everyone to move back. "Give them some room for takeoff. They'll kick up a lot of dust."

Vangar and Finch both pumped their wings and ascended, two draconic air fliers, into the sky with elegance and muscular grace.

Finch flamed the sky, a plume of fire erupting from her mouth.

Keelie couldn't help a smile. "Show-off," she whispered.

Everyone was transfixed by the dragon spectacle above them.

Keelie was amazed that no one had run to hide in their shops, hopped into their vehicles, or run for the mountaintops when Finch and Vangar revealed themselves to be dragons. Maybe the faire's fantasy ambiance had made them comfortable with any possibility.

She'd been right. The humans needed to know what they were up against, and the people of the High Mountain Faire might just be able to hold their own against the goblins. Still, they needed help. She hoped Dad arrived soon with reinforcements.

She nodded to Sir Davey. "You stay here and control the crowd. I have something to do."

She had to find the Compendium, and with the goblins trying to find a way through the magical shield, she had to act quickly. Keelie moved away from the crowd, looking for a place to work undisturbed.

She held out the aspen branch and envisioned the book of elven household spells and charms. If this worked, the branch would lead her to the Compendium. She had to get this right, and fast.

twenty-two

Keelie held the image of the Compendium in her mind as she walked purposefully through the jostling crowd—some racing to their shops, preparing for battle—and stopped next to the art gallery near Galadriel's Closet. Standing in the road in front of the booth, Keelie pointed Hrok's branch to the east, west, north, and south. She recalled the Compendium's elegant calligraphy and the numerous spells within it, including the hay-fever charm she thought she'd never use and the protection charm she'd cast over the Redwood Forest.

If the book had developed a consciousness and wanted

to find her, she wanted to open herself telepathically to help it.

Here I am, she thought. *Where are you, Peascod? Where did you go with my book?*

Keelie felt a tingle touch her mind. It wasn't green, but a different kind of magic—something young and fresh.

But it disappeared as soon as she tried to lock onto it.

Then, nothing.

Around her, the performers and shop owners ran through the streets, gathering swords and other weapons as Sir Davey bellowed out orders. The armory and forge had made their wares available, and Keelie was pleased to see able-bodied men and women arming themselves. It looked like a fantasy movie set as everyone rushed to and fro.

Knot sat at her side. "Meow any luck?"

Lowering the branch, Keelie shook her head. "What's the status on the goblins?"

"Meow skulking in parking lot, and at the front gate."

Keelie wondered what the normal people of Fort Collins would think if they drove by the faire and saw the goblins gathered in the parking lot. They'd probably think it was part of the show, until it was too late.

In the sky above, the dragons attacked and hurled flames at the goblins. Their magic was now combined, as Finch and Vangar shared their power and strengthened the bond between them. Keelie knew they were keeping the goblins at bay, but the dragons would grow tired, and then what? It would be up to her.

Knot wriggled his tail in agitation. "Shield will break soon."

"Let's just hope the dragons can hold out."

A wind began to blow in the faire and she leaned into the cool breeze. It lifted the curls on the back of her head. Swirls of dust danced in the road. Then the cool air transformed into a cold wind and a discordant jangle rang all around her, obliterating the chaotic sounds and preparations.

Keliel. You summoned me.

As the whirlwind of dust disappeared, Peascod spun up from the ground dressed in torn motley clothes, the lower half of his mask shattered, pieces dangling, revealing mottled goblin skin covered in bleeding sores. The Compendium was under his arm, and Toshi floated beside him like a chewed and torn ghost. Crumbs of dirt fell to the ground from the book binding.

"Yes, I summoned you. You have something that belongs to me," Keelie told her nemesis. "I want it back."

"I'm afraid I can't let you have this. Why is it that all the magical goodies seem to come to you?" Peascod's puppet mimicked his actions spastically, patting the green, leatherbound book. Creepy even for Peascod.

"Just luck, I guess." Keelie crooked her finger, motioning for Peascod to hand the Compendium over. She didn't like him having his grubby hands on it.

"I'm afraid I can't do that," Peascod said.

Toshi waved its hand in a no-no gesture.

Peascod opened the Compendium. "Very interesting reading. Have you read the section on dimensional travel?"

Leering at her with its fixed grin, Toshi gleefully rubbed its hands together.

Keelie had never seen a section on dimensional travel, and she didn't like the sound of it.

"Did you see the pages on goblin magic?" Peascod's eyes watched her from the hollows of the mask.

"The information on goblins was limited," Keelie replied.

"There are layers upon layers in this book, and if you know the right words of persuasion, you can get access to them."

"So I've heard." Keelie thought she saw the book shudder when Toshi touched it. "Give me the book," she said, forcing the fear out of her voice. The branch tingled in her hand. Lot of good it was—maybe she would need to get rid of it.

Toshi's flat black eyes stared at her as if he could see straight inside of her, and knew she was afraid.

Hrok's voice popped into her mind.

Whatever Peascod does, hang on to my branch because it will be your way back to this time and place.

What do you mean, it's my way back?

I sense the one named Tavyn. I must break our connection, for he watches you through me. He has the little aspen tree. You must save it if you can. Be safe, Tree Shepherdess.

Sweat trickled down Keelie's back. She had to keep Peascod distracted until she figured out what she was going to do to stop him.

"Why does Tavyn want this book?" she asked Peascod.

At first, Peascod scowled; then he laughed, revealing jagged teeth. "Keelie, you know as well as I do—for the power."

She'd guessed as much, but she had to keep Peascod talking until she had a chance to grab the Compendium and run for it.

"How long has Tavyn been your master?" she asked.

Peascod hissed. "He thinks he is my master. I only played along. Isn't that right?"

Toshi nodded.

"Rather convincingly," Keelie said.

"It's all your fault," Peascod spat out. Toshi turned to Keelie and floated within two feet of her, waggling its hand in front of her face like she'd been a naughty child.

"What?" Keelie watched the poppet to make sure it didn't do anything else, but it drifted back to Peascod and hovered beside him.

"Tavyn and me. That night in the Redwoods, he captured me and forced me to swear allegiance to him. Linsa was dead already, and he knew about the leaking wild magic at the rift. He wanted to control it. He wanted more magic."

"Why? What gave him the idea the Compendium would give him power?"

"There are signs the old gods are returning, and Tavyn wants to be part of the old pantheon, but with a new edition—himself as a goblin god. Doing that takes magical power and a magical army.

Peascod's jagged teeth chattered as if he were chilled

from fever. Toshi patted the jester's shoulder as if trying to comfort him. In fact, Peascod didn't look well—pocked with sores, skin dry, lips cracked and bleeding. He'd looked like a normal, albeit down-on-his-luck person back in Northwoods, but now he was changing into a monster. Maybe using magic for evil was taking a toll on his body.

"It's time Tavyn faced me, one-on-one." Peascod turned to Toshi, who grinned a fixed smile at the jester. "This time I have an assistant."

A thundering crash behind Peascod signaled that the goblins had smashed their way into the faire. The magical shield had broken. Keelie looked up in the sky, but she didn't see the dragons. Exhaustion must have claimed them. The goblin horde marched down West Road, brandishing swords, spikes, and axes.

One giant goblin led the others. "Humans, surrender, and we'll let you live," he bellowed.

The other goblins roared in unison. It was a primal noise that rippled like a bad vibration through Keelie's body.

She stepped to the edge of the lane, but her head throbbed as the trees all called to her at the same time. *What will you do to protect us?*

Mental overload. She inhaled to steady herself. Concentrate, she advised herself.

Focusing on the trees, she sent waves of comfort. *Be brave. They aren't here to hurt you.*

Sir Davey had rallied the shopkeepers and performers, and they had formed a ragtag army that now faced their foe with Finch's deadly weapons. Keelie was proud of them, but she knew they wouldn't be able to vanquish the goblins. She wished Dad would hurry up with the reinforcements. Where was he?

The humans rushed at the goblins, who ran to meet them. The sound of screams and clanging metallic weapons filled the air.

Keelie turned to Peascod, who was flipping through the pages of the Compendium, ignoring the mayhem. Not a good thing—she had to get the book from him. She walked closer to the unstable jester.

"The book belongs to me, Peascod. Can't you feel it? If you released it, the pages would fly into my arms."

"It may want you, but I need it," Peascod hissed. "I have a way to free myself from Tavyn. Why do you always interfere with my plans?"

Toshi nodded and pointed its wooden hand directly at her, then floated back to Peascod.

The poppet wasn't just scary, it was irritating. Keelie noticed that a nearby candle shop had a bucket of warm dipping wax in the window; she wondered if she could grab Toshi out of the air and dunk it in wax.

Toshi stopped and turned slowly to look at her. Had it read her thoughts?

"Is it time, my friend?" Peascod asked Toshi.

It nodded, painted eyes still on Keelie.

Hrok's branch, still in her grasp, began to twitch. She remembered Hrok's advice. *Keep the branch.*

Light burst from the pages of the Compendium. Magic was about to be used.

Keelie had to distract Peascod. He already seemed to be having a hard time concentrating, so if she talked, maybe it would keep his attention focused on her.

"Maybe we can work together to stop Tavyn," she suggested. The idea of cooperating with Peascod appalled Keelie, but she would do whatever it took to get the Compendium away from him.

"I have a better idea." Peascod began reading in a strange language Keelie didn't understand. She'd read elven words, and she knew they didn't sound like this. Yet it still sounded familiar, sort of like the guttural language she'd heard spoken between the goblins.

The pull of magic began, enveloping her in skin-tingling waves.

Keelie didn't know what to do. The goblins seemed to be winning the hand-to-hand combat against the faire folk. The dragons were flying overhead again, but they couldn't blast the attacking goblins because they were too close to the humans.

The trees screamed in her mind, and she started to fall, weakened by the magical onslaught. She reached out and clung to one of the Galadriel's Closet support beams.

Then, in the chaos of the fighting, Keelie saw a face she hadn't seen since the Redwood Forest. Tavyn was striding purposefully toward her, ignoring the fighting all around him and looking more like the goblin on the tarot deck and less like an elf. He was carrying the pot with the goblin tree, which smirked at her.

Keep cool! Keelie knew she couldn't show fear. "Done lurking in the woods?" she asked calmly.

"You are finished, Keliel Heartwood," the little goblin tree said.

"I wasn't talking to you." Keelie glowered at the traitor treeling. "You staged your own tree-napping."

Tavyn extended a taloned hand toward Peascod. "The book, vermin."

Peascod ignored the goblin-elf and continued to read from the Compendium. A high wind blustered through the faire and the sky darkened as if the sunset was on fast forward.

Tavyn cried out, growling commands to the armored goblins behind him. He got no response—his army was cowering as the sun split into two, then four, then again and again until it seemed as if many setting suns surrounded them. The pull of magic was stronger, too, and reminded Keelie of the magic at the rift.

Keelie held tightly to the aspen branch and closed her eyes against the disconcerting light. She sent out her tree sense, trying to anchor herself with the truth of the forest. Green, unchanging... and suddenly—gone.

The bell on the jester's hat rang loudly, and its distorted jangle filled the entire faire with the weight of discontent and unhappiness.

Gravity started to pull sideways, and she felt as if every molecule of her body was being disassembled. Her last thought, before all the air was sucked out of her lungs and the world turned inside out, was that she would love to have that purple and blue dress with cap sleeves hanging in the window of Galadriel's Closet.

Whoosh!

She was being transported somewhere, but much faster than in her whooshing travels with Herne or Dad. It was like being in a swirling vortex, or a spinning carnival ride on hyperdrive. Her shoulder banged painfully against a solid surface, and she opened her eyes a crack. She'd hit the door of Galadriel's Closet.

She gripped the wood (oak, from Georgia) of the shop support tighter in an attempt to stay in the faire. Dresses and costumes from within the shop zoomed out of the windows and door as the increased pressure pulled them around Peascod, who seemed to be at the center of the vortex. Clanking armor sailed toward the conjuring jester, along with statues of dragons, wooden swords, and chickens from the nearby petting zoo. If an object wasn't nailed down, it was making its way toward him. Hapless goblins flew through the air.

Opposite the deluged jester stood Tavyn, his feet squarely on the road, an arm across his face to protect it from the Renaissance Faire objects pummeling him on their way to Peascod. A turkey leg hit him on the forehead, and he let go of the goblin tree. It was sucked away as if by a giant vacuum cleaner, screaming, "Save me, Master!" before vanishing into the spinning tornado.

Tavyn didn't even look in the little goblin tree's direction.

Tarl the mud man held on to a post of the Wing-A-

Ding shop while two goblins shielded their heads as pewter wine goblets and fairy wings from the shop assailed them. The shopkeepers and performers clutched counters and were flattened against walls, unable to stand. Dulcimers and flutes from the music shop whirled around the goblins; more turkey legs smacked them, and one goblin howled with fury as a Steak-on-a-Stake drove into his thigh and stuck there like a meat pincushion.

Above it all, Finch and Vangar flew, spouting flames as they winged their way over the fairground, prepared to attack. Another wave of turkey legs rushed toward Peascod, but he couldn't see them because of the accumulated Ren Faire souvenir T-shirts flapping around him.

The trees in the faire spoke in a wave of green.

Where are we? We do not feel the sun, nor feel the dirt in our roots.

Shepherdess, this is wrong. We can't feel the Earth.

Stay calm. Keelie sent reassuring waves of magic their way, glad to feel them in her head once more.

Tavyn motioned with his hands and uttered a word that reverberated all around and sounded, gong-like, in her skull. Keelie had underestimated the amount of magic the half-goblin could wield. She wouldn't make that mistake again.

Everything stopped whirling and dropped to the ground, including the turkey legs.

"It worked," Peascod said.

"Of course, you fool." Tavyn scowled at the jester.

Keelie looked up at the sky and around the faire. They were encircled by an eerie darkness, and a strange pink moon cast a weird, dusky glow on the faire. Some stars twinkled in the background. The sky was not a Colorado sky, but the ground around her was the same. The faire was a mess—the path covered with debris, the windows of the shops broken by flying merchandise.

Something was missing, and when Keelie realized what it was, her heart skipped several beats. There were no Rocky Mountains. It was all empty horizon.

Peascod made an elegant bow, one leg extended. Then he rose and lifted his hands outward and spun around, shouting, "This is my faire, where the jester shall rule, and the subjects shall be loyal to me."

Mimicking Peascod's moves, Toshi circled around him.

"What did Peascod do?" Keelie gasped. She remembered Peascod mentioning "dimension travel."

Tavyn peered down his nose at her. His pointed ears peeked through his thick, silver-shot dreadlocks. "I thought you had studied the Compendium." He used a condescending tone of voice that reminded Keelie of Niriel.

"I did," Keelie said. "It seems to have layers it decided not to reveal to me." Like moving an entire faire to a different dimension. She definitely hadn't read that chapter—she would have remembered it.

"The book reveals what it wants when it wants." Tavyn flicked his eyes over at Peascod, who had an idiotic grin on his grotesque face. His mask was gone, shattered by the debris, revealing the necrotic skin beneath.

"The fool has lost his mind." Tavyn turned to Keelie.

She pointed at Peascod. "So, I take it he used goblin lore to …"

"Move the High Mountain Renaissance Faire to a different dimension." Tavyn yawned, as if not caring about the danger he, too, was in. It seemed Peascod would do anything to get his freedom.

"What dimension?" Keelie asked, as if she knew one from another.

"It might be the one between the human world and the spirit world." Tavyn looked around. "Hard to tell. Far from the reach of human, fae, or elven intervention."

"Can you send us back?" Keelie wanted the Rocky Mountains, and she wanted to be back on good ol' Earth. She'd had enough of spirits and gods. She didn't want to meet up with whatever lived in this neighborhood.

"I'll need the Compendium."

"Well, you know where to get it. Your jester has it." If Tavyn could move the faire back to the Earth, maybe she could do the same. It was a stretch, but she was desperate. She didn't trust him. He had aspirations to become a god to the dark fae.

A line of fire landed near Tavyn's feet and he jumped back. Keelie did too.

She looked up in the sky at Finch flying overhead. The dragon circled around, coming in for another attack.

The goblins went on the rampage again, taking advantage of this latest distraction. The shop owners and performers were losing the battle, despite the fresh dwarven troops fighting valiantly alongside them. Fatigue, despair, and confusion seemed to be written on the humans' faces. The dwarves fought on with grim determination.

Thomas the Glass Blower staggered toward Keelie, blood bubbling from a wound in his chest. He collapsed on the road, and the goblin behind him waved his bloody sword and roared in victory.

"No," Keelie shouted. She started to run toward the fallen merchant, but Knot leaped in front of her, causing her to trip. She landed hard on her knees but still managed to keep from breaking Hrok's branch.

"Meow too dangerous."

Thomas lay crumpled in the clutter-strewn, dusty lane, and his eyes dulled as life faded from his body.

twenty-three

Peascod glared at them from the road in front of Galadriel's Closet. Toshi shook its head, but smiled as it looked directly at Keelie, and then clapped its little wooden hands.

"Seems as if we have our first human casualty." Tavyn arched an eyebrow.

"Tsk. Tsk. The first of many casualties, including you, Tavyn," Peascod called out. He clung to the Compendium, looking drawn and pale as his puppet soared toward the goblin-elf. "Although I should thank you for giving me that idea about moving the faire to this dimension. We can take care of our business unimpeded."

Keelie sent a "thanks a lot for nothing" glare at Tavyn.

Tavyn held out his hand and the puppet stopped. It couldn't move, immobilized by magic.

"Peascod. I tire of your games." Tavyn's voice deepened. He pushed his hand forward, and the puppet zoomed back and slammed into Peascod.

Keelie didn't know what was wrong with Peascod, but it really looked like the jester needed to be in the hospital. He appeared to have aged in the past hour. But she couldn't feel sorry for him—he had brought this fate onto himself. Remembering Cricket, Keelie couldn't forget that it was Peascod who had killed the harmless little goblin.

Toshi floated in front of her.

Keelie recalled Sally saying that a poppet could store magic. What if Peascod had put his own life essence into the puppet?

Destroy the puppet. Destroy Peascod.

But how?

Tavyn's eyes flared with pure disgust as he glowered at Peascod. "I will deal with you later."

He turned to Keelie, and his eyes widened when he saw the branch. "I think I will take that gift from our friend Hrok."

He'd recognized the branch. It was all suddenly clear to Keelie. "You *are* a tree shepherd."

"Surprise!" Tavyn grinned, showing sharp goblin teeth. "My grandfather was a tree shepherd. Who'd guess the power would arise in me when I embraced my goblin side?"

A goblin tree shepherd. Hrok had read it right. Keelie stared at Tavyn, horrified.

Fire poured down from the sky, nearly hitting the goblin. Finch had zoomed in. Tavyn aimed a blast of magic up toward the retreating red dragon.

"I have work to do. Call off the dragons, or I will order my goblins to kill each and every human found within this faire, children included." Tavyn kicked Thomas's body.

Repulsed, Keelie wanted to blast Tavyn with green magic—but what if he could turn it against her? He was a tree shepherd too. Dad was right; she didn't know enough about her own magic to be able to fight with anything but luck.

"I don't know how to reach Finch or Vangar when they're in dragon form." She shot a dark look at the goblin-elf. To think that people made comparisons between the two of them. Except for that halfblood thing, and being tree shepherds, they had nothing in common.

"I suggest you find a way, *tree shepherdess.*" He flashed a smile at her, as if he found the situation amusing. He beckoned the goblins to bring Mara and her daughter forward. A goblin ripped the toddler from her mother's arms. Little Ava screamed and Mara reached out, crying for her daughter.

Keelie had to do something.

"It's up to Keelie—she has to call off the dragons," Tavyn yelled above the terrified shrieks of the little girl.

Keelie hadn't been able to stop the rampaging goblins,

and so far, she hadn't regained the Compendium. But she had other ways to fight.

She thrust Hrok's branch into the dirt and called on the green that surrounded them. As the trees answered, desperate for help themselves, she thrust her power into the ground. If Under-the-Hill was still there…

The dark coolness of the Under-the-Hill filled her head, but it wasn't the abandoned mustiness of the one under the meadow. It was the spicy-scented warmth of Herne's dominion.

A roar came from the end of the road and chimes rang loud and clear, filling the air. Keelie turned in the direction of the noise.

Tavyn frowned and pounded his fist into his hand. "What have you done?"

A pulsing swirl of light, like the Aurora Borealis, formed in the middle of the path. It looked like the vortex at the Quicksilver Faire turned on its side. It separated the lines of fighting goblins and humans.

Tarl and Sir Davey scurried out into the lane to carry Thomas's body out of the way while the goblins were distracted by the light. A pirate grabbed a discarded goblin sword and came to stand at Keelie's side, ready to defend her.

A ground-shaking crack, like thunder, split the air. Literally. Where the pulsing whirl of light had once been was a pulse-edged sliver of darkness, a door into nothingness in the middle of the road.

It widened, and a row of gleaming, prismatic-armored knights, lances ready, rode out of the dark sliver of doorway into the faire. Keelie gasped, recognizing the High Court's fairy army. Humans, dwarves, goblins stood frozen, staring at the beautiful beings, and then the goblins charged.

The armored knights lowered their lances and attacked. The dwarves followed, howling battle cries. Keelie was startled to see Knot, wielding a lethal-looking short sword, to the left of King Gneiss.

Tavyn screamed and ordered more goblins into the fray, while the humans threw themselves onto the rear guard of the goblin army. About fifty armored goblins split off from the fight and ran down the road to circle Keelie, Tavyn, and the pirate. The pirate hacked at arms and legs as they came near, wounding many, but to no avail. The goblins seemed impervious to pain.

Keelie called upon the trees again, and they bent, their branches hitting some goblins on the head and sweeping others aside like ugly croquet balls in a crazy lawn game.

One of the fairy knights turned his mount and galloped down the lane toward them. Tavyn screamed and leaped, landing on the roof of Galadriel's Closet. Peascod grabbed Toshi out of the air and whirled underground in a spray of dirt.

The knight reined in his horse and leaped to the ground, yanking off his helmet. Brown hair tumbled down the shining armor, and around her father's grim face.

"Dad!"

He ran to her and swept her up in his arms.

"How…?" Keelie asked.

"Bruce, Deuce, and Zeus have a mutual friend in common

with you, and I thought we could use his help," Dad said as he turned her around. "We brought reinforcements."

"The High Court, yes. What mutual friend?"

Another knight removed his helmet, and Keelie saw that it was Salaca, the fae lord. He bowed to her from atop his war horse, then put his gleaming helmet back on, wheeled his mount, and attacked the goblin army. The fae army kept marching out of the doorway—now standard bearers came, holding aloft great silken flags with strange symbols on them. Behind them rode King Fala, the crown of the High Court fae bright on his brow.

And at his side, antlers proud, was Herne—with his Wild Hunt behind him.

Herne caught Keelie's eye and winked. And then the fae warriors, light and dark, fought side by side for the first time in millennia.

Keelie looked for a weapon, ready to join the battle, but Tarl grabbed her up and held her fast to his broad chest.

"Don't let her go till the battle's over," Dad yelled, mounting his horse again.

"Dad, come on, I want to help!"

He rode away, intent on the endless hordes of goblins that seemed to spin out of the ground everywhere.

"Sylvus take me," Keelie whispered. Even the fae might not be enough to stop them.

Tarl suddenly cursed and turned around. Raven was standing behind them, a pike in her arms. "You hit me!"

"Sorry, Tarl. I saw Keelie and thought you were an ogre." Raven shrugged. "You okay, kiddo?"

"I will be if he puts me down," Keelie said, but her eyes were on the carnage around them. "I think we're losing. Even with the fae, we're losing."

Raven pushed her hair out of her dirt-streaked face. One of her nails had broken, and blood stained her tank top. "I have an idea, but it's a little crazy."

Keelie cocked her head. "Yeah? Tarl, let go of me. I'm not going to run or fight." *Yet*, she added under her breath.

As Tarl released her, Raven grabbed her arm and pulled her toward the ruins of the King's stage. Tarl joined Merk the Troll and what seemed to be a real troll; the three whirled giant war axes and charged a group of rampaging goblins.

"Remember when you drew on Earth magic in the Wildewood?"

Keelie nodded. "I can't do that here, though. We're in another dimension or something, and I have no connection to the Earth."

Raven smiled. "No, but I have a connection to my husband. Remember him? The unicorn lord of the forest?"

Keelie felt her eyes widen as she realized what her friend was saying. "We can link to the Wildewood through Einhorn?"

"And through my Lord Einhorn, to every forest on Earth."

The two friends grinned at each other and joined hands. Then Raven closed her eyes and Keelie opened her tree sense. The image of Einhorn, the silvery-haired lord of the Wildewood, appeared.

Raven, what's happening? My forest screams.

"Hang on, hubby. This is going to be a wild ride. Ready, Keelie?"

Keelie pushed on her power and Einhorn immediately responded, their mental link showing him what was needed.

Behind them, on the hills of the stranded faire, green power surged up from the ground, surrounding the fighters in tendrils of power. The fae and humans were untouched, but the goblins screamed as the power swept over them, leaving them vulnerable to the faire's defenders.

Channeling the magic took every ounce of Keelie's strength. After a while, it was too much. She and Raven fought to keep the conduit open, but then everything winked out into a starless dark.

When she opened her eyes again, Herne was standing over her. Fala stood nearby, talking to someone she couldn't see.

"Am I dreaming?" She touched her forehead. The aftermath of the magic hurt, like a dozen hangovers must hurt. Keelie vowed to never drink. She didn't want to ever feel like this again.

"Keliel, you're back." Herne bowed his head. "We were just discussing where we could be." He studied the area around him. "Where are the mountains? I thought we were near the Rockies?"

"Peascod used the Compendium to move the faire to another dimension."

Fala snapped his fingers. "That's why we were rerouted here. I thought we'd hit an interdimensional exit when we neared Earth."

"Did we win?" Keelie immediately knew that the fighting was not over. She heard the clash of steel against steel further into the faire.

"I thought we might have a time continuum problem," Herne said to Fala.

"Will you two stop talking like Dr. Who?" Keelie struggled to her feet. Raven was already standing, a little wobbly, nearby.

"There's Tavyn." Keelie pointed toward the goblin, who now fought at the head of his remaining goblin faction, and then she saw Peascod, now sitting on the peak of the candle shop roof, nodding his head as he conferred with Toshi. He lifted his eyes and glared at Keelie.

"We've defeated most of the army. Peascod is in a much worse state than I'd realized," Herne said. "Like random chaos—you're not quite sure what he's going to do."

Finch and Vangar landed, and with a burst of flames, transformed into their human forms. They looked like a draconic biker couple in iridescent black and red leathers.

"Glad for the reinforcements," Finch said, her red-gold eyes flashing at Herne and Fala.

"What a happy family reunion. Too bad it won't help you in the end," Tavyn declared as he walked toward them. Wild magic flowed in and around him like a captive cirrus cloud.

Fala sneered disdainfully at Tavyn. "Who is he?"

"A goblin-elf hybrid," Herne explained. "He magically enslaved Peascod when I sent him out into the human world."

"I am no longer magically enslaved to him," Peascod called down. His eyes blazed with crazed fury, and he was still clinging to the Compendium. Keelie knew she had to get it, and soon, before the jester did something destructive to it. Hrok's branch twitched in her hand as if it was coming awake, or reacting to the magic.

Fala turned to Herne. "Was he one of Vania's allies?"

"Yes," Herne said.

Fala drew his sword.

Tavyn narrowed his eyes. "So you choose war rather than surrender."

"The fae do not parlay with goblins." Fala glowered.

A swirl of energy surrounded Tavyn. "You will. Goblins, attack!"

The goblins roared and leaped forward, fearsome weapons slashing before them.

Fala held his sword aloft. "Knights!" Fala and Herne led the charge for the good side. This time the odds were more even. Peascod scurried down from the roof and turned to flee, and Keelie bolted after him.

"Not so fast," she shouted. "Like I said, you have something that belongs to me."

Peascod whirled around and glared at her, the single bell left on his hat jangling discordantly.

Thrumming with energy, the branch in Keelie's hand pointed itself toward the Compendium. She realized the finding spell she'd cast before was still working. Time for the next step. She took a deep breath and grasped the branch more tightly. "Return to me what I have lost."

Energy from the branch flowed to the Compendium, and the magical book sailed out of the jester's tight grasp and flew toward her. She caught it by the edge of the cover.

Peascod shrieked in rage, picked up a turkey leg, and threw it at Keelie. It missed her head by inches.

She had the Compendium. In shock, Keelie turned to Dad, who was running toward her. "I have the book!"

"Keelie, watch out!" Dad shouted.

Toshi was surging forward, a small knife in its hands, murderous intent in its eyes. As the puppet zoomed toward her, Keelie smacked it in the head with the Compendium. Toshi hovered back in surprise.

"No," Peascod screamed.

To Keelie, it seemed as if everything was happening in slow motion. Peascod rushed past her to attack Dad. The jester's bell rang out as they fought in a blur of arms, legs, and jester hat.

Toshi rounded on her. Dropping the Compendium, Keelie grabbed an abandoned goblin sword and swung it at the puppet flying toward her. She smacked it with the side of the sword, batting it away. Toshi recovered swiftly, and, knife outstretched, returned like a puppet arrow.

Keelie felt time slow as it drew near. She noticed every detail of Toshi's tattered clothes, the painted eyes, the glint of the lethal little blade. With one swift move, she sliced off the head.

It fell, bouncing, as the puppet's body flopped to the ground.

Dark energy flowed from Toshi like greasy smoke. It

drifted toward Peascod, enveloping both the jester and Dad, hiding them in a dark shroud of noxious vapor. A loud gurgling emerged from within the miasma.

"Dad?" Keelie took several deep, ragged breaths as she picked up the Compendium. As she touched the book, a wind blew and cleared away the dark fog. Two bodies lay, crumpled together, on the ground. She didn't dare think about the impossible.

"I'm fine," Dad said, his face still in the dirt.

Relief flooded through her. Keelie clutched the book closer to her chest.

Dad pushed Peascod's body off him. The jester's decapitated head rolled away like a gory bowling ball, nose eaten away, mottled skin pale and pocked with oozing, infected sores.

Keelie's relief was colored with the need for a hot shower and lots of antibacterial soap.

Dad stood up. His face was red, but other than that, he seemed fine. Stepping back, he breathed heavily, trying to regain his wind. Keelie blinked back tears and threw her arms around her father, clasping the Compendium and the branch as he embraced her.

The branch began to tremble.

Dad stepped back. "What is this, daughter?"

"It was a gift from Hrok, who said we may need it to get back to our own dimension."

"Indeed."

The battle continued all around them. The goblins numbered fewer now, as the fae knights and the army of shopkeepers and performers battled the remaining goblins. The dragons worked the rear, picking off goblins as they broke ranks to run away.

Blue and red blasts of magic glowed and burst over the magic maze, where Tavyn and Herne were battling. Keelie wished there was a way she could help Herne—he was a nature god, sure, but Tavyn was wicked and devious and wanted Herne's job. Maybe part of Tavyn's plan was to steal Herne's power; she couldn't underestimate him.

"Dad, I need to go to Herne."

Dad put an armored arm out to stop her. "Herne is powerful. He can fight without your aid."

The Compendium in her arms began to bounce as if it wanted to say something.

"I think I need to be there," Keelie said, holding tight to the book.

Dad started to speak, but seemed to reconsider. He puffed out a breath. "I want to protect you, but it's futile. You're powerful enough to be of help. Let's go together."

They rushed to the site of the battle, which had moved out of the maze, near the candle shop. Melted candles and overturned candle stands were scattered everywhere, left in a mess from the magical tornado that had swept through. Tavyn launched a blast at Herne, who stepped aside; the bolt of dark, inky magic hit the side of the pub, leaving a huge hole in the wall.

Tavyn cut his eyes over to Keelie. "I'm glad you have brought me the book."

"Keelie, do not let him have the book, whatever you

do." Sweat trickled down Herne's face as he hurled another ball of magic.

The Compendium bounced in Keelie's arms again, slipping loose enough for the cover to flip open. Pages flew, landing open at the Gods of Old section. An illustration of Herne filled the pages—the horned hunter, mounted on a fiery-eyed horse.

Keelie read, *The nature god and all gods of Earth pull their power from the magical core of the planet.*

But they were now in a different dimension, so Herne couldn't refuel by tapping into the magical core of anything. Keelie suddenly realized that Peascod had been played like a puppet—Tavyn had always planned to fight Herne this way, and he was the one who'd planted the idea of another dimension in Peascod's mind.

She looked again at the battle. It seemed that Herne's powers were diminishing, while the goblin-elf appeared to be growing stronger.

The pages in the book turned.

Transporting to an Original Location Spell:

Secure an object from a living thing such as a tree, a flower, or even shrubbery, and place it in the ground. With this object and the power from the Compendium, the chosen one must visualize the original location and call upon the power of the Great Sylvus, the original author of this Compendium.

Sylvus had written the Compendium. Cool!

Keelie knew what to do. She lowered Hrok's branch to the ground, placed her hand on the Compendium, and visualized the faire.

She'd never called upon a god before, but she would now. As Keelie pushed the branch into the ground, she felt for Earth magic, the place she had touched when calling on the forests. The branch vibrated. Stretching tall, it grew until it towered above her head. She smelled the spicy scent of Herne's domain, but his energy was not hers. She couldn't draw on it.

Dad's eyes widened. "Daughter, what magic is this?"

"Sylvus's," she whispered. "Hold on, Dad." She started to read from the book, supplying words that fit their situation: "Oh Great Sylvus, return us to our original home. Hear my cry. Hear my plea to return the faire and everyone within it to the Earth," she concluded loudly.

In her mind, she saw a misty realm, and slowly, an image emerged of many hooded beings gathered around a circular hearth. She couldn't see them clearly. She noted that some of them yawned as if they'd been awakened from a nap. Could these be the old gods?

She heard the deep-toned laughter of a god, one that was green-tinged and smelled of life. It had to be Sylvus.

Visualizing the High Mountain Renaissance Faire, Keelie recalled the many friends and memories she'd made there since arriving almost a year ago.

A strong wind blew all around her, and the noises of the battle faded in the background. Keelie heard Tavyn shouting "no."

Green magic filled her and the ground rumbled beneath her feet.

She heard a deep voice in her mind.

You have been chosen to watch the green of Earth. To be messenger and arbitrator to the gods of old and the magical beings of the new times.

Keelie swallowed. She didn't need another job. *Why me?*

You are one of the chosen.

The chosen? Keelie didn't know if that was good or not, but she didn't think she should argue with Sylvus. But, given that he was the god of the elves, she wanted to make sure he didn't do things the elven way, not explaining things and situations to her.

Could you send me instructions before you send me out to do something? I'd really appreciate clear communication.

You have the Compendium. Fare thee well, Keliel Heartwood, until we meet again.

Greenness enveloped her, and then she felt the furnace-like heat of Herne's kingdom. She drew up great armfuls of it and tossed it, like a heap of rope, toward the forest god.

She felt Herne's surprise, and saw his melting chocolate eyes see her. He knew what she'd done for him. And then she knew no more.

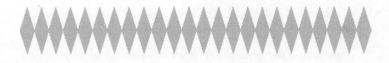

twenty-four

When Keelie awoke, she saw Herne hovering next to her. He looked worried. Dad's face floated next to Herne's. Fala waved at her from the side, his outfit sparkling clean as if he hadn't been in battle.

She tried to sit up, head aching. "Why am I on the ground? Are we back on Earth?"

"To answer your first question, you fainted when you called out to Sylvus," Dad said.

"To answer your second question," Herne said, interrupting Dad, "yes, we're back on Earth. You did well, Keelie Heartwood."

"Keelie?" Dad asked. "Are you really okay?"

"Yeah, I think so."

Suddenly, she remembered what Herne had been doing before she fainted and looked around wildly. "Where's Tavyn? Did you get him?"

"He escaped in the chaos when we returned to Earth." Fala frowned. "But we will catch him in good time. Do you recall that Peascod is no more?"

She nodded, shuddering at the memory of his death, and then grabbed hold of Herne's breastplate and pulled him toward her. "I saw the old gods, and Sylvus, too. He spoke to me, Herne."

"They must trust you, to allow you to see them," Herne said. He didn't seem surprised at her revelation.

Dad's face appeared above her. "What did Sylvus say? Did he answer the riddle of the tree ring's focus? Or about Lord Mariel's Compromise?"

"I don't know about the riddle or any compromise. He said that I'm to be a go-between for the old gods, and for magical beings too." Fala and Herne exchanged glances. Keelie couldn't read what passed between them.

"Things are going to be interesting from this point on—for humans, fairies, and elves," Fala said.

A helicopter flew overhead. "Have the elves come back to the faire?" Keelie asked.

"No, that's the media. They're our other problem," Herne said. "Seems the human newsfolk arrived here after reports of dragons and goblins, and they saw the entire mountain vanish."

Fala nodded. "Then they saw it return."

The Compendium opened its pages.

Dad's eyes opened wide. "Did you do that, Keelie, or is it moving on its own?"

"It seems to have a mind of its own, for sure. I can't wait to tell Elianard."

"News reporters are all over the place, asking questions," Herne continued. "Even worse, Homeland Security. Once, when I took a human flight over the Adirondacks, my magic responded to the land and my antlers appeared. The air marshal on board was quite upset."

Keelie bolted upright. "So the mountain is back where it belongs?" What if it had landed in downtown Fort Collins?

Herne nodded. "Once you jammed your staff into the ground, you collapsed, and the faire and everyone within it was transported back to Earth. It seems the Compendium augmented your tree shepherd magic, allowing you to return us to this dimension." He paused, looking troubled. "Before that, of course, you opened the portal between worlds and allowed our armies to travel to the faire. Then you used the Compendium to tap into my magic from Under-the-Hill and link it to me." Herne frowned. "Keelie, there may be an after-effect from such magic use—"

His words were interrupted by a woman with a microphone who rushed up to Keelie, followed by a cameraman.

"Honey, can we have a word?"

Keelie recognized the woman—Teresa Smith, the news

reporter from a national cable news channel. Teresa tossed back her perfect hair and looked into the camera.

"We're here live at the High Mountain Renaissance Faire, where we're about to talk to an injured girl waiting to be transported to the hospital for emergency surgery." She shoved the microphone in Keelie's face. "Can you tell me what happened? The world wants to know what you saw. Did you see dragons?"

Here was Keelie's chance to tell humans everything. Should she expose the magic? Before the battle, she'd wanted to tell humans about the magical world so that they could protect themselves from the goblins, but now, what purpose would it serve? If this hysteria was any example of what could happen, learning about magic would tear apart society. People would be afraid, and some would covet the power. She glanced at Herne, and then at her father.

Herne's antlers had retreated into his skull, and Dad had pulled his hair back over his ears. Fala's fairy glow was muted as he attempted to blend in with everyone else.

She saw Vangar and Finch in the distance, back in human form, rushing around trying to help injured people.

What would the world do with the knowledge that there were live dragons at the faire? She loved and cared for these people. If they wanted the secret revealed, then it would be up to the many magical races to make that decision. It wasn't her secret to give away.

Keelie smiled. Guess they would have to call a Council meeting.

She looked into the camera. "I thought it was an earthquake," she told Teresa.

The reporter looked frustrated. "Come on kid, you don't have a brain injury. You remember what you saw."

"There's dragons and fairies all over the faire, but you don't believe they're real, do you?" Keelie frowned at the woman as if she thought she was nuts.

"Come on, Herb," Teresa said. "There's got to be livelier interviews somewhere else." The two hurried off.

Dad dropped back to his knees. "Keelie, are you really okay?"

"I'm fine."

Fala turned to Herne, his forehead creased with worry. "What are we going to do about this situation? Was this Peascod's intent all along? Revealing the world of magic to humans will upset the balance."

"Elves will be in peril," Dad said. "We'd be an object of scientific curiosity. I've seen this behavior before, when humans are confronted with something new and different. Fear compels people of all forms to do dangerous things. At least the fae live in another realm."

Okay, Sylvus. A little help here. Keelie searched the trees for a message from Sylvus, but there was no answer.

The pages of the Compendium opened. Talk about an answer from above. She remembered Sylvus implying that it was her instruction book.

Ancient Oblivion Spell:

Have you done embarrassing things at parties that you wished everyone would forget? Made embarrassing speeches at a Council meeting? This spell will erase selective memory and not harm the participating subjects.

Important note: If used to make humans forget, and if more than one race was present at the time of the gaff, all races must be represented at the time of the spellcasting.

Keelie smiled.

Thanks, Sylvus!

She stood and held the Compendium. "I think I have an answer to our problem, but I need a dragon, an elf, a dwarf, and two fae—one dark and one High Court. Do we have everyone we need?"

Herne stood next to her as Finch, Vangar, Dad, Sir Davey, and Fala formed a circle near the Admin building. Nearby, reporters trawled the faire seeking people to interview.

Keelie stepped into the center and read the Oblivion spell. As she read, a pale gray mist appeared from beneath her feet and crawled to each of the members of the circle, who looked apprehensive but didn't break ranks. When all had been touched by the mist, it expanded, then burst, and flowed like waves across the fairegrounds.

"Everyone will remember a strong earthquake," Keelie said as she completed the spell.

She cut her eyes over to Herne. "I hope it works."

The mist traveled through the faire, touching reporters, shopkeepers, and performers. A glazed look formed in their eyes when the magic settled on them.

Teresa Smith stopped nearby, her curious expression replaced by blankness. "What am I doing here?" she asked herself.

Finch winked at Keelie. "I've got this."

Tarl the mud man walked up to Teresa. "You're here to cover the earthquake."

Several other High Mountain Faire folk joined them. "I was in my shop when all of my pottery went flying out the window," Sam the Potter said. "I found one of Hob's masks all the way down here." He lifted a broken, bone-white mask, then tossed it on a heap of trash and wiped his hands. "Creepy thing."

Finch joined the gathered group, and the cameraman swung his camera toward her.

"Can you tell us about the faire?" Teresa Smith held the microphone up to Finch.

Finch smiled. Her eyes sparkled, and she looked directly into the camera as the magical gray mist drifted around it. "Despite the earthquake here at the High Mountain Renaissance Faire, I'd like to reassure the public that the faire will be as good as new this weekend. The Middle Ages will be alive and kicking and everyone is invited to come join in the merriment."

Teresa Smith nodded. "You heard it here first. The High Mountain Renaissance Faire will be opened to the public after the unusual earthquake that hit the Fort Collins area."

Keelie hoped the oblivion spell would spread across the airwaves, into the minds of any people who'd seen earlier newscasts.

"Hey, where did that tree come from?" Tarl was looking

up into the branches of an aspen that now spread its branches over the Admin building.

Uh oh. That one would have to remain a mystery.

Keelie juggled the Compendium from one arm to the other. It was heavy and awkward. So cumbersome. It was past time to get this thing online—the Dread Forest elves must never lose their lore again. She also wondered if she could talk to Sylvus about maybe transforming the book of knowledge into something more modern, like a tablet computer with a wooden case.

The book rose and hovered in midair, and the pages opened to a new section.

Object Transformation:
You will need a wooden staff…

This was more like it. Keelie headed to the meadow to talk to Hrok.

◆ ◆ ◆

The next day, Keelie found Sally examining her tarot booth. The structure wasn't in too bad shape, except for a sagging corner. It looked like the support post had suffered some damage.

"Do the cards say anything about Tavyn?" Keelie asked.

Sally shook her head. "No sign of a goblin wizard, but the cards reveal that new powers and new magic have been awakened.

Mara joined them, holding little Ava's hand. Ava

reached up to Keelie with her chubby fingers, then laughed when a *bhata* landed on Keelie's shoulder.

Its twiggy face bent in a grin, and its berry eyes radiated happiness. It climbed down to Ava.

Keelie looked at Mara. "Can you see that?"

Mara nodded.

Keelie turned to Sally. "You?"

She nodded as well.

"The humans with magic in their blood can see and feel the magic all the time now," Mara said.

"Then you remember?" Keelie whispered.

Mara winked.

Ava laughed as the *bhata* danced around her. Knot strolled out into the open area. Ava squealed with delight. "Kitty."

Knot's tail bushed out. His eyes widened with fright when he saw the toddling little girl coming after him, squealing "Kitty, kitty, kitty" at the top of her lungs.

"Are you going to tell anyone?" Keelie asked Sally.

She shook her head. "The faire folk keep their secrets. It's an unwritten law amongst us."

Keelie knew the secrets of the faire would be safe.

In the woods behind the tarot booth, a huge antlered stag was watching her.

"If you ladies will excuse me, I need to go and check on something."

Herne stood there, in his deer form, head straight and chest expanded. "What do you think?"

"You make a great buck. I don't know if I'd hang out here during hunting season, though."

"Good point." Herne narrowed his eyes. "I hadn't thought of that." He transformed into his human form. "I think there's something you need to see." He held out his arm. "Milady Keliel, if you will accompany me."

Keelie mentally prepared herself for the whoosh.

A cool breeze brushed against her face, and then she stood before the spruce trees Bruce, Deuce, and Zeus. Their tangy scent filled her. She could look down and see all of Fort Collins below and the Rocky Mountains before her. Flowers grew around the stones where Cricket had been buried.

Sadly, she looked at the grave of her little friend, but she knew he rested in peace.

"Why did you bring me here?"

He pointed. "Watch."

King Gneiss and Sir Davey stepped forward. Vangar and Finch landed in the meadow, their dragon forms huge and muscular. Dad was riding on Vangar's back, balanced casually like an expert rider, with Sally in front of him. She looked thrilled and terrified at the same time.

A swirling vortex of light appeared and Fala stepped through, hands held high as if he were about to perform in front of an audience. He wore a gold circlet on his forehead and a glittering chain mail shirt.

Herne arched an eyebrow. "Bit overdressed?"

"What's going on?" Keelie asked. She wondered why her magical friends were here.

Finch and Vangar shifted into human form.

Herne pointed to everyone gathered. "Keliel, since it is important for all races to work together, we have come together this day, and in this meadow, in honor of you and one whom you loved despite his differences. I decree this the first council meeting of the Circle of Magic." He rested his hand against his chest. "I represent the goblins and the dark fae."

Fala bowed his head. "I am here on behalf of the High Court and the Shining Ones."

Dad smiled at her. "For the elves."

Sally motioned with her hands. "For the humans."

Sir Davey and King Gneiss removed their hats, both with snowy plumes. "We represent the dwarves."

Finch and Vangar stepped up to her. "We represent the magical beasts and shapeshifters of this world."

"Keliel Heartwood, you have done what others thought would never happen. You have brought us together in peace."

In her mind, Keelie heard Hrok's voice. *You, my dear Daughter of the Forest, represent the Great Sylvus and the trees.*

Keelie looked at her friends and wiped at the corner of her eye. Not that she was getting teary or anything. "Then I guess it's time to open this meeting of the joint council, the Circle of Magic."

epilogue

Keelie sat on her narrow bed in the newly repaired Swiss Miss Chalet. Their salvaged belongings were packed up, and they were ready to head out as soon as Dad finished the business paperwork. Insurance adjustors had been crawling all over the faire the last few days.

She pressed the tree app on her newly transformed Compendium. She loved the wooden finish (hawthorn, High Mountain Renaissance Faire).

Words scrolled across her screen.

It was Hrok. She had the best connection to him.

Hello, milady.

She keyboarded her answer.

You know you'll be able to keep in contact if you need me.

Yes, Keliel.

She loved how Sylvus had combined forest magic and technology. She'd used the object transformation spell he'd shown her to turn the Compendium into a tablet computer.

After the fires and the magical confrontation with the goblins, Dad had decided they needed a break. He'd been in contact with the Dread Forest, and when Alora, the Queen Tree, asked to see Keelie, they'd decided to skip the Wildewood Faire and head back to their home forest. Keelie hated saying goodbye to her friends, but Dad said they would pick up the Ren Faire circuit again in a few months. They needed to replenish their stock of furniture to sell, in any case.

Keelie looked forward to helping Dad, and of course she had to adjust to monitoring the forests of the Northern Hemisphere on her tablet computer. She would miss her friends, but Zabrina was in Edgewood, and Elia was close to her delivery date.

Sean and the Silver Bough Jousting Company had booked Ren Faire gigs year-round, so he wouldn't be returning to the Dread Forest anytime soon. Although saddened at the loss of their relationship, Keelie knew they would become friends in time. And didn't she have lots of time? Maybe it was for the best.

A loud ding from her tablet pulled Keelie out of her thoughts. She looked down and saw that a new icon had appeared on her tablet's menus: an antlered deer head.

She recognized that deer. She pressed the dark nose.

"You called?" a familiar voice said. A tall, handsome man appeared before her, dressed in green that complimented his curling chestnut hair and, yes, the deer antlers coming out of his head. Herne, hottie god of the hunt.

"Did I call you?"

"You did." He looked around the tiny camper cabin. "Very cozy. Like a turtle, but with a hotplate and a bookshelf." He smiled at her. "If you ever need me, just press my app and I'll be at your side."

"A god with an app. Gotta love progress," Keelie said. "But I don't think I need the Herne app."

Herne pretended to look hurt, but then smiled sunnily, with more than a hint of mischief. "Don't delete it, Keelie. You have a tendency to find yourself in misadventures."

"I don't think I'll be having any more adventures. I'm going to be working as a messenger and spending time with my family."

"Ah, family. You'll find that the definition of that word will change drastically for you, and soon."

At Keelie's wary frown, Herne smiled and spread his arms wide. "My dear Keliel, your adventures are just beginning."

Keelie looked down at her tablet, where other mysterious apps were popping into existence.

She grinned. Herne didn't know the half of it.

About Gillian Summers

A forest dweller, Gillian was raised by gypsies at a Renaissance Faire. She likes knitting, hot soup, and costumes, and adores oatmeal—especially in the form of cookies. She loathes concrete, but tolerates it if it means attending a science fiction convention. She's an obsessive collector of beads, recipes, knitting needles, and tarot cards, and admits to reading *InStyle* Magazine. You can find her in her north Georgia cabin, where she lives with her large, friendly dogs and obnoxious cats, and at www.gilliansummers.com.